W9-CBT-915

Contents

The Lord is my shepherd; I shall not want.

He maketh me to lie down in green pastures: he leadeth me beside the still waters.

He restoreth my soul: he leadeth me in the paths of righteousness for his name's sake.

Yea, though I walk through the valley of the shadow of death, I will fear no evil: for thou art with me; thy rod and thy staff they comfort me.

Thou preparest a table before me in the presence of mine enemies: thou anointest my head with oil; my cup runneth over.

Surely goodness and mercy shall follow me all the days of my life: and I will dwell in the house of the Lord for ever.

Psalm 23

Acknowledgments

I am grateful for a grant from Judy Blume and the Society of Children's Book Writers, which materially assisted the completion of *Kate of Still Waters*.

I am indebted to the staff of the Bourbon County Library— Beulah Diamond, Susan Eads, Carol Merringer, and Anne Rogers—and to the Bourbon County Extension Agents Doug Teague, Bernie Milam, and Betty Overly for help on this and other books. Some of the people whose willingness to give me the benefit of their professional experience and/or special skills enabled me to write *Kate of Still Waters* were Dr. Guy L. Chappell of the University of Kentucky Animal Sciences Department; Renee Earlywine; L. H. and Marilyn Fischer of *Sassafras Meadow;* Lynn and Page Mayfield; Henry Myers of *Pleasure Ridge;* Laurence Simpson; Jane Bennett Wells of *Many Pines* and *Innisfree;* and Laura White. My respectful thanks to each.

To the generous people who read all or parts of my manuscript and gave invaluable suggestions and encouragement— Bettie Cannon; Col. G. P. Groves; Elizabeth Leal; Professor Anne Young McConnell of the University of Kentucky Library and Information Science Department; Diana and Katherine Mears; Jean Naggar; Anne Robins; Catesby Simpson; Gloria Whelan; Judith Whipple; and my husband—my deepest thanks.

CHAPTER 1

Supernova

"It's okay," I told Hetty Anne as I came down the school bus aisle. "Mom and Dad both said yes." Hetty Anne gave the victory sign, and I took my seat beside her as always.

A stranger getting on at the next stop and seeing us would have thought Hetty Anne was my older sister. We are both pale-skinned, and we wear identical straw-colored pony-tails. In reality, Hetty Anne's only sister is through school already, and mine hasn't started yet. In reality, who got on at the next stop was J. M. Stanley, the worst pain on the bus. J.M. hardly looked at us; he was too busy carrying on yesterday's argument with the other boys about which Reds pitcher would win the most games.

The Reds' next game was going to be televised exactly when PBS was scheduled to show "Anne of Green Gables," so anybody who knows my dad knows what my chances were of seeing "Anne of Green Gables." Fortunately the only sport that interests Hetty Anne's father is horse racing, and she had invited me to come and watch "Anne" with her.

Hetty Anne's ancestors built her house themselves with their own stones before Kentucky was even a state. The oak tree that shades it is older still. The Engles' farm is very different from ours. Dad raises steers and lambs; Mr. Engle breeds horses. The horses are more beautiful—also more dangerous. Dad's cousin was killed by a mare that hadn't even meant to kick him. "He just happened to have his gut where her hoof happened to fly when she got ready to take off," Dad says. "You be careful around Matt Engle's horses, Kate."

I am so careful around horses that Hetty Anne laughs at me sometimes, but I enjoy feeding them through a fence. I've learned just which weeds they like best.

I didn't expect to do much tidbit-feeding on "Green Gables" day. Last spring was hotter than usual, and those April showers never did come along. By May, choice weeds weren't easy to find even outside the pastures. As for where animals grazed, everything edible was cropped right down to stubble, and where they stood or walked the most, like along fences and around gates and water fountains, the bare hard dirt was covered with half an inch of powdery dust.

All along our school bus route, Hetty Anne and I saw tree-high jets of water circling our neighbors' struggling tobacco—those of our neighbors who have irrigation pipes and deep ponds, that is. All the ponds were low. Our cattle still could drink at ours, but the stream that crosses the Engles' pony paddock, way at the back of their farm, was dry as a saltine, Hetty Anne told me, and Mr. Engle had to bring the pony up and put him in one of the yearling paddocks, where he'd have a fountain.

"Green Gables" day was 80 degrees in the shade by three-thirty, and hotter on our old bus, so Hetty Anne and I were looking forward to a cold glass of milk in her kitchen. Maybe if we'd guessed how long it was going to be before either of us swallowed a drop of anything, we would have told our driver to let us off at Tom Allen's tobacco plot and run

2

straight for one of those beautiful jets of sparkling pond water. Instead we got off at the foot of the Engles' long driveway.

We knew there was trouble before we took our first step. Clouds of dust were billowing up from the paddock to our right and the one just beyond it. In the first, the Appaloosa pony was racing at top speed along his fence, and in the next, the Engles' best colt was matching him stride for stride. "Oh, no!" Hetty Anne exclaimed. "Pops was afraid of this. And he's not even home!" She dropped her books on the grass and started climbing the pony's fence. "Get a shank, Kate!" she begged as she jumped down into the paddock. "Bring it to his gate!" She was off running after the pony. He and his rival had galloped as far as their fences let them and were reared up on their hind legs, flailing the air.

Had it not been so frightening, it would have been beautiful—two challenging males, one thirteen months old, the other thirteen years, both in prime condition. I dumped my books beside Hetty Anne's and started running up the driveway toward the barn. I knew where the rope shanks hung.

Neither animal paid the slightest attention to Hetty Anne. At the same instant, both began to race back toward the corners they had just run from. Faster and faster their hooves pounded. The dust swirled behind them. As each approached his corner, neither slowed. Hetty Anne's scream froze me.

Where the pony's fence met the driveway, it curved and continued smoothly toward me. The colt's ended in a steel-barred gate as tall as I am. Perhaps the pony heard Hetty Anne and the colt did not. Perhaps the pony, as Hetty Anne claims, is wiser than any thoroughbred even without twelve years advantage and remembered. Perhaps the wide black planks of the curving fence were easier to see than the steel gate. At any rate, I watched helplessly as the pony braked into a skid that I did not believe had possibly commenced in time to save him from crashing. The colt never tried to stop. I was screaming with Hetty Anne.

As the colt hit the gate at top speed with a thousand pounds of bone and muscle, the gate bent like a clothes hanger and the colt catapulted over its top. He landed a body's length beyond, on the grass. Nobody knows how he could have done this, and Hetty Anne and I can't tell anyone; things happened too fast. There his body lay, spread out dead still on the ground. Thirty seconds before, that colt had been the Engles' best hope of running their farm another twelve months. Hetty Anne stood motionless in the pony's paddock, her hands clapped to her cheeks. I, too, stood disbelieving. Between us, the lather-dripping pony snorted and pawed the dirt. Behind us, traffic hummed. People who knew nothing of our anguish were driving unconcernedly by on the Clermont Road, while we stood in easy sight of them, staring at disaster.

The colt's neck rose slowly and slowly lowered. His legs began to struggle and went on struggling. The colt stood up, shook himself, and looked around. This was not possible, and I did not believe it. I did not move, and I don't believe Hetty Anne did, either. The thousand-pound colt began trotting down the drive toward me.

I didn't know how badly the colt had already hurt himself. I did know that once he made it to that busy road, there would be no chance of getting him back on the farm without mortal injury. Tossing his head and walling his eyes, he pranced toward me.

I knew this colt. I had never been on the same side of his fence with him, but I had often fed him clover across it. He was called Supernova, thanks to Dad. Dad had happened to be there when the colt had tried to be born upside down, and Mr. Engle had been obliged to reach into the mare and turn him over. Dad had held the mare's head. "Well, Rales," Mr. Engle had said, once the colt was on the straw and whickering. "What shall I call him till he sells?"

"Supernova," Dad said. "May he shine like his namesakes. May he, too, travel a hundred thousand miles a second!"

Yes, I knew this colt, and I knew he was the best bred and the best-looking on the farm and that the Engles could not afford to lose him. If he ever got where he was heading, no one would catch him till he got hurt. He would run until a bone broke or his heart burst or a car hit him. I stood my ground.

As the colt drew closer, I stretched my arms out wide. "Whoa, Super," I said, and he stopped. His whole body shone with sweat. He drew back his head and turned it to look at me sideways. I glanced around, trying to see without moving what there was I might offer him. I was afraid to turn my head enough to see where Hetty Anne was, dreading that any movement would make the colt bolt. Afterward she told me that she had stood stock still, afraid of the same thing.

Nothing green was within my reach but ragweed. Not a horse on the farm would glance at ragweed. Cautiously, I put out my hand as if I had something. Cautiously, Super's nose crept forward to snuffle it. Twice as cautiously, my hand eased back to take hold of his halter. His ears pricked. His skin shivered. My heart was pounding. My hand closed on his halter.

I had led some of the Engles' quiet old mares by the shank from time to time. I had never led any yearling. Even if I'd had a shank, there wasn't a chance I could take Supernova anywhere he didn't want to go. Dad says he must have been a little dazed from hitting that steel gate. With my hand gripping his halter as if it were a rope dangling me over a cliff, I turned him quietly around, and we walked up the drive and into the barn and into the first stall I saw open.

I bolted the stall door and leaned against it. My legs felt like ginger ale. Later Hetty Anne told me that she had climbed the fence into the drive behind us so that if Super shook me off and started back toward the road, she might have some prayer of heading him. "Prayer! Kate, I never prayed so hard in my life!" She came into the barn behind me just as Super started running around that strange stall as if he thought it was a space rocket about to take off with him. Hetty Anne and I closed the barn's end doors and she got a shank and moved him into his own stall. Then she buzzed the house on the intercom, and Mrs. Engle came running over.

Mrs. Engle got the horse vet on his car phone, and he said he would turn around and come immediately, but it seemed to take him forever. Hetty Anne and I showed Mrs. Engle the smashed gate and the gouged earth where the colt had landed. Mrs. Engle turned away and leaned against the fence, and I thought she was going to be sick.

Finally we heard Dr. Hornigan's tires in the driveway. "Supernova, eh?" he growled, striding into the barn. "It's never the cheap ones. You couldn't hurt that pony out there with an earthquake." He knelt on Super's straw and began feeling the leg with the most scrapes. His expression told us nothing. He moved from one leg to the next, and back to the

6

first. Finally he stood up. "Walk him down the aisle for me once, Laura."

Mrs. Engle walked the colt up and down the aisle. He did not limp. Dr. Hornigan nodded. "You can put him away. I'm going to give him some penicillin; he's got those little cuts. You won't get any scars, though. He'll be all haired over by sales time. I can't find any breaks." I saw the tears well up in Hetty Anne's eyes. Mrs. Engle sighed, a long sigh. "Come on back to the house, everybody," she said. "I just made doughnuts."

Dr. Hornigan smeared salve on Super's scrapes. "That knee is going to swell. Have Matt hose it. Looks like you haven't got a problem." For the first time Dr. Hornigan grinned, a great big grin.

I had never been such a heroine before. First Hetty Anne had to tell her mother and Dr. Hornigan how I had saved the colt's life, and then, after Mr. Engle got home, she and her mother told it all over to him.

I had to tell my parents myself, so I wasn't such a marvel in the version they heard. Even at that, I wasn't so impressed with myself as they were. Bravery, when you don't have to see anything suffering, let alone hurt it yourself, and there's no mess, and you only have to be brave for two or three minutes, isn't enough to prove you're tough enough to be a farmer. All the fuss people made over me was nice, but it doesn't soothe my worries about my future. But at that time, I wasn't worried.

CHAPTER 2

The Stabbing

*L*ast May the pastures turned lion-colored. The only green field on our place was the alfalfa Dad was raising for hay. The cows lowed to get into it, but turning cows loose on alfalfa is dangerous. I learned that the day they broke down a couple of fences and got into ours.

I was helping Dad mix grain in the barn. After a while, I started hoping Dad would send me to the house to fetch the two of us some ice water. "Boy," I hinted, "this would be thirsty work even on a *cool* day."

As usual when physical comfort crosses Dad's mind, he thought of his animals first. "It *is* extra hot, Kate," he agreed. "Maybe you better go out and check the cows' and ewes' fountains. Make sure they're functioning."

I headed for the cows' fountain first, but I didn't get around to putting my hand in it that day. One look at the empty field and flattened fence, and I yelled for Dad. We drove the cows into a paddock where they could stay till we got the fence mended, and Dad went to get his tools. I walked over to be sure the fountain in the paddock where we'd put the cows was running okay, but I didn't wet my hand there, either. I never got more than halfway to it. Out of the corner of my eye, I saw that something was on top of one of the cows. I knew—even as I stopped in midstep and jerked my head around so fast I felt fire shoot up my neck, I knew—that this could not be true. As my head turned, the cow toppled over. I screamed, and in that same moment saw that the cow's distorted shape was entirely her own. Nothing was on top of her; she was just incredibly swollen. She was so ballooned out, she looked as if she must explode. Her neck struggled, but her body was bloated and stiff-legged as a corpse.

Dad turned around and came running for the second time. Halfway to me, he looked where I was pointing and stopped momentarily. Then he dashed for the barn. Seconds later he was out again and racing toward us. In his fist was a sharp-ended metal tube as long as my hand.

I opened the gate to save him that half minute. By the time I could fasten it behind us, Dad had inspected the cow. I joined him fearfully. "Now watch this, Kate," he said. "I'll explain later." Without another word, he leaned against the prostrate cow and stabbed her in her side.

Green froth spewed up higher than his head. I gasped and swiveled and clapped both hands over my eyes.

"Pay attention!" Dad snapped. I pressed my hands harder against my face. Dad's strong grip closed on both my wrists, pulled them down to my sides, and turned my body to face the cow. "Kate, I would not have told you to watch if this weren't something you needed to see. You may have to do it yourself some day and nobody near to tell you how."

Green bubbles foamed out of the tube that protruded just below the cow's loin. The cow was deflating like a punctured tire. "That tool is a trocar," Dad said, holding me so I couldn't run or even turn away. He had to let go, though, when I began to throw up.

9

The tube was still draining viscous green foam from the cow's side. I turned my head away. "Kate," Dad said warningly, and I began to cry. Dad shook me, not hard, but angrily. I was astonished by this, and furious, too, which stopped my sniffles, but my neck wouldn't move. "You can get this lesson now," Dad said, "or you can get it twenty-four hours from now, but we're going to stand here till you get it. Do you want to work for other people all your life, or do you intend to farm this farm?"

I spat a couple of times, wiped my eyes with the back of my hand, next my nose, and finally my mouth. Then I faced Dad with what probably would have looked like a murderous scowl to any third person but which Dad accepted for attention.

"What I have done is puncture the cow's rumen, her paunch. That green stuff is nothing but chewed-up alfalfa. She's overstuffed her rumen, and it's quit working and filled with gas. If you hadn't seen her fall, it would have gone right on swelling till it put so much pressure on her lungs that she suffocated. Now come and see how to put a trocar in."

I had seen him put a trocar in. He had held its point against the cow's side between his left thumb and forefinger, then before I even had time to wonder what he was doing, he had slapped the other end with the palm of his right hand and driven it deep inside. I would have thrown up again just from remembering, if there had been anything left inside me. Instead I took a deep breath and moved closer to the cow. I don't think it would bother me to work for other people, but I do want to farm this farm.

"The trocar," said Dad, "has a little hole near its point; I'll show it to you when we take it out of her tomorrow." I heard that "we" like a little stone dropping in my stomach, but I tried not to change expressions. "All that gas she's collected is going to go into the tube through that hole, and out, as you're seeing, through the top. If we'd had time, we could have accomplished the same thing by running a tube down her throat, but once a cow goes down with bloat, you don't have minutes. She is about to die.

"Now. The important thing to remember if you puncture the wrong thing and kill your animal is that without you, she was going to die, anyway. She can't be any deader than she was going to be if you hadn't stuck her at all. But, you can learn the right place. Put the heel of your right hand here." He placed his own against the cow's backbone far enough toward her tail so that when my hand followed his, I felt no ribs under my palm. "Now put the heel of your left hand against her hip bone. Now touch your thumbs together. Where they touch is the place to puncture. Learn the place now, by sight, because you can't expect to feel those bones when the cow is bloated. The trocar lives in the barn medicine cabinet. You'll always find it there."

Up till that afternoon, I had taken for granted that Becky and I would take over running this farm some day. Since that afternoon, I have worried.

CHAPTER 3

A Test

I was lucky Lowlands County 4-H Clubbers got to go to camp in July last year, because by August, the drought was so bad, nobody was allowed to put water in a pool. Swimming in the pool was one of the three best things about my weeks at camp.

The other two: (1) Hetty Anne was my cabin's Junior Counselor; (2) When the ribbons were awarded on our last day, I got the one for archery.

I'd begun as early as Day One to believe that I might be Best Archer this year. I remember on Day One nocking the final arrow of my very first set and thinking, *This one will hit the bull's-eye,* and it did. Everyone who ever claps, clapped. (That means all of the girls, and those of the boys who aren't afraid they'll seem childish.) I stepped back under the pine trees with somebody else to let Rubylee Barlow take her turn.

Rubylee stood with her ankles together. Someone must have told her her legs look better that way, but it's no way to shoot. Hetty Anne had shown everybody the right way, but I wasn't surprised that she didn't correct Rubylee. Rubylee rides the same school bus we do, and goes to the same church, so Hetty Anne knows that she goes to pieces easily.

In addition to her feet not being planted sensibly, the camp's bow was too long for Rubylee. Her first shot rose in a limp arc and went piffle not even halfway to the target. "Way to go, Rube," her boyfriend called. First day at camp and Rubylee already had a boyfriend. Hetty Anne gave him a look, and he laughed. Rubylee mugged a hopeless expression back at all of us and tried to laugh herself. Her second arrow got as far as the target, all right, but about two yards to the left of it. The third was no better, and it was Morgan Culverhouse's turn. Rubylee didn't go sit by her boyfriend but came and stood by me with her back to him. "This is my least favorite class," she griped. "I hate myself when I flub up like that, and as soon as I flub the first shot, I know I'll miss with the others, too, because flubbing up in front of everybody turns my arms to sticks."

"I'm the same way," I said. I'm not always going out of my way to say reassuring things (or anything else) to Rubylee Barlow, but I didn't want to watch Morgan Culverhouse shoot.

"You!" said Rubylee. "You never miss the bull's-eye twice the same day."

"I practice with my parents all summer. You only shoot the week you're here. I bring my own bow, too. It's a big help, not being a stranger to your bow. I've used this one forever. Dad used to bring it to 4-H camp when he was my age."

"It's generous of Dad to let me have the bow Granddad made him," I remarked to Mom the summer he gave it to me.

She smiled, but she seemed to have something else on her

13

mind. "Your father would like you to have everything," she said, "so long as he is the one giving it to you."

I didn't think about that then—I was thinking about my new bow. Ever since this Easter, though, I have thought about it a lot.

Rubylee fingered my bow's smooth surface enviously. I'd been careful to give credit to how familiar I was with the bow, not the bow's superiority, because I didn't want Rubylee to ask to borrow it. Rubylee breaks things. "Where my arms and legs turn to sticks if people watch me is swimming," I told her. Like her and Hetty Anne, I grew up swimming in my neighbor Tom Allen's lake. I'd never been in a swimming pool till the first year I went to 4-H camp.

When Dad used to come to this camp, most of the kids were from farms, like him. Now farm kids like Rubylee and Hetty Anne and me are the exceptions. Clermont's 4-H'ers have been taking swimming lessons all their lives at the Y (and a few, like Morgan Culverhouse and her brother, at the country club). "The first time I jumped in that pool, I felt as if somebody'd kicked me right in the nose," I told Rubylee. "Nobody'd warned me about the chlorine. I just clambered out gasping, the quickest I could. All the town kids were laughing at me. I wanted to crawl under the cabin."

"Yeah, that stuff stangs," said Rubylee. She rubbed her nose. "But I still don't hate it the way I hate this old Robin Hood stuff."

"*I* hated it so much that first year, I even told the JC I was sick so she'd excuse me."

Rubylee grinned. "Did it work?"

I shook my head. "She laughed at me. She said more swimming was exactly the prescription for my ailment."

"That was *mean.*"

"Yeah, because I was so humiliated by the way I'd

14

thrashed and splashed that first day, I really did feel halfway sick."

I didn't tell Rubylee the whole story. I'd been nine, the youngest you can come to 4-H camp. I'd taken the JC aside and told her very low-voiced that I couldn't go in the water because I had my period. I didn't know what that meant. I'd heard one of the JCs say it the day before, and it had worked for her. When I tried it, though, my counselor looked startled and then her eyes widened like somebody trying not to smile. "You have what?" she asked. I told her again, and she went ahead and laughed.

"I don't think you look so bad swimming," Rubylee said.

I was encouraged to hear that, because I had decided to ask Hetty Anne to move me out of Beginners into Advanced. After the freedom of the Allens' lake, piddling around the shallow end of that pool was frustrating, and the other Beginners got younger every year. Also, you have to be in Advanced before you can use the diving board. I had decided it would be good for my character to make myself try to learn diving. Diving takes courage. Everybody thought I had courage the day I caught Super, but I found out otherwise the day that cow fell over. "Wish me luck," I begged Rubylee.

I went to the pool a little early for class. Hetty Anne was there even earlier, picking up anything someone might slip on. I was lucky to have Hetty Anne for swimming counselor, I thought, because she'd already seen what I could do in the lake. She wouldn't have to test me. That was important, because I knew I wouldn't do so well in the pool. I never have got used to the chlorine and crowding. I'm sorry for town kids who have to do all their swimming in squinchy little acid baths. In the Allens' lake, your eyes never get bloodshot; your hair never turns into Excelsior. It's so user-friendly, I've seen ducks swimming around the far edge when I was just quietly floating.

I helped Hetty Anne gather up forgotten towels and sun-glasses. At the far end of the pool another JC, Morgan Culverhouse's brother, Hume, was practicing diving. He had a figure like one of those Greek statues the *National Geographic* publishes photographs of, and his tan was all one color from the top of his forehead to the soles of his feet. He climbed up the steps to the diving board with his back perfectly straight, walked to the end in about four steps, raised his arms, bounced lightly once, and plunged with scarcely a sound. After he surfaced, he did it all again. He never glanced our way. He never looked left or right, just at the diving board or the water. Over and over. Someone should have been filming him. He was perfect.

"I'm glad you want to move up, Kate," Hetty Anne said. Across the pool, Hume Culverhouse surfaced, shook the water out of his black hair, and pulled himself easily onto the concrete. "I'll get somebody to check you, and if you pass, you can start with the Advanced group this hour. Hume?" she called.

I nearly fell into the pool. "*Hush*," I croaked. I grabbed her arm, turning her so that her back was toward Hume, who fortunately hadn't heard her. "I don't need—I don't need a *boy* to check out my swimming! You do it, for pity's sake!"

"Oh, Kate. Hume's the best swimmer in camp. All I could say would be, 'Great, Kate, you made it to the side!' or, 'Tough, Kate, you didn't make it.' What good would that do you? Hume can give you some pointers." She called Hume over and asked him to okay me for Advanced. Talk about arms and legs turning to sticks.

"Sure," said Hume.

I might have drowned.

"All they want to be sure of is that you can take care of yourself in the water," Hume said. "Let's just see if you can swim the pool's length."

I had to do something more ambitious than my usual dog paddle. I tried to coordinate the kicking of my legs with the reaching and pulling of my arms. Hume swam along to my right, using the sidestroke so he could watch me. This made me feel very funny all over. It's the kind of situation I might think about a lot afterward but cannot stand while I'm in it.

My head kept wanting to turn from side to side as I used first one arm, then the other. Thinking of how straight Hume's neck had been on the diving board, I tortured myself keeping mine stiff, my face toward him always. That made my ugly tongue a problem. I didn't want to show it to him the whole length of the pool, let alone spit water into his face with every stroke. Breathing with my mouth shut was hard, and once in a while I had to gasp, but I always clamped my teeth together again instantly. I couldn't believe it when we got to the end of the pool. I tried not to huff and puff climbing out, but I was about to die.

"Pretty good, Kate," Hume said. "You pass."

"I do?"

He smiled. "Couple of little things will make it easier for you. If you'll let your head turn with your stroke . . ." He showed me, reaching out first one arm, then the other, his neck twisting with each reach the way mine had tried to do. "And if you breathe through your mouth, you can take in more oxygen and you won't tire so fast."

"Oh," I said.

Across the pool, J. M. Stanley, who also was a JC last July, arrived with his cabinful of boys. He ran shouting up the diving board ladder, bounced hard four times, and plunged into the water yelling, *"Wahoo!"* The minute he surfaced, he wahooed again. The boys he had shepherded all stood at pool's edge watching him.

J.M. is the last one I want around when I'm wearing a bathing suit. He's the kind of smart-mouth who told Hetty Anne's sister Ursel right to her face that she is "stacked like a brick outhouse." (I would have pushed him smack in Tom Allen's lake, but Ursel just looked at him the way you look at something marked down that you've already got six of.)

Hetty Anne isn't shaped anything like Ursel; she looks more like one of those arrows we shoot. I am in between. I wondered if Hume noticed that kind of thing.

Standing so close to Hume, I could see that he had dark hair on his legs. The water running down them made paths in it. The boys in my class hadn't started growing hair on their legs yet, and I had thought that all crinkly straw-colored growth on J.M's was just one more sign of how common he is. I was a little sorry about Hume. It made him less like those Greek statues.

But not a lot. "That J.M. is such a show-off," I said. What I was saying but not out loud was, He's not even on the same planet as you.

"He's a pretty good diver," Hume answered.

I wished I hadn't said anything. Maybe now Hume thought I was catty. Maybe he would agree now with what J.M. had called me the first time I ever spoke to him: Prissface. Did he really believe J.M. was a good diver? (I didn't think J.M. could be good at anything.) Or do boys just stick together? I know that if J.M. had said to me, "Morgan Culver-louse thinks she's something," I just would have smiled. I hardly took any pleasure in having passed my swimming test. All afternoon, half my mind was worrying about what Hume thought of me now, and lying on my bunk after lights out, I was free to worry 100 percent.

As soon as we campers were in our bunks and the Adult Counselor was sound asleep (we always knew, because she snored), Hetty Anne and our other JC went to meet Hetty Anne's boyfriend for root beer at the Rec Hall. Only the AC slept. Some of the girls pulled their bunks together so they could talk, and Morgan Culverhouse played "La Traviata" on her tape deck. That wasn't the kind of music any of the other girls would have chosen. I think I was the only one besides Morgan who likes opera, and I didn't say anything, because why should I take up for Morgan? "If you listen to it once, you'll like it the second time," she told the others sweetly. She says everything sweetly. I was glad she was in my bottom bunk so I didn't have to see her. Morgan has beautiful clear brown eyes, and her eyelashes are thick as woolly-worm fur. I'm so fair, I have to blink for anybody to know my eyelashes are there, and my eyes can't make up their minds what color they want to be. They turn whatever the weather or what I'm wearing suggests to them—gray or green or various blues. It's embarrassing when I have to fill in a form. The blank left for *color of eyes* is always small.

"Things could be worse," says Hetty Anne, whose eyes are the color of cornflowers, night or day, drought or tornado. "If you had one eye one color and the other another, now *that* would be something to complain about. If you had one brown eye and one blue and lived in the Dark Ages, you'd have to choose one and wear a patch over the other. You couldn't ever get a husband. People thought a woman with different colored eyes was inconstant, and the only way to keep her from committing adultery was to lock her up in a convent all her life. Compared to that, now, you haven't got a problem."

I have, though, and my eyes are only part of it. Morgan sits right across the aisle from me in homeroom, and she keeps a tan all year. I don't complain to Hetty Anne about my skin, because hers is almost as pale, but mine is so skim-milky you can see my veins right through it, some places, and I can't get a tan even in August, and there are my arms on my desk every day right across the aisle from Morgan Culverhouse's. Morgan goes to the beauty parlor at least once a month and looks it. She has black hair cut way up the back of her neck and pointy over her ears, and bangs. She also has an older brother who will probably never look twice at any girl who isn't at least as pretty as his sister. Let alone one who forgets to sound *sweet* all the time.

Anyhow, I had passed my pool test, so that's how I moved from Beginners to Advanced Swimmer at 4-H camp last July. Camp this summer will be different from ever before: one of my two favorite JCs will not be there. Hetty Anne has a paying job lined up in Lexington. There's no way I would ask the other one his plans.

CHAPTER 4

Opals and Crystals

Dad grows the sweetest watermelons in Kentucky. He plants the seeds in little hills and then spreads so much straw around that no weed has a possibility of competing with them. We never have to hoe. All we have to do is count the gorgeous sun-colored blossoms, and watch the little melons replace them. And watch the little watermelons balloon. Morgan Culverhouse claims you tell a ripe melon by how it sounds when you thump it. Morgan took a 4-H seminar last summer called *Consumerama* that teaches you how to shop. Now she knows which sunblock she should buy before she goes to lie all afternoon beside the country club pool and how to choose the melon she's going to eat when she gets home. Dad says that thumping melons is for the unfortunate people who have to buy them at supermarkets. "Sometimes it works, and sometimes you open your melon and find it's as pink as the rose of Sharon and tastes like gelatin. People who grow their own don't run that *awful* risk," he congratulates us.

The time to pick a watermelon, Dad shows my sister, Becky, and me every summer, is when the top is the beautiful dark green of the grass that grows in the barn shade and the bottom is sort of whitish greenish yellow. Dad has never chosen us a melon that wasn't sweet as honey and red as cranberry juice. When he pushes Mom's French chef knife into a melon he has picked, that melon will just split the rest of the way open, it is so near to bursting with sweet juice. When Becky and I are waiting for the first watermelon to ripen, eagerness gets us near to bursting ourselves.

One morning last July, I rode to town with Dad. He had stuff to buy at the hardware store, and Mom gave me a list of things like envelopes and Duco cement to get for her at the Sundry Store. By the time I had found everything, Dad had his hardware and was waiting for me at the cash register. He was putting something in his pocket as I came up to him, but I thought nothing of it.

When Dad stopped at the gas station and bought ice, I had a good idea what we were going home to. Sure enough, the first watermelon of the year was waiting in the bathtub for that ice. Dad had sneaked out and picked it just before we left.

By the time that melon was cold, Dad had spread a bale of straw in the back of the pickup for Becky and me and the watermelon to ride on. "Late-twentieth-century hayride," he declared. Dad and Mom rode with the cab windows open, and we sang things like "Bill Bailey" and "On, On, U of K" together all the way to the pond in our woods. Sometimes Dad blew the horn, for emphasis. Of course by the time we piled out of the truck, there wasn't a frog in sight.

There is nothing like the year's first melon, and there is nothing like knowing that you can have absolutely all you could possibly want. We hadn't brought forks or plates: the knife was all that was going to need cleaning. Mom and Dad sat on a log to eat their wedges, but Becky and I sat right on the pond bank. The water was low from the drought, but we took off our shoes and socks and paddled our feet and spit our seeds into it. On about our third pieces, we were ready to slow down a little, and we tried to see if we could make our seeds collide in the air. We never succeeded, but somehow trying seemed hilarious.

When we had all eaten as much as we could dream of eating, I thought I might just lie back right where I was and sleep like a boa constrictor, but that's when Dad took the sack out of his pocket—the one he'd been stuffing there as I joined him in the Sundry Store. The sack's contents were: three jars of Magic Bubble Soap and four wands. Dad gave each of us a jar and a wand. He sat back down on the log beside Mom, and he and she took turns dipping their wands into Mom's jar. I unscrewed the lid on Becky's jar for her, and we all blew bubbles—huge, slow, shimmering bubbles, stately as the Goodyear blimp; little, gay, shining bubbles, quick, quick, quick, one right after another. I felt like one of those heroines in the fairy tales whose mouth pours forth roses and pearls every time she speaks.

Our bubbles floated out over the pond, rejoicing in the sunlight after being shut inside those jars. "When I was a little younger than Becky," I confessed, "I halfway believed that a soap bubble was to a fairy what a web is to a spider, and I was always trying to see the fairy fly away when a soap bubble popped."

"If she's there, you'll see her," was what Mom had answered when I had asked her about this notion. Mom never lied to Becky and me when we were little the way some parents do, not even about Santa Claus, but she didn't always nail us to the floor with the truth, either.

"My bubbles are not fairy cocoons," Dad said. "They are planets. I am creating a new solar system." Dad has been interested in astronomy ever since he took a course in it at the University of Kentucky about twenty years ago.

"I am blowing opals and crystals," Mom said, "for the girls to wear at their weddings."

Dad began giving his planets funny names, and Mom got to giggling so hard she had to forfeit some of her turns. Becky and I got to giggling just from listening to her. Pretty soon we were all helpless.

That was one of the few melons we got last summer. Dad had been keeping the vines alive by hand watering, but finally the drought got so bad he just had to give up. Come August, we didn't get enough rain to make a cactus bloom. The creek beds dried right down to rocks. The wheat that had shot up so green and straight drooped like summer candles left standing in their holders all week. We didn't harvest any wheat straw; Dad had to buy all the sheep's bedding. Our corn never got any taller than I am, and finally, like the wheat and soybeans, it just died. Everybody's did around here. Tom Allen turned his pigs into his cornfields. We don't have pigs. Our cornstalks just stood there, rattling.

Hay was the same story. That May first-cutting Dad and I drove the cows out of was all we got. By second-cutting time, the alfalfa was dead as everything else. Dad had to buy his winter hay off a truck from Michigan. So did Hetty Anne's father and everybody else around here.

I get a safe feeling every summer when I see the winter hay stacked high under shelter. Even last summer, knowing we'd paid for them with borrowed money, seeing those rows of meadow-smelling bales made my shoulder blades relax. As the drought went on, though, Dad began throwing hay to our sheep and cattle. By August, he was feeding more hay than he usually feeds in January. Finally he just had to sell the cattle. He got less than we had paid for them, but he would have lost more if he had gone on feeding them bought hay and bought corn. "How are we going to pay the bank back?" I asked Mom.

"Things will pick up," she said. "We don't have to pay them right away. We just have to make interest payments every six months. Don't worry about it."

She might as well have said, "Don't get sleepy." Paying interest is like renting money. Ten percent interest means that if you borrow one thousand dollars from the bank on New Year's Day, you have to pay them one hundred dollars by next New Year's Day, and you still owe them the thousand. Our interest is 12 percent right now, but the bank can raise that any time it wants to. How do I not worry about it?

"Maybe interest rates will come down, and we'll have less to pay than we think," I heard Mom encourage Dad.

Dad grinned, which he used to do a lot. "Maybe the Milky Way will come down," he said, "and we'll have star-spangled sheep."

CHAPTER 5

Orange-Coconut

Mr. Engle always sells all his yearlings in September. "We've got three fillies, a couple of chestnut colts, and Super," Hetty Anne told me. Super is a bay. "Super's the only one we expect to make much profit on." We were talking in the churchyard with one eye each on our parents. Services were over, but we didn't have to head for our cars till they quit talking to their friends. "The sales company hasn't told us what day they'll auction our six," Hetty Anne said. "I'm rooting for a weekend date, so Ursel and I can both help. If we sell on a weekday, Ursel can take a day off work, but I don't know if Pops will let me miss school."

Ursel Engle is a paralegal; she works in Lexington. I pulled my skirt and slip away from my hot legs. Even warm air cooled them. "How much does your father want for Super?"

"All he can get," Hetty Anne answered grimly. "We weren't in the best shape even before the whole state of Kentucky dried up."

We both fell silent, remembering rain. The grass we were standing on was bronze, and the velvety petunias that usually bloom around the church steps all summer were little sticks.

Two days later, Hetty Anne telephoned. "We heard from the sales company," she said. "Monday."

Crossing my fingers I asked, "What do your parents say about school?"

"I have to go."

I uncrossed my fingers. Maybe they did some good, though, because, come September, we learned that our county was having what they call an In-Service the second Monday. Only teachers had to come to school. This was good luck for me as well as for Hetty Anne, because she invited me to come out to the Keeneland Company's sales establishment and watch the excitement. "We might even get a little work out of you," she suggested straight-faced, "if Super gets loose."

Now I was the one to wonder what my parents would say. There was a good chance Dad had some all-day project in mind he needed my help with.

Mom grew up in Alexandria, Virginia, where my grand-mom still lives. She met Dad at the University of Kentucky. In their UK yearbook, she is wearing lipstick and a sorority pin, and her hair is curled. Her father was a stockbroker. He died before I was born, like Dad's parents. He was surprised that Mom chose to be a farmwife, she says. He thought it would be too hard for her to learn how, at her age. Dad says she learned fast, though, and was a help from day one. Then I came along and started learning from the time I could walk. That's the best way to learn anything, and now Dad depends on me for a lot.

I waited till halfway through supper. About the time Dad was ready for second helps, I mentioned Hetty Anne's invitation. "Fine," Dad said. "I'll drive you out to Keeneland right after breakfast Monday."

"I have to go to Lexington for my dental appointment that morning," Mom reminded us. "I can't take Becky, so . . ."

"I'll look after Becky," Dad promised. "Kate deserves to see Super sell."

Keeneland assigns horses they are going to auction to numbered barns, and the horses arrive there a few days early. People who like a horse's pedigree can come to his stall and ask to see him walk outside. Monday morning I ate a big breakfast. There's a lot of work to showing potential buyers yearlings. I didn't have to tell Hetty Anne that I wasn't eager to go in the stalls of a bunch of excited horses. We had agreed that inside chores were hers and outside chores were mine. That meant that things like filling water buckets and removing manure from the straw in the stalls were her job, and things like filling hay bags and removing any deposits that got dropped in the walking ring were mine. I figured I was going to need my strength. As I swallowed the last of my eighth waffle, I saw that Becky hadn't finished her first. I knew Mom would say the two remaining waffles were Becky's, but Becky said she didn't want them, so I ate those two also, and was ready to go.

"Come along for the ride?" Dad asked Becky.

I had thought the reason Becky seemed mopey might be that I was going to the auction and she wasn't, so I was surprised when she answered, "No, thanks."

Dad was surprised, too. He and Mom have the rule that if they *ask* us, we're entitled to say no. Having given Becky a choice, he couldn't turn around and say, "Hop in the truck!"

I tried to help. "Don't you want to say good-bye to Super?"

"*No*," Becky answered, and pushed her chair away from the table.

"Hey," I told her, "you really got up on the wrong side of the bed!" She didn't look at me.

"Wouldn't you like to see Keeneland in September?" Mom asked her. "The dogwoods will be gorgeous!" They were, too, all wine colored.

"We have a dogwood in the front yard," Becky said in a muffled voice, and we do: one small young skinny dogwood. A puppywood, that's what.

"It won't just be Super," Dad told her. "There'll be hundreds of yearlings, from all over the country, and hundreds of people, from all over the world!"

I didn't quite catch Becky's answer. "It makes me scared," was what I thought she said. I don't know what Dad thought.

"We won't be there long," he mentioned, "just long enough to drop Kate off. Then I thought I might go to Victorian Square and buy ice cream. If you come along, we'll do that, and then take a ride on the merry-go-round."

Becky adores the merry-go-round at Victorian Square. She didn't smile, though. She opened her mouth, but before she could say anything, Mom spoke over her head to Dad. "Careful what you promise, unless your pockets are jingling. This week's household recreation budget has enough to pay for either ice cream and the merry-go-round *or* for LaNelle Barlow to sit Becky while you're gone, but not both."

Rubylee's older sister, LaNelle, is Becky's least favorite sitter. Mom wasn't exactly threatening Becky. She was just making the point that Becky couldn't stay home alone.

If Dad had any money he didn't say so. He stuck his hand out at Mom palm upward, and she counted him out some dollars. He put them in his wallet and turned to Becky. "Which will it be?" he asked her cheerfully.

"I guess I'll come," she whispered.

29

I was too intent on my own doings to wonder about Becky's gloominess very long. To begin with, Dad let me drive the pickup from the garage to the road.

Three years from now when I'm old enough for my learner's permit, I'll be more than ready for it. I thought about what a good one Dad is to teach a beginner how to drive—or anything else—after he took the wheel. Dad never makes fun of a mistake or gets cross at having to show somebody twice. He never gives half an explanation because he's too busy to give the whole. The only time he gets impatient is when he is disobeyed (if I don't look at the bloated cow he's told me to watch him treat, for example). Then he becomes a different man.

I had expected Dad just to pull up and let me out behind the barn where the Engle yearlings were, but he parked. "I need to speak to Matt about something," he explained. "You come, too," he told Becky pleasantly. He wasn't making the same mistake twice!

Usually Becky keeps up pretty well, but that morning she seemed to be hanging back. I thought probably it was because I was keeping hold of her hand. She hates that, but I was afraid a colt would get away from somebody and start racing around. The people who show yearlings are never any bigger than Hetty Anne. ("A big groom dwarfs the horse," Mr. Engle explains. "You want your *yearling* to look big; *he's* the one that's for sale.")

I caught a glimpse of Ursel, hurrying into one of the stalls, but I didn't see Hetty Anne. Mr. Engle was standing in the middle of the walking ring beside the barn talking to a couple of men in bush hats and open-collared shirts. Dad joined them while Becky and I were still only about halfway there. He was the best-looking of the four, I thought. Trying to cheer Becky up, I asked her didn't she agree.

"I guess so," she said, not looking at him, or me, either.

When we finally caught up with Dad, I learned that the men were Australians waiting for Ursel to lead Mr. Engle's only gray filly out for them to inspect. So that's where Hetty Anne was—making sure the filly had no straw in her tail, making sure the mane was all hanging on the proper side. I thought Hetty Anne would be as glad as I was the Australians weren't looking at Super. Both of us were hoping Super would run his races in America, where we could read about them in the sports section.

"Such a long face for so early in the day, mate," one of the Australians, a chunky man about Dad's age, teased Becky. Becky said nothing.

"I think she's a little chilly," I said, embarrassed for her.

"Chilly!" he exclaimed. He and his friend were both wearing short-sleeved shirts. "Well, we can take care of that. Just hop in my pouch!" Becky stared. "Didn't you know all Australians had pouches?" he asked her. "That's where we carry the little Australians."

"That's kangaroos," said Becky.

The other man laughed, but the chunky Australian just widened his eyes. "Well, I *am* a kangaroo, mate." He held his right forearm up for Becky to see how hairy it was. "See my fur?"

Even in a good mood, Becky detests being talked to as if she were a little girl. She turned her back on both Australians and asked Dad if she could wait for him in the Engles' tackroom.

"You'll be warm there, Becky," Mr. Engle said. "Those

comfort-loving daughters of mine brought a space heater."

By the time I got back from shepherding Becky across the barnyard, the Australians were gone and Ursel had joined Dad and Mr. Engle. Ursel was wearing jeans and T-shirt like Hetty Anne and me, but her eye makeup was perfect as always. Ursel wears green and blue eye shadow, and lots of mascara. Hetty Anne was in Super's stall, slicking him up for two business-suited Japanese men. "The one wearing the camera is the golf champion of Japan," Ursel whispered to me, "and the other is his interpreter."

I never see anything about Japanese racetracks in the *Herald-Leader*.

Mr. Engle had hired a young man to show the colts. "These daughters of mine are strong enough to keep me in line," he said to Dad, "but they're not quite a match for a stud horse like Super. He's grown a little bit since Kate led him by the nose this spring." Dad snorted at that "keep me in line" bit. "It's true," Mr. Engle protested. "I believe I'm the most henpecked man in Lowlands County!" He said this trying to look beaten down, but laughing. "I realize you're just as outnumbered as I am, Rales, but your girls are smaller. You're only chickpecked." Then he had to go tell the Japanese golf champion—or rather, his interpreter— that one of Super's brothers had won a race since the catalog was printed.

I knew that Mr. Engle also was hoping Super would be bought by an American—not for sentimental reasons, but because he had to think about trying to auction Super's little sister next year. More Americans come to Kentucky auctions than anybody else, naturally, and Americans will know more about Super's victories if he wins them in America.

Mr. Engle didn't come back right away. We could see that

the golf champion was asking the interpreter questions which the interpreter was asking Mr. Engle, and Mr. Engle was answering the interpreter, and the interpreter was telling the champion what Mr. Engle said, and then the champion was asking another question. Meanwhile, the groom hadn't even closed the stall door on Super when a thin-lipped man in a white Irish linen snap-brimmed cap walked up, caught his eye, nodded with his head toward Super, and lifted his eyebrows.

The groom led Super back to the walking ring. The thin-lipped man watched Super walk, felt his legs, measured the bottom of his right front foot, nodded, and walked away. I sighed. "He may be back in thirty minutes," Hetty Anne said, "with a millionaire client."

"Way to talk," said Ursel.

The big farm showing yearlings out of the barn across the yard from Mr. Engle's stalls was using the same walking ring. They had lots of help, all wearing red jackets with the farm's name stitched in white letters across their backs. Ursel seemed to know one of them. They were passing their customers trays of dainty little beaten biscuits and ham, and the one who knew Ursel brought a tray over and offered us each a biscuit. He must have been someone who knew Ursel from college, because I don't think anybody who knew her from her law office would have recognized her—not from a distance, anyway. For the office, Ursel rotates five identical blue-gray shirtwaists with three suits: one black, one gray, and one navy blue. The jackets are boxy, and the skirts come below the knees. Her makeup is the same, though, whether she is chasing barn cats or insurance fraud. When Ursel blinks, her eyelashes remind me of a monarch butterfly I watched emerge from its chrysalis and then just sit for a long time, fanning its sticky wings dry. Ursel butter-flied her lashes at the fellow in the red jacket, and I could see he'd rather have been working for Mr. Engle.

I decided to take my biscuit to Becky. Dad still hadn't been able to talk to Mr. Engle.

Becky didn't even have the space heater turned on. She was sitting on a bale of hay. She turned her face away as I came in. "I don't want any," she said.

She was crying! I sat down on the hay beside her and put my arm around her. "What's the matter, honey?" I coaxed. "Don't you feel well? What is it?"

"It makes me sad," she sobbed. "It makes me sad."

I hugged her. "We'll all miss Super, but there'll be more yearlings next year." She sobbed harder than ever. "Super has to go to school," I told her, "to learn how to win races. He can't stay home forever any more than you and I can. What if Mom carried on like this come August when you start school?"

She lifted her face. Where she had wet me felt cold. "Go to school?" she said.

She thought all the yearlings were going to be *eaten*. We all supposed she knew that what Keeneland sells is race horses, but somebody in her Sunday School class the day before had told her about his older brother who raised a calf for a 4-H project. The calf had been sold at auction to a fast-food chain. Any animal sold at auction, this boy assured Becky, went straight to the butcher. She couldn't bear to tell Super good-bye; she couldn't bear to look at any of the yearlings. She could hardly bear to look at any of us, we all seemed so hard-heartedly happy. I had to tell her the truth three more times to convince her of it. Then I offered her my ham biscuit again, and she ate it in two bites.

I felt awful that Becky had been so miserable. I felt awful until I reflected that now she was on her way to ride the merry-go-round, and now we were all going to have ice cream for supper, and neither would have happened if she hadn't been mixed up.

Becky hopped up from her hay bale, and we rejoined Dad, who was still waiting to talk to Mr. Engle. The white-capped man was back, with a red-haired woman in wrap-around sunglasses, who was saying something to Mr. Engle. Mr. Engle was looking very attentive. Held by the groom, Super stood before them like a statue titled *Nobility*. The woman with red hair talked and smiled; the man with thin lips never moved them. When they left, the groom started leading Super to his stall, and Mr. Engle joined us. "Well, Rales, I think she's sold on him. She's got money, too. Did you get a look at that emerald?" The red-haired woman had worn three or four huge rings on each freckled hand.

Just then Super made a deposit, right in the path. Then all three fillies started whickering for hay. By the time I had another breathing space, Dad and Becky were gone.

I began to try to keep a list of who-all looked at Super.

A Californian in a corduroy jacket and a silk maroon scarf around his neck. (Good.)

A couple of Irishmen who talked to each other intently the whole time Super walked around the ring in front of them (as if he owned it) without ever taking their eyes off him. (Not so good.)

The red-haired woman. "She told me she liked his action," Mr. Engle said happily. (Since I never heard her speak, I didn't know whether she was a Good or a Not-so-good.)

The Japanese golf champion took his picture. (N.S.G.)

Six tall Arabs and a little Texan, all in blue jeans. The

Texan also wore boots and a big hat just the way you'd expect. The Arabs wore running shoes. "The Texan trains horses for the Arabs," Hetty Anne told me. "He used to be a jockey." He was the only one who talked to Mr. Engle. The Arabs stood back watching with one expression on all six faces, one expression which never changed. "The one scratching himself is a prince," Hetty Anne told me. "When he comes to an auction, he brings all his nephews and parks his jet across the road at the airport. One of his nephews talked to me last time Pops had a colt as good as Super, but he isn't here today. He told me he was studying petroleum engineering at the University of Oklahoma."

"Will Super go to Arabia if the prince buys him?" I asked.

"No, to England."

"Well," I said, "that's closer than Australia."

The next looker was a Kentuckian in a blue turtleneck and a tweed jacket with leather elbow patches who scribbled on Super's catalog page for at least three minutes before he went away. I watched him hopefully. "Wouldn't you like to know what he wrote?" I asked Hetty Anne.

"Not necessarily," she said. "Might be bad."

I got too busy to keep up my list, but I know that Super had lookers from Mexico, New York, Arkansas, Canada, and Puerto Rico. The Puerto Ricans came back three times, so I was more worried about them than any of the others. "You girls are worried about what's only the second most important question," Mr. Engle said. "The most important question isn't where Super goes, but what he brings." As usual, he was laughing, but Ursel and Hetty Anne weren't.

Finally the time came to show Super in the walking ring inside the sales pavillion itself. People who had never come to his barn leaned on the ropes around the ring and looked at him now. Then Keeneland's groom took him from ours and led him backstage. We hurried to get seats inside, just in time to see Super led out on the stage between the auctioneer's raised booth and the audience. Now Mr. Engle looked just as sober as the rest of us. I was sitting between him and Hetty Anne. Ursel had been right behind me, but had peeled off at the last minute. I figured the excitement had sent her to the bathroom. I hoped she wouldn't find a line! Keeneland can sell horses like lightning, Hetty Anne had told me.

Several men in green jackets stood on the floor with the audience. Each man's job was to watch his part of the room for bidders, and yell up at the auctioneer when he found one. Ursel still hadn't shown up when the auctioneer finished his spiel about what a gorgeous yearling Super was and asked for bids.

The auctioneer's chant was unintelligible to me now. All I ever made out was the "who'll gimmes." He asked that over and over because not one spotter saw a single bid.

The spotters gripped their sales catalogs and nervously searched the room. I searched it even more nervously. I saw at least eight white caps, most too far away to identify, or to see what color hair the people sitting beside them had. ("She's a sure bid," I had heard Mr. Engle tell Dad.) I saw the Puerto Ricans; I saw several people who had seemed to like Super. None of them was moving. Hetty Anne and Mr. Engle weren't moving, either, just staring up at the board on the wall where bids get posted in lights, and where nothing was posted. I heard myself swallowing.

Way down in front, a couple rose and started walking up the aisle toward us. My heart stopped beating, and my hands tightened on the arms of my seat. It was the white-capped man and the red-haired woman. Mr. Engle saw them, too. His back went rigid.

They walked right past. They came near enough to touch and never seemed to see us. They weren't paying the least attention to the auctioneer behind them, begging for a bid. Mr. Engle didn't turn his head as they went by, but I did. They went right out the door. They never glanced back.

Mr. Engle's face had broken into a sweat. The groom began another turn around the stage with Super. Suddenly one of the spotters yelled. Lights blazed on the board. A bid! Almost before I could react to what a small bid it was, three more came in so fast I couldn't even tell which spotters had seen the bidders, let alone see the bidders myself. Ursel slipped into her seat beside Mr. Engle. "Good girl," he told her. I didn't speculate why: the number on the board was changing again. The Puerto Ricans were leaning forward. One nudged another, and a spotter shouted. The six Arabs were staring at Super with the same expression they'd worn back at the walking ring, and the little Texan had his hat pulled down low over his face. The Californian ran his finger between his neck and his silk scarf. The lights kept dancing. The auctioneer seemed as excited as I was. He punctuated his gibberish with a gloating number every time the bid went up another thousand. The Engles began to grin.

At last only two people were contending to buy Super. One was somewhere to the left of us, and one I believed was somewhere in the back. Before I could identify either of them, both stopped. The auctioneer gabbled faster than ever. The spotters pounded their catalogs and waved their right hands in the air, first with five fingers up, then four, finally just one. One spotter, who didn't know Mr. Engle, even caught *his* eye and beckoned frantically at *him* to bid. The auctioneer read the number on the board in a warning voice and said, "Once!" Three times and Super would be gone to the bidder on our left. Everybody in the auditorium seemed to be holding his or her breath. "Twice!" said the auctioneer. The room was hushed. Then somebody raised the bid—not one thousand but five thousand dollars. The audience gasped. The auctioneer named the new price three times and pounded his podium with his hammer. Sold! The audience broke into applause.

The groom led Super off the stage. People were looking all around to see who the winner was, but the auctioneer's man who usually ran to photograph the buyer and get his signature didn't appear. A strange sensation in my spine seemed to be telling me that that last big raise was a joke. Super would have to be brought back onstage because no one had bought him yet. How far back would they roll the numbers? Mr. Engle saw my face and patted me on the arm, laughing once more. "It's okay, Kate. The bid came from the walking ring, that's all."

Nobody had explained to me, when we'd been watching our groom show Super off to those rope hangers, that the men in green jackets watching them, and us, too, were bid spotters.

The four of us hurried back to Super's stall to find out, when the new owner came to claim him, whose colt Super was now.

It was the red-haired woman, still in her wraparound sunglasses.

Super brought far more than any of Mr. Engle's other yearlings. I was in a daze the rest of the day, but I do remember that the Australians bought the gray filly. They told us they would name her Waltzing Matilda. They told us they bought only gray horses—so Super never had been in any danger of going to Australia. Hetty Anne explained Ursel's brief disappearance, too. "What'll frequently happen is, everybody waits for the other fella to stick his neck out first. The smart owner has somebody like Ursel planted to get things started for him, if she has to." Like the red-haired woman, Ursel had bid from the walking ring.

"I was scared to death the spotters wouldn't notice a female in jeans!" she told us. She has a laugh like her father's. "I had my breath all drawn to *scream* if nobody saw my arm waving!"

The Engles drove me home, and the eight of us sat around eating ice cream, and I got to hear all over again what a heroine I'd been back in May. Dad and Becky had bought a gallon of a kind we'd never had before, orange-coconut. All my life, if I ever eat orange-coconut ice cream, I will think of Supernova.

Dad and Becky must be psychics, because what nobody could have told them was, Super was going to Florida.

CHAPTER 6

Burlap and Sequins

The red-haired woman paid so much for Supernova that I thought the Engles' money worries were over. In December, I found out just how wrong I was. Our school bus is cold all winter, but it got much colder as Hetty Anne told me. Mr. Engle wasn't able to pay the bank all the interest he's supposed to pay them every six months, and Mr. Culverhouse told him they wouldn't lend him any more money. "That's not what Mr. Culverhouse said, of course," Hetty Anne went on. "He said they *couldn't* lend him any more. The bank added the December interest payment to what Pops already owed them and started charging interest on that, too, of course. They gave him three months to pay them all he owed, by which they mean, to sell out, because of course there's no other way we can pay them off."

"Where will you *live?*" I finally asked.

Hetty Anne didn't look at me. She looked at the books in her lap, but I didn't think she saw them. Maybe she was seeing her big old comfortable stone house, and the oak tree shading it that was there before Daniel Boone shot his first Kentucky squirrel. Maybe she was seeing her mother's face when her dad came home from the bank and told her what they said. "Pops is looking for a horse farm that needs a manager," she answered me at last. "A house on the farm always goes with a job like that, and they might let him keep some of our mares with theirs—the best ones, anyhow. Otherwise we'll have to sell them all, and nobody's getting what he paid for mares right now. Trouble is, the old farms already have managers, of course, and nobody's starting any new farms *now*. Why would they, with average thoroughbreds selling like snowplows in August?

"We might buy a mobile home, if our place brings enough, so we'll be ready to go wherever Pops finds work. Where will the horses live? that's the real question. Can't put *them* in a camper."

The Engles put their farm up for sale. They also advertised for B&Bs—bed-and-breakfasters. Hetty Anne moved out of her room into Ursel's, and Mrs. Engle put her great-grandmother's best quilt on the bed, and a picture of Secretariat on the wall. "The day Super wins a race," Hetty Anne said, "Secretariat's coming down and Super's going up."

I had thought it would be awful to have strangers in the house, but not to hear Hetty Anne's stories. You'd think B&Bs were the greatest thing in entertainment since satellite dishes.

"You should brood less and take what comes more, Kate," Hetty Anne says. She reminds me of times that something I thought was bad turned out to be good—like when I read in the *TV Guide* that the Reds had a game the same time as PBS had "Anne of Green Gables." The first thing that had popped into *my* mind was, Morgan Culverhouse has her own set. She can go in her bedroom and watch any program she likes. Hetty Anne's reaction was, "You and I will have more fun watching together."

I can't deny that, and then, Super got loose. If I'd had my

own set like Morgan, Hetty Anne and I wouldn't have caught Super and saved his life. "See, Kate," Hetty Anne had said, "you never know what good luck is, so you might as well take what you get." Dr. Hornigan was driving away before we even remembered that we *both* had missed "Anne of Green Gables." But the last Friday before Christmas vacation, PBS showed it again. Our TV wasn't working, and we were waiting till we sold our spring lambs to get it fixed, so the Engles invited me again.

"We hope Kate can stay for supper Friday," Mrs. Engle told Mom. "Matt can deliver her home when he picks Rales up for Club." The Lowlands Club was having its monthly evening lecturer Friday. Hetty Anne's wrong, I thought. Sometimes you do know when you're having good luck. Now besides watching "Anne of Green Gables," I was going to get some of Mrs. Engle's pie, and I was going to get a look at Hetty Anne's newest undertaking.

When Hetty Anne and I signed up for 4-H this school year, we both chose Sewing Modeling projects. Everybody expected us to make dresses, but I got busy making a tool apron, and Hetty Anne set to work on a dazzling pure white coat.

I remember helping Dad fence when I wasn't even Becky's age, carrying his bag of staples for him from post to post. "She'll make a farmer," he bragged to Mom when we came in for lunch the first day. "I never have to tell her when I need a staple. I just lower my hand, and there it is."

I remember how proud I felt, but I also remember how the ringing of the hammer on the steel staples hurt my ears, and how I couldn't spare either hand to put over them. I wished then I had pockets for those staples so that one hand would be free. The apron I was making had plenty of loops and pockets and was for Dad. I want him to know how I appreciate that he has never complained about not having sons to help him farm, the way Rubylee Barlow's father complains—not even in a jokey way like Mr. Engle.

A coat, though—that was a different world of difficulty. Especially pure white. I imagined Hetty Anne was having to keep her workplace as clean as a surgeon's.

Tuesday morning as I took my bus seat, Hetty Anne was smiling. "We've got a B&B for the whole week: an artist." I pictured somebody setting up his easel in one of the Engles' pastures and painting mares and foals, but no, Hetty Anne said, horses didn't have anything to do with this artist's coming. "We're cheaper than any place he could get in Lexington, any place with room for his supplies, I mean. He doesn't paint pictures, he *creates* them, and that takes lots of supplies. He's going to wrap the Energy Tower in silver-sequined burlap."

"Wow!" The Energy Tower is the tallest building in Lexington—thirty-two stories. "That's crazy."

"Isn't it?" Hetty Anne agreed cheerfully.

"I don't see how he can do it in one week, either."

"I hope he can't," said Hetty Anne.

The bus had reached the Fletchers' stop, so I turned my head away from our window. The Fletchers had their plastic Santa Claus on the roof already, including the reindeer with the red light bulb in its nose. "Better get used to it"; Hetty Anne giggled. "It'll be there till Easter."

"Maybe if your artist has some burlap left over, he could wrap the Fletchers' house," I suggested. "What's his name?"

"Cheops."

"Well, let's ask Mr. Ops—"

"Not Ops, *Key*-ops."

"Oh. Cheops Somebody, or Mr. Cheops?"

"Your guess is as good as mine. He's already paid cash for the week, whichever. He said his last creation was in Louisville, so Mom called Uncle Frank before she took his money." Mrs. Engle's brother manages one of the biggest department stores in Louisville. "Uncle Frank said Cheops was a sound businessman and wouldn't cut our throats or burn the house down, and he sent Mom this article from the Louisville paper."

Cheops, the *Louisville Courier-Journal* said, was born in Cairo during an air raid, but moved to New York at five when his mother became an interpreter at the UN. During his first five years as an artist, no one bought his drawings, and he almost starved. Then he persuaded Egypt's government to let him put yellow polka-dotted slip covers on the Great Sphinx. The idea was to promote Egypt's tourist industry and demonstrate the superiority of her cotton with one gesture. "Make no small gestures!" the article quoted Cheops.

Photographers came from all over the world to record the new art form. Whatever this did for Egypt, said the *Courier-Journal*, it made Cheops famous. Now his drawings and collages and his scale models of his projects sell for thousands of dollars apiece. He spends all of it on his creations, the *Courier-Journal* said, such as covering Louisville's newest fountain with an enormous river-colored tarpaulin that it took six helicopters to drop in place.

There was a color photo of Cheops with the article. I was surprised that he had curly red hair. "His father was Irish," said Hetty Anne.

We had reached her driveway. The FOR SALE sign was as ugly as a swastika. I had learned not to ask if there'd been

45

any lookers. Nobody else had been making any more profit breeding thoroughbreds lately than Mr. Engle.

Hetty Anne was going to get her coat-work out and show it to me after we saw "Anne of Green Gables," but the closing credits were still running when we heard a car drive up, and we hurried to the front hall. Hetty Anne wanted me to get a good look at Cheops.

The person who opened the door and came in carrying a suitcase was Ursel, back from four days of reading Cincinnati hospital records for an insurance case. She set her suitcase down. "Hi, Kate. Hi, Sweetie. Anything new?"

"We have a B&B," Hetty Anne answered. "Come take a look at my old room."

I followed the two of them upstairs to hear what Ursel would say.

You couldn't see Mrs. Engle's antique quilt for the drawings on the bed. There was a model of the Energy Tower on the bureau, and a model of the Statue of Liberty in the middle of the floor. Secretariat's portrait was draped with burlap. "He didn't waste any sequins on it," Hetty Anne pointed out. The wastebasket was also wrapped, and the room's one chair.

Ursel stood in the doorway, her blue-and-green eyelids raised almost out of sight. "What is going on?"

"Art," Hetty Anne replied.

"Art." Ursel picked up the burlap-wrapped wastebasket. "What's it supposed to be?"

Hetty Anne slapped one hand flat on her chest, the way she had told me Cheops did when he made a pronouncement. " 'My art is *nonrepresentational!*' " she quoted. " 'Cheops does not paint bowls of daisies or scowling gentlemen surrounded by their julep cup sets!' Too bad you're not a member of the Lowlands Club." Hetty Anne's hand and voice dropped again. "Our nonrepresentational artist is tonight's speaker."

"Oh, too, *too* bad," said Ursel.

We had just finished supper when Cheops arrived. Mrs. Engle was cutting a big pie made from the Engles' own cherries, and Ursel had hung her four-in-hand and boxy jacket on the stair rail and gone down to the basement to get some ice cream out of the freezer. I was nearest the door to the front hall. "Step out and see if he'd like some pie, Kate," Mrs. Engle asked.

Cheops wore horn-rimmed spectacles, just like his photograph; chambray jeans; a light green turtleneck; and no shoes or socks. His feet hadn't shown in the photograph. His toes were hairy. "Won't you join us for dessert, Mr. Cheops?" I asked.

"*Cheops*," Cheops corrected me. "Cheops has no titles. Americans are hung up on their Doctor, their Judge, their Sister, Brother, General. Cheops needs no titles." His right hand clapped his chest. "Cheops is Cheops." The hand fell to his side, and he stuck his curly head into the dining room. "Thank you so much, Mrs. Engle, but no time. Lecture preparations to make, and my assistant hasn't even arrived!"

"There's lots of time," Mr. Engle declared. "Come on—take a seat so I won't be so outnumbered."

"Thank you, but I"—Cheops paused as Ursel emerged from the basement with the ice cream—"would be delighted." He followed his head into the dining room and held Ursel's chair for her, the chair she sat in every night with no help from anybody. Ursel butterflied her eyelashes. Soon Cheops was telling her, while the rest of us listened also, how he got fifty thousand dollars for a scale model of what the Statue of Liberty would look like in a red, white, and blue Orlon shroud. The millionaire buyer had donated the model to the Smithsonian Institution in Washington, D.C., he boasted. "With his money, I bought the fabric for my Lexington creation."

"Fifty thousand dollars for fabric?" Mrs. Engle murmured.

Cheops shrugged. "For this creation, money hasn't been the hard part. Those *mossy fossils* who supervise inhaling and exhaling in Lexington have been the problem. Imagine: in the heart of this city of little two-story period-piece houses trying to look as if great-great-grandmother just finished tea, soars my offering to the Artistic Spirit in the Bluegrass *Today*. From its summit calls Madonna's dynamite song, 'Express Yourself.' *Fantastic*, no?"

"*Fantastic*," Hetty Anne agreed with a straight face. I had to cover my giggle with my napkin. Hetty Anne thinks Madonna belongs in a zoo.

"Very *today*," Ursel seconded. Her office is in the building next to the Energy Tower. I could see her whole firm locking its doors for a two weeks' vacation at about the third "Express Yourself."

Cheops turned delightedly back to Ursel. "This has not been grasped by Lexington's dinosaurs. Even though Madonna's beautiful music would play for two weeks only, still it would violate this, it would violate that.

"I tell those dinosaurs, 'Make no little plans!' I ask them, 'Are you going to sit back and let Louisville be the *big-shouldered* city in Kentucky, while Lexington stays the *little old lady*? Accept the gift of my total creation, and Lexington will be CBS! She will be NBC, ABC, *PBS*!'"

Cheops's glasses were getting steamy. "Have some more pie," Mrs. Engle said soothingly, cutting a big piece. "Where will your next project be?"

Cheops stuck his plate at Mrs. Engle, but answered her question as if Ursel had asked it. Ursel blinked carefully. "Tonight, I ask this Lowlands Club for help toward my Fourth of July creation, my 'Statue of Liberty *Today*.' The banks will lend me the monies. I give them a few drawings for security." I saw Mr. and Mrs. Engle exchange glances. "What I need is letters—hundreds, thousands of letters, to overpower unappreciative opposition. The traffic policemen, the D.A.R., the Pigeon Roost Preservers of America—dozens of organizations must be convinced that my art is the will of the people."

"Have you ever had a project turned down?" Hetty Anne asked.

"All my projects are turned down. Cheops never gives up. In the end, either Cheops has won, or he is still going to. Well. Sometimes I have to give in on a detail." He muttered something.

"Have some more ice cream," Mrs. Engle said.

Cheops held his plate out. "Petty disappointments never depress me," he told Ursel. "In discouraged moments, I am borne up by my dream, the one I come back to after every successful creation, the *ultimate* creation, the goal of my artistic career." He waited for Ursel to ask him what that was.

Ursel often seems to be more interested in you than she is, because she wears contact lenses. They make her stare straight at you while you answer questions, and they make her eyes shine. Before I caught on, I used to make my answers longer and longer. She went right on looking fascinated until one day she sat down while I was still answering, and I realized I had worn her out. I sympathized with Cheops. "What is the goal of your artistic career?" I asked him.

"Ah. What is the super colossus, the greatest artifact of all? Fifteen hundred miles of brick and stone—"

"The Great Wall of China," Hetty Anne said quickly.

Cheops beamed. "I will cover the Great Wall of China with flowing folds of Chinese-red silk."

We all fell still. I felt a little dazed, and I guessed everybody else did, too. Mr. Engle cleared his throat. Just then the telephone rang with a call that turned out to be for Cheops. He left the room, and Mrs. Engle said, "Matt," in her warning voice. Mr. Engle's grin broke surface.

"Have some coffee," Mrs. Engle said severely.

When Cheops came back, his hair looked as if he had been running his hands through it. "My assistant is in Nashville, Tennessee!" he announced. "He missed the exit! What is to be done? Cheops must have a demonstrator at his lecture. To prepare this demonstrator takes half an hour at least. It is impossible to drive from Nashville, Tennessee, to Clermont, Kentucky, in twenty minutes. Beautiful lady!" He flung himself into his chair beside Ursel. "Would you assist in this emergency?" Ursel stared at him. "Do it for art, if not for Cheops!"

Ursel's page-boy bounced on her shoulders. (Ursel takes a curling iron in her briefcase so her page-boy will never lose its bounce.) She blinked regretfully at Cheops, whose right hand splayed on his chest as he waited for her answer. "Any other evening, I'd just be honored, but not this evening," she said.

Cheops didn't even move his hand. "Perhaps you?" he said to Hetty Anne—and to me!

I looked at Hetty Anne. Hetty Anne looked at her father. It was his club. Mr. Engle looked at Mrs. Engle. Say yes, I begged silently. "You'll be back before eleven like usually?" Mrs. Engle asked Mr. Engle, frowning. We would be back well before eleven. "What sort of things would they be demonstrating?" she asked Cheops, still frowning.

Cheops smiled reassuringly. "Cheops is no magician, going to saw the beautiful daughters in two. He is no mad chemist, going to blow off the beautiful noses with explosive mixtures. Cheops is an artist! Only to display his work is all that Cheops is needing from the beautiful girls, and the father is there every moment like the father bird, ready to fly to his chicks' defense."

"See what your mother says, Kate," Mrs. Engle said. I flew to the telephone.

Mom asked all the questions mothers have to ask so they won't have to blame themselves forever if they never see their child alive again. Then she said yes, if the Engles were letting Hetty Anne.

Probably the assistants' costumes were in Nashville with the assistant, I thought regretfully. Hetty Anne could wear whatever she looked best in, but I would have to go in just what I'd worn to school. Hetty Anne is too tall for me to borrow her clothes.

"You have time for one more piece of pie while I change for my lecture," Cheops told us. "Then we have to leave, because with two assistants, backstage preparations take twice as long." He jumped to his feet and ran up the stairs.

"If I changed clothes, I wouldn't have time for more pie," Hetty Anne said, settling back. "Wonder why two assistants take twice as long instead of half?"

We didn't have time for more pie, anyway. Cheops was

back downstairs before Mrs. Engle finished cutting our pieces. He had changed his light green turtleneck for a dark green turtleneck. He was still barefoot. His loafers, though, turned out to be beside the front door.

Cheops never had told Mrs. Engle what he was going to ask Hetty Anne and me to do. I figured we would ride in with him, and he would explain to us as he drove. "You must ride with the father," he said. "My car is packed full with my demonstrating materials."

So when Mr. Engle picked Dad up, and Dad wanted to know what sort of debut Hetty Anne and I were going to make at the Lowlands Club, we couldn't tell him.

What Cheops wanted Hetty Anne and me to do turned out to be well within our range of talents.

There was a cold draught across the stage, but I was toasty by the time the curtain rose, and I knew Hetty Anne was, too. I stood on one side of Cheops, Hetty Anne on the other. I couldn't see her, because I couldn't move my head, but I saw Mr. Engle's eyes bug and Dad's face stiffen. Then they turned to each other, then back to us. I knew they were trying to figure out which was Hetty Anne and which was Kate. I would have giggled if the wrap around my mouth had been looser. (If we'd known in advance, we could have arranged that Hetty Anne would wink at her father and I would wiggle my nose at mine.)

The lecture Cheops gave turned out to be exactly the things he had said at table. I watched Mr. Culverhouse when Cheops got to how the banks would lend him all the money he wanted because his sketches were so valuable. Mr. Culverhouse scratched his neck and scowled at his knees. Dad and Mr. Engle stared straight ahead.

Cheops never mentioned Hetty Anne and me. We were

demonstrators of his technique. "You are art," he told us, as we stood in our stage places and he wound his wrapping round and round us. (Once he was finished, we couldn't have walked.) "All art has to do is *be*."

Though Cheops didn't mention us, next morning the *Clermont Clarion* published a picture of him lecturing to the Lowlands Club with what looked like two mummies, one on each side of him. So did the *Lexington Herald-Leader*, and our names were in both captions. The *Herald-Leader* got us backwards. The *Clarion* didn't, because as I realized halfway through the lecture, anyone who knew us could tell Hetty Anne from me in an instant; she's half a mile taller. We thought the evening was well spent whatever names the papers printed. When Cheops finally got the last band of wrapping unwound from around us, he paid us for our evening's work: ten dollars apiece.

He also gave the Engles a good-bye present. They found their picture of Secretariat, no longer draped, under the bed. In its place hung a carefully wrapped rock—and this time, there were sequins on the burlap.

"How much do you think Mr. Culverhouse would lend Pops for that?" Hetty Anne asked me. Hetty Anne can joke about anything.

CHAPTER 7

Night Duty

Mid-January, I doze on the school bus, coming and going. By February, Hetty Anne's lucky if I don't go sound asleep and fall over on her. January is the month our ewes mostly have their lambs, usually in the middle of the night. Mom and Dad and I take turns checking the flock every three hours, because somebody has to be there to help a lambing ewe. If the checker is Mom or me and a ewe is getting down to business, we waken Dad. Some nights so many lambs come, it takes all three of us to keep up with them. For weeks we see more of the barn than we do of our beds. I love lambing, though. To me, it's more fun than Christmas, the lambs are such darlings, and their mothers are so glad to see them. Mom and Dad get more cheerful by the lamb, too, because selling lambs is how we pay our mortgage.

Helping at lambing gives me a feeling that I don't think my town classmates ever get. When your parents go off to work that you never help with or even see, you don't feel a part of what feeds your family the way Hetty Anne and I do. I sympathize when my classmates gripe about their chores. Lawn mowing and vacuum cleaning aren't like taking a tiny newborn creature in your arms and guiding it to its mother for its first drink. I want to raise my children on a farm, this farm.

This year, lambing really stretched out. Hearing Hetty Anne say, "Your stop next, Kate; wake up," became an almost daily thing. I would straighten up, look around, grip the books in my lap, and lean forward, waiting for the first creak of the opening door. On our bus, you're not allowed to so much as lift your bottom off the seat till Mr. Ormsby has finished braking, but if you take five seconds beyond that to start down the aisle, he's grouching at you. He knows just where to swivel and glare, too, because we don't get to choose our seats according to how we feel that day; we take the seats he has assigned us. On our Bible School bus, kids can sit anywhere they want and we sing all the way, but when we get on Mr. Ormsby's bus in the morning, we have to march straight to the farthest empty seat and sit there and nowhere else, and no yelling. (That means no singing, too, because Mr. Ormsby can't seem to tell the difference.) Coming home, we have to sit in those same seats. Kids grouse about what a stickler Mr. Ormsby is, but I forgive him because of Hetty Anne. Hetty Anne being two grades ahead of me, I never would have sat beside her except for Mr. Ormsby's rules. How much taller she is than I am doesn't show when we're sitting down, and she is the sunniest person I know.

On the other hand, if it weren't for Hetty Anne, Mr. Ormsby's rules would put me beside J. M. Stanley. J.M. is the kind of boy who gets behind you at the water fountain when there are a lot of other kids around and asks you loudly, "Are you finished?" and when you say yes and get out of his way, he tells you even louder, "Then wipe!" He's the kind of boy who smells as bad getting on the bus Monday morning as I do leaving the barn Saturday afternoon. I'll never forget the first time I spoke to him. I was only in first grade and J.M. was a jug-eared third grader. I got on the school bus one afternoon and as I passed his seat, I saw that he was drawing locomotives all over the margins of his English book. Mom and Dad had impressed on me that our schoolbooks belonged to the Lowlands County School System. I was so shocked by J.M.'s vandalism that I stopped right beside him in the aisle and demanded loudly, "Don't you know you shouldn't draw on school property?"

"Who's paying you to mind my business, Prissface?" J.M. retorted, just as loudly. All over the bus, kids laughed.

J.M. claims he is going to quit school. Nobody should hope that for anybody, but Hetty Anne will be transferring to Lafayette High School this fall. I am making the most of her shoulder while it lasts.

Sometimes I daydream that Hume and Morgan Culverhouse ride our bus, but if they did, they would probably sit together.

The day I was finally able to tell Hetty Anne, "Those last two ewes will lamb tonight," the groundhog had already seen his shadow and gone back to sleep for six weeks, and I was ready to do the same.

"I'll cross my fingers for you!" said Hetty Anne.

After I got off, I turned to wave. Sure enough, Hetty Anne's pale face was at the window, and she had both hands up where I could see them. One had its middle and forefinger crossed, and the other had its thumb up.

Becky was waiting on the porch to open the front door for me. She was thinking of every possible useful thing she could do, trying to show us older three that five was not too young to help with lambing. Becky adores the little soft lambs. In the cutest picture we have of her—the one Mom sent Grandmom last Christmas—she and I are sitting close together with our backs against the barn wall and our laps spilling over with day-old triplets. One lamb is nibbling Becky's chin, and Becky is grinning so hard her eyes are squeezed shut.

Becky closed the door after me carefully, demonstrating that she is now much too grown up to slam it. "I'll take your books upstairs and put them on your desk for you," she offered. I have to go to my room first thing, anyway; house rule is no snack till school clothes are hung up. Becky knows that, but as I had come in from helping Dad give the sheep their breakfasts, I had thoughtlessly told Mom in Becky's hearing that the last lambs were sure to come before morning. To five-year-olds, "last chance to help this year" means "last chance."

"You only *think* it's fun to freeze your hands and feet off," I told Becky. "The barn really and truly is no place for you tonight."

Becky made a face and stumped off to offer to pour the milk for Mom. If Mom saw through her, she didn't let on.

Mom has always been a good sport about letting Becky "help" her. She was the same with me when I was five. She would let me cut out doughnuts for her, after she'd rolled the batter. I know she could have made doughnuts twice as fast if I had cleared out of the kitchen, but she always looked pleased when I offered to help.

Mom has a very nice face when she is pleased. I don't look at all like her. She would be pretty if she would get a permanent like Mrs. Culverhouse. Mom puts her hair in a ponytail like mine only with pins instead of elastic, then wraps it around itself in wider and wider circles and pins those down till she looks like a pioneer.

Well, I was only half-right about what I'd said to Hetty Anne and Mom, but I was 100 percent right about what I told Becky.

Dad and I both went out to the barn right after supper. Sure enough, Sheena was digging in the bedding. We looked at each other and Dad grinned, and my heart started to beat a little faster. We put Sheena in a lambing pen. She started digging there, too, of course, but after she finally had herself a nice nest dug and lay down in it, she didn't have more than a couple of contractions before she got up and started making another one. This was her first lambing, and first-time mother sheep are like that. Sheena dug three nests before she was satisfied. Then she lay in the last one, and her contractions got regular.

Each time Sheena had a contraction, she would grunt, and shove on her lamb with her inside muscles. Mom says contractions hurt. I keep reminding myself that if Becky and I are going to take over this farm some day, we have to learn to accept what can't be changed, like sheep and cows having labor pains. I, especially, have to learn this, because Becky watches me. I don't want to turn Becky away from farming.

At last the sack that the lamb had been floating around in all winter ruptured and fluid gushed out from under Sheena's tail. Then Sheena had another contraction, and two little hooves came peeping out the same place. Dad and I exchanged excited smiles. About that time, I was still hoping the other ewe was listening and would get the idea and get started, and we would be through for the year by nine or ten o'clock. Before very long, I was hoping the opposite!

Often a ewe will deposit her lamb on the straw only seconds after her sack ruptures, but we weren't that lucky with Sheena. She grunted and shoved so hard that I felt my muscles straining with hers the way I feel my seat and thighs tighten, trying to help pull the car Mom is driving up an icy hill. Still the lamb's head didn't pop out. Sheena stared at me. Becky underestimates the difference between five and thirteen. As recently as two years ago (maybe even last year), having Sheena look at me like that when I couldn't stop her pain would have made me physically sick. Now I have learned to keep reminding myself that a farmer who is unnerved by pain or mess is useless, that I mustn't let sympathy for an animal's suffering tie me up so tight I'm helpless. Our animals need me to do those things I *can* do, even though I can't do everything we'd both like to have done.

First lambings are usually the toughest, because the ewe has never been stretched that way before. I had known that Sheena might have a harder time even than most first-timers, because she was the smallest ewe in our flock. She struggled and struggled without result. Dad's face showed nothing. My own broke into a sweat. When we finally saw a little black nose, I felt a thrill all the way to my elbows.

After that nose, though, the lamb just didn't make any more progress. "It's a big one," Dad said. He knelt and with one forefinger, gently tried to push Sheena's taut skin back from over the lamb's eyebrows so as to let the head out, but he couldn't do it. "Hand me the Vaseline, Kate," he said. Even more gently, he eased his vaselined forefinger inside Sheena and lubricated the lamb's head. Sheena grunted and groaned, but the lamb didn't budge. Suddenly Sheena stopped groaning and the hind leg she wasn't lying on sank.

My view of the lamb was blocked, and Sheena didn't seem about to move anymore. "She needs help!" Dad said. "Get twine!"

I ran to cut some off a hay bale. In my mind was a picture of Dad tying it to those two little wet legs, but by the time I got back, Dad had Sheena lying on her spine, her four hooves pointing at the ceiling, and she was grunting again. "Straddle her," he said, "and take hold of her hind legs!" Then he tied one end of my twine to the leg in my left hand, led it behind my back and down across my right shoulder, and tied it to the leg in my right hand. I was relieved to feel some of Sheena's weight shift from my arms to my shoulders. I was a lot more glad, before Dad was done. "Keep her legs wide apart," he told me, and went to work.

What Dad began to do looked a little like milking, except that what he had hold of was the lamb's forefeet. "You don't want to just jerk a lamb out," he told me. "You'll hurt the lamb; you'll hurt its mother. What you want to do is walk it out." First he gently pulled the right foot with one hand and gently pushed the left foot with the other, then he did the opposite. Push, pull, each time Sheena grunted. Where my calves touched her sides, I could feel her contractions. With each one, Sheena grunted and Dad's hands went push, pull, but the lamb's head did not budge. Dad's face was intent: push, pull.

My face must have betrayed how my arms ached. "Hang on, Kate; it's coming," Dad said to comfort me. Suddenly the lamb's big head popped out.

For a second, relief relaxed my whole body, but the knot came back inside me almost as fast as the tension came back to my arms, neck, and legs. Nothing followed that glistening head. Sheena sounded desperate. "It's the shoulders," Dad said. His seesawing push, pull resumed. "Hang on, Kate. You're doing swell. She can't pass both shoulders at once. I'm trying to pull one by at a time. Which one is up to them."

When the shoulders finally did pass through Sheena's pelvis, the lamb came out so fast Dad sat *whump* down on the straw. For a second, grinning up at me, he looked more like a surprised high school boy than a father who's been farming all his life. Then he gave his slimey hands a quick scrub on the straw, and hopped up and freed me from my harness. We laid Sheena on her side again, carefully, so as not to break the ropy umbilical cord that was still carrying the lamb its oxygen. The bad part was over, I thought, because there is one compensation to first-time mother sheep. They rarely have twins.

The lamb was a ewe. Dad wiped the mucous from her nostrils and laid his hand on her ribs. I was a little jealous that he, not I, was the one who would feel that miraculous moment when the cord breaks and the lamb swallows its first air.

Trouble was, apparently this one didn't. Sheena made a scrabbling movement as if to get up. She sank back exhausted, but her attempt had been enough to splash the bedding with bright blood from the rupturing cord. Now the lamb's oxygen was all up to its lungs. I saw Dad's fingers on her side splay just perceptibly, then pluck a straw from the bedding and poke one end of it into the lamb's nostril. I didn't breathe myself, listening. We heard the faintest, faintest sneeze! She was not dead.

Dad shook the lamb; he raised her a couple of inches above the straw and dropped her. I'd seen him do these things before—not often, but they'd always worked. This time, they did not. Cold spread through my own body. Suddenly Dad grabbed the lamb by her hind legs and lifted her as high as his arm would stretch, and swung her around his head.

Never in my life had I seen such a terrible sight. Grief and rage that the lamb had died after all his labor, all Sheena's suffering, had put him out of his mind. His mouth was stretched in a grimace and his eyes were wide and unseeing. I cowered out of his way as he swung the poor little limp body around his head a second time. I had been shocked speechless, but as his arm began to lower, I finally cried out, imagining that he was about to dash the lamb to the floor. Instead he held her tenderly in his arms for one moment only, then laid her down and without pausing even to glance at me, began to massage her rib cage. The lamb gave the tiniest of bleats, and Dad turned to me with a wonderful smile.

"Doc Spivey says when you swing one like that, the gut first falls away from the diaphragm and then against it, and pushes air out of the lungs," he told me. "He says once that's happened a couple of times, the lungs will keep going on their own, provided there's not something else wrong with the lamb. All I know is, it's worked for me a few times." Doc Spivey is our vet. "I'm sorry I scared you," Dad said. "I couldn't wait to explain. The lamb's brain can be damaged if it goes without oxygen many seconds, and the one thing a lamb does not need is to be any stupider."

I had stopped breathing myself while he was whirling that tiny body through the air, but now we stood beaming at each other. We still had a few little jobs to do for the new couple, and there was still a chance that the other ewe would come through before dawn (she didn't), but just for half a minute we let ourselves stand still and silently congratulate ourselves, the lamb, Sheena, the state of Kentucky, the world.

I got a towel and helped Sheena dry her lamb so it wouldn't get chilled. Sheena licked the lamb and talked to it, and I rubbed. I beamed up at Dad and he beamed back at me. I could feel cold wet seeping through the knees of my coveralls, my jeans, my long johns. I'd be nearly as big a mess as Dad before I got up. "You were a big help tonight, Kate," he said.

Morgan Culverhouse never has a hair out of place or a nick in a single fingernail or a spot of any kind on any part of her clothing, let alone both entire knees. I have a dream about Morgan and Hume sometimes, the same dream, over and over. I'm with Dad in the barn looking like something the pitchfork picked up, when I hear a car door slam. I look out and see Morgan and Hume getting out of the car, carrying a box of red paper poppies to sell for disabled veterans. I hide. From my hiding place I hear Dad say, "I don't have a nickel on me, but Kate does. Kate? Kate!" he calls. I pretend not to hear, but he goes on calling till I have to come out. When I hand Hume Culverhouse some money, we both look down at my hand and it's as yellow and lined as a chicken leg, and my fingernails are black. Then I wake up, and don't get back to sleep very soon.

Kneeling beside Sheena's beautiful healthy ewe lamb, I wasn't worried about wet knees or dirty fingernails. I've come a long way since last May. All that blood and slime and gushing mess and all that scare and I hadn't shed one tear and my stomach felt just fine. I felt great. I was tired, but I'd never felt better. I laid my towel aside and helped the lamb find Sheena's udder.

CHAPTER 8

The Night of Orion

Supernova has a different official name now, but we will always call him Super. This February, word came to Mr. Engle from Florida that Super had won his first race. "Didn't I predict that colt would outshine the brightest planet?" Dad demanded. "Do I know my astronomical bodies, or do I?" He had been in a good mood even before Mr. Engle telephoned. Our last lambs, twins, had come a few nights before (without any of the trouble Sheena's one had given her). Now Dad and Mom and I were just about caught up on our sleep. Dad was whistling as he went out to give the ewes drinking water for the night.

I heard the back porch door slam as he came back in. "Helen!" he called to Mom. "Kate! Get Becky up! Come out and look at Orion, everybody!"

I was doing my homework, and Becky was already tucked in sound asleep. I turned off my desk lamp, and Mom put Becky's snowsuit on her right over her pajamas, and we all went outside to see Dad's favorite constellation. The moon wasn't up yet and the stars were the whole show. "Look due south," Dad said, pointing with his binoculars. "See those three stars? In the straight line? See, Becky? Those are the belt of the mighty hunter Orion. Now look—"

Dad wants to share everything that is wonderful about our farm with Becky and Mom and me, like having a sky full of stars instead of that blur city people see. Our sky gives city people neckaches when they visit us at night because they can't stop looking at it.

My sister Becky knows more about stars than I did when I was five, because I have explained some things to her. When I was five, Dad showed me a book full of drawings of the marvelous pictures you would behold in the sky if you looked in the right seasons. I was thrilled. I never had seen any of them, but I expected to. "I'll show you all of them," Dad promised. One night he got me out of bed: "Come see Sirius!"

I jammed my feet into slippers. I was still tying my wrapper when I got to the front yard. Dad had his binoculars, and he hunkered down to my height and focused them. "Now *you* look," he said, holding them still for me. "See that bright star?"

I saw a lot of bright stars. "Mmm," I said.

Dad looked again, to make sure I hadn't bumped the binoculars out of position with my forehead. "Yes, there it is," he said. "The bright one, the brightest in the sky!"

I looked again. Maybe one star did look brighter than the others. I let out my breath and said yes. Then I started holding it again, because I didn't have anything on my head or hands, and my neck was cold, and my ankles, too.

"Sirius is thirty times brighter than the sun," said Dad. That really confused me. I certainly didn't see anything anywhere as bright as the sun. I opened my mouth. "You wouldn't know that, just looking at it, because it's so much farther away than the sun," Dad explained. I closed my mouth. Nobody I knew knew as much as my father. "Sirius," he said, "is Canis Major's nose. Remember Canis Major?"

In the picture in Dad's book, Canis Major is very plainly an animal, sort of like a short-tailed mother lion. I didn't see anything like that in the sky, without the binoculars or with.

"Now, see two stars?" Dad asked. "One on each side of Sirius?" He positioned the binoculars for me again. "Those are his ears. See them, Kate?"

I squinched my eyes and I wiped them, and I rubbed my feet against each other to warm them, and I looked at Dad to see if he were joking. Dad positioned the binoculars for me again, and I put my face against them and said yes, I saw Canis Major's ears.

"Good!" said Dad. "Now left of him is the other dog, Canis Minor. You remember him from the book. Over their heads is their master, Orion, and just to the right of Orion is Taurus the bull. Look."

Again he bent his knees till he was my height, and I put my face up to the binoculars and steadied them with my hands. My ears, fingers, and toes were asking me if I wanted to take them inside before they froze solid and broke off, and my father was asking me if I saw a man and three animals, and I said yes to all of them.

The truth is, there aren't any star pictures in the sky; only in people's imaginations. People who want to, look at six or seven stars and imagine pictures around them sort of like those connect-the-dots puzzles Becky likes to work. It's not really crazy. It's like hearing music in your mind when no music is playing. We all do that. The crazy part is expecting somebody else to see the picture you're imagining. I wouldn't think the Blue Danube Waltz to myself and expect Dad to hear it.

I have explained to Becky that she won't really see a bull or a swan in the sky, that it's just pretend like the tooth fairy, so she wasn't disappointed that night Mom got her out of bed to come out and let Dad show us Orion. She smiled and Mom and I smiled, and we all pretended to see the mighty hunter. We all went to bed happy and we slept so well, none of us even thought about Canis Major and Canis Minor, the two animals that always come with Orion, the big dog and the smaller. We slept so well, none of us has slept well since.

I have accepted that I will never be as strong as Dad, will always be smaller. "Farmers come all sizes," Dad says. The day he stabbed that bloated cow, I realized that the question was not, would I be strong enough, but would I be brave enough, tough enough? I worry about that a lot. You can see why I was so pleased not to have wailed or passed out or something when the dark liquid gushed out from under Sheena's tail, when she suffered so long, when the cord bled the lamb's blood all over the straw; when the lamb almost died. But it's not enough to be a brave, tough onlooker. Could I have done the things Dad did? The answer that night was no. The question now is, is it in me ever to be able to make that answer yes? When I think the answer is no, I feel myself sinking into darkness like Sheena's lamb.

I don't know if I heard the shots the night of Orion or not. I must keep reminding myself that this doesn't matter. By the time Tom Allen fired his gun, it was too late.

Did I hear anything before that? Tuck it into a dream, explain it away for myself in my sleep? Or did I do worse? Did I wake up, but because my room was too cold, my blanket too cozy, did I just tell myself that I hadn't heard anything? Did I shove my chilled hot water bottle to the edge of the bed and turn over and go back to sleep so fast I forgot all about hearing something? I can't remember anything now, and yet when I keep trying, I seem to.

Dad and I went to the barn before daylight as usual. There were dead sheep all over the field. Some were scattered, lying where the dogs had ripped their throats. Some were piled up in a huddled bunch, not even bitten. They had died of fright, fright and running. We have bells on their collars so we will hear them if they run like that. Why didn't any of us hear anything?

Becky wakes up sometimes with a nightmare. She'll pad down the hall to my room and beg to get in with me. Then we're both awake, at least long enough to hear a dog growl or a ewe bleat or a lamb scream—or a neighbor shoot two wild dogs nobody around here ever saw before he saw them jumping his four-foot fence in the moonlight. He killed them both, a big one and a smaller one.

Mr. Allen had set his alarm clock so he would check the only one of his ewes that hadn't lambed yet, but instead of finding her lambing, he found a nightmare, a real one. Why couldn't Becky have had a dream one and wakened me?

Before Mr. Allen telephoned to tell us about his tragedy, we had discovered our own. Lambs were bleating for dead mothers. Ewes were standing over dead lambs, nudging them with their noses, trying to get them to stand up. The dead lambs were already frozen stiff, but the dead ewes' wounds steamed in the pale cold moonlight.

The ewe that had lambed last was still in the barn in a claiming pen with her twins. This had saved their lives. Sheena had been spending her first night back outside, and it had become her last.

Mom had Becky stand beside the mailbox and tell Mr.

Ormsby, "Kate won't be coming to school today." I was helping Mom and Dad sort out whose lamb was dead and whose was alive; whose mother was dead and whose was alive; which living animals were so hurt they would have to be slaughtered. We had slept too well.

CHAPTER 9

Orphans

We stood in the barnyard, Mom and Dad and I. Silently, each of us was counting. We knew without counting that we had more lambs than ewes. The motherless ones pushed their little black noses into us, trying for something to drink. "We've got three sound ewes with dead lambs," Dad said. "We'll try to get each to adopt one. We can't save the others."

"I could bottle-raise them!" I cried.

Dad shook his head. "You're a good farmer, Kate, but there aren't two of you. Orphan lambs are a job by themselves. You're in school, and Becky isn't old enough, and your mother already has more than she can do." He didn't say anything about himself. I believe he already had decided he would have to take outside work. "They're *worse* than a job," he corrected himself. "Instead of getting paid, the worker pays. By the time you raise one, you've spent more on it than it will bring at the stockyards."

I looked at the little lambs, bleating for their mothers, who were lying stiff on the hard ground. My own mother's face was almost that stiff. A long time ago she told me that I shouldn't make Dad's job harder at stockyard time by letting him see me cry, so I am pretty good about swallowing and holding my eyeballs still so nothing spills, and rubbing my nose when Dad is looking the other way. I did all those things, but Sheena's lamb was nibbling at the tip of one of my glove fingers. I wanted to cry out. Dad couldn't mean that the lamb he and Sheena and I had struggled so hard to get—he could not mean to butcher her? "We have to replace the ewes the dogs killed some way," I argued desperately. "Maybe we could raise *ewe* lambs cheaper than we could buy—"

"No," said Dad, "not really. Anyway, as I pointed out, we haven't got the manpower. But you're thinking like a farmer, Kate. The three we try to graft will be females. Help your mother take the smallest three into the barn, and get the sheep paint." I carried Sheena's lamb with my face half submerged in her wool, so my tears wouldn't show.

We number our ewes with paint as they lamb, and we paint each mother's number on her lamb. This helps us keep everybody straight, which sheep are not always smart enough to do for themselves. We have little claiming pens for the same reason. Even to their mothers, lambs all look alike. Ewes recognize their lambs by smell, and it takes them a few days to get a fix on what their new lambs smell like. If you leave a mother sheep with her new lamb in a little pen for two or three days, she will come out with such a strong sense of that lamb's unique smell that she will let that lamb nurse her even if she is dying, and she will never let any other lamb in the world nurse her, if she has to kill it to stop it.

I ran to the house for the paint. As I stepped onto the back porch, the telephone was ringing inside. "Kate?" The voice was our neighbor Tom Allen's. That's when I learned that some of Mr. Allen's sheep had been savaged, too, and that he had shot both dogs. "Ask your dad to come over later and see does he know whose they are," Mr. Allen asked me, "because if it can't be proved they've had rabies shots, I'm going to have to take their heads to Frankfort."

In the end there was some good for somebody in Mr. Allen's also losing lambs, because Dad was able to give him the rest of our orphans to graft onto his lambless ewes, just the way we were doing with the three we kept.

Mom and I bedded three claiming pens and put one lamb in each. I was glad Dad had given us an inside job. I knew what he was going to do outside, and I didn't want to see.

My avoiding watching Dad skin three dead lambs didn't prove I'll never make it farming. Jack Estep, our county agent, doesn't like to see it done, either. "They didn't teach you that at UK," I heard him say to Dad once. He and Dad had been classmates at the University of Kentucky.

"My dad taught me that," Dad said, "and it's a lot more effective than any wet towel." Mr. Estep thinks you should just rub the dead lamb with a wet towel and then rub the orphan with it. He claims that will bring enough of the dead lamb's smell onto the orphan to fool the dead lamb's mother. I find that hard to believe, but when Becky and I inherit this farm, we are going to give it a try. I haven't told Becky yet, but I will as soon as she's old enough not to blab to Dad.

The number on the first lambskin Dad brought in was Eudora's. I held the biggest of the three orphans while Mom painted Eudora's number on beside its old number, but bigger. Then I sat the lamb on its bottom so Dad could fit that dead lamb's skin onto it like a coat. The skin's underside was slippery, and even the woolly side was damp from frost, and the live lamb seemed to think Dad was trying to kill her. She was so terrified, I was afraid she would die just sitting there with her legs stuck out in front of her, and Dad and Mom and me all trying to tell her we were her friends. Finally Dad got all four legs in the leg holes. Then Mom took over holding the lamb while I tied a piece of twine around its middle and Dad went out and got Eudora.

For hours Eudora had been anxious for her lamb to nurse, and she didn't waste more than ten seconds smelling her own lamb's skin on top of that orphan. She talked to the orphan excitedly in deep sort of chuckle grunts, and shoved it to her udder with her nose, as if it needed urging. I felt my own stomach relax, listening to the orphan drink, and in spite of all that had happened, I smiled at Mom and she smiled at me.

It was the same with the second ewe, Sheba. The third one, though—Sadie—was bad-tempered. Only our ram had knocked me down more often than Sadie had. I am sure her mean disposition was what made Dad bring her last. He knew she would give trouble.

We had saved the very smallest lamb for Sadie: Sheena's lamb. Sheena wouldn't have died if we hadn't been in such a hurry to get her out of that claiming pen and back with the flock. I already felt like a murderess, and to make things worse, the lamb kept looking at me as if she were certain I could find her mother for her if I just would. She kept rubbing against me and smelling behind my knees and calling Sheena. She had called so many times she was hoarse.

Sadie didn't want anything to do with Sheena's orphan. You would have thought she was a dog. The instant we put her in the orphan's pen, she scuttled as far from her as she could get. When she stumbled after her, she butted her. Her own lamb's skin was tied on over the orphan's, but that didn't help, because she scarcely sniffed it. She just tried to hide under the water bucket, just tried to knock the poor little hungry lamb down.

Then Dad shoved Sadie against the wall and held her, and Mom put the little lamb up to Sadie's udder to nurse, first from one side and then from the other. When Sadie's hind legs stopped trying to dance, Dad's face relaxed some. "Maybe her udder had got so tight she didn't want to have it touched," he said. "Let's see if that was it." Cautiously he let go of Sadie's head.

Sadie hadn't changed her mind at all.

That's when Mom tied her to a ring on the wall. Sadie might be ready to let the lamb nurse the next time. Till then, all she could do was dance and kick; she couldn't butt. The lamb might stay hungry, but she could dodge Sadie's feet.

I put a flake of hay in front of Sadie, and Sadie grabbed a bite. Dad picked up the orphan and held her bottom up to Sadie's nose. The lamb's bottom was covered by Sadie's lamb's skin, but Sadie wouldn't even sniff it. She wouldn't even chew while Dad held that orphan in front of her face. The hay she had grabbed just sat in her mouth like a cigarette that's gone out. Dad put the lamb down. "Breakfast time," he said.

The poor little lamb lay down at once. I guess she was full, but she was also exhausted. She looked so cold lying there with no mother to cuddle up to her, I wanted to hold her myself. I imagined her dreaming about dogs. "I'm not hungry," I said, and that was true. I couldn't imagine when I would be hungry again. "Could I just stay and—"

"Breakfast time," Dad repeated. "Extra trouble calls for extra food, not less. Nobody's brave on an empty stomach, or smart, either. Inside."

"We'll buy more cattle when we sell our lambs," Dad had said. Now we'd lost the lambs.

CHAPTER 10

One-One Thousand

"Shouldn't wonder if the Allens put their farm on the market come spring," I heard Dad tell Mom as the Allens' truck bumped away with our extra orphaned lambs. "He's been talking all winter about retiring, and this might be the last straw."

"Dorothy wants them to come to Louisville where she can look after them," Mom answered. Dorothy is the oldest of the five Allen "children," the only one who lives in Kentucky.

I don't know how easy it was for Mr. Allen to fool his ewes with our substitute babies, but next morning when Dad and I got to our barn, Eudora and Sheba were feeding the orphans we had given them. Not Sadie. We had to leave her tied. Dad held her hind legs and I guided the hungry lamb to what we could tell was the first drop she had tasted since Mom and I had come out and helped her the same way at midnight.

"The other four can go back to the flock," Dad said.

"Do those skins come off?" I asked. I tried to look neutral.

Dad glanced at me. "I'll do it. You go along." I guess I didn't look so neutral.

Keeping my mind on the blackboard was hard that day.

Ever since Dad saved that bloated cow, I had been worried that when the time came, I wouldn't be tough enough or brave enough to take on this farm. Now the question was, would there be any farm for Becky and me to take over?

If there weren't, what would we do?

Riding home, Hetty Anne and I thought of all the famous orphans we could, and chose three lamb names. Sheena's, we called Little Orphan Annie. When I got home, Mom said, "I need you to help me nail up a board in Sadie's pen. Your father had to go out."

She spoke casually. I didn't ask where Dad had gone. I was more concerned about Little Orphan Annie, because I knew what that board meant. Sadie still wasn't accepting her.

Sadie couldn't just stay tied. For the time being, standing her along the wall and nailing a board between her and the rest of her pen was the answer. I held the board high enough for Annie to be able to stick her head under it and nurse, but too low for Sadie to be able to kick her away, and Mom hammered in the nails. Then Mom went in to start our supper and left me to see that Annie got hers.

At first, Annie was afraid to put her head under the board. Fortunately I was stronger, and once she found out what was waiting for her, she forgot the board. That was a problem, too, because she nursed so enthusiastically that she sort of bobbed up and down, and once she had bumped herself on the edge of that board, she was twice as scared of it as before. I had to start trying to teach her all over again. By the time Mom called me to supper, Annie and I were both ready to lie down, but at least Annie was full.

Dad didn't eat much. He didn't say much, either. I didn't find out where he had been till after supper. "I'll do the dishes, Kate," Mom told me, so I knew there was something she and Dad meant to talk about that I needed to hear. My room is right over the dining room, where they were having coffee. I sat down to read my history assignment beside the open hot-air register in my floor.

"After that, I went to Southern States," Dad said. "They aren't hiring, either. They told me that if many more customers quit paying their bills, some of the help they've got now will have to be let go.

"I talked to Jack Estep about maybe doing custom work for other farmers—say somebody's got a job I own the equipment for and he doesn't, like combining, say, or if his combine breaks midjob and he can't get the new part fast enough. Jack said it's a good idea; several guys have talked to him about doing that kind of work. He said he'd mention me along with them if anybody asked him about getting that kind of help."

"A lot of guys," Mom repeated.

"Several."

"If anybody asks him."

"I haven't told you the worst," Dad said. "Tinsley Mills is closing."

"Oh, *Rales.*"

" 'I'll do anything you'll pay a man to do,' I told them. 'If I don't know how to do it, I'll work for nothing till you've taught me.' They said next payday would be their last. They've been bought by a bigger company, and the big company is closing them down."

I couldn't believe it. Tinsley Mills had been making sports clothes in Clermont all my life. A weekday without their whistle is like a spring without meadowlarks.

"Too small to be efficient," Dad was saying. "Koreans can make clothes and ship them all the way across the Pacific and truck them all the way across the desert and over the mountains and sell them to Kentuckians cheaper than we can make and sell them right here in Clermont. Anyhow, next I went to IBM. It's fifteen miles, but I figured I could carpool." I heard that past tense, and my heart felt like lead.

"I made them the same offer I made Tinsley. Seems they've got two hundred robots and six miles of conveyor belts, and they don't need *me*. There's a freeze on all blue-collar jobs. I'm going to write to Ralston Purina." Dad studied agriculture at the University of Kentucky and did very well (better than Jack Estep, Mom says). When he graduated, Ralston Purina wanted to hire him to travel around the middle west selling their feed. "I'd rather stay home and buy your feed," Dad told them. His parents were still living then, and having him off at college had left my grandfather short-handed.

"Meanwhile, I asked at the quarry. They said they would add my name to their file."

Dad's voice was so toneless, I couldn't bear to listen to it anymore. I got up without making a sound and took my history book back to my desk.

Farm work is hard, but at least it's varied. How many days could Dad last just loading rock? I tried to read, but I kept getting to the bottom of the page and finding that I hadn't noticed anything I had read. Then I remembered that I hadn't cleaned my teeth since supper.

Our dentist says people should clean their teeth as soon as they get up in the morning and immediately after every meal. After breakfast I'm in a hurry to meet the bus and at lunch I'm at school and nobody wants anybody spitting in the girls' room sink, and at night, sometimes I used to be in bed before I'd remember, and then maybe I'd think about how cold the floor would be on bare feet and fall asleep before I talked myself into getting up. Not anymore. My parents can't afford for me to get cavities right now. A long time ago, our dentist told me, "You should brush your teeth six minutes a day, Kate; it's good for your gums," and I just laughed. The night Dad told Mom he'd tried to get a job at the quarry, I closed my history book and went to the bathroom and counted seconds while I brushed. (One second is the time it takes to say "one-one thousand." You don't have to say it out loud, which is a good thing if you are brushing your teeth.) In the time it took me to brush my teeth once on each side, I had counted only to twelve-one thousand. Since it takes twelve seconds to brush each tooth once (that's front and back, plus their bottoms and the exposed side of the four end molars), and since twelve seconds goes into two minutes ten times, if I brush each tooth ten times on each side, three times a day, that makes six minutes. Starting that night, that's what I do.

That night I dreamed Dad was breaking rock in prison, and after I wakened and got back to sleep, I dreamed it again.

"Dad tried to get a job at Tinsley Mills yesterday," I told Hetty Anne on the bus the next morning. "They told him they'll be employers in Clermont for only three more weeks."

Hetty Anne stared at me.

"Mom said it will kill some of their workers," I said. "Some of them have worked there all their lives."

Hetty Anne couldn't think of any bright side to that. We didn't say anything the rest of the way to school.

When I got home, Mom had my snack on the table. I didn't ask her where Dad was because I thought I could guess. I changed clothes, drank the milk, put the apple in my pocket, and took the mackerel sandwich in my hand out to the field to see how Sadie was treating Annie. The two older orphans were napping with the other lambs on a sunny slope, but Annie was following Sadie. I jammed the last of my sandwich into my mouth so I could take hold of Sadie's collar and feel her udder. She had plenty of milk. My apple had been in our basement all winter and was soft and wrinkled. I held it for Sadie to eat, and Annie started to nurse. Her little tail flipped back and forth. Watching Annie drink made me so happy, I stood there till she had finished, praising Sadie for taking good care of her.

When Annie finished, she went over and lay down with the other lambs. Maybe if I had thought about that "like a farmer," the way Dad is always reminding me to think, I would have realized something important about Sadie.

CHAPTER 11

Wait'll Next Year

Sunday was one of those warm sunny days when nobody can believe we still face another month of winter. Driving home from church, Dad glanced at the rest of us and said, "What about it, merry men?"

"Yayyy!" Becky and I cried.

"Now, marry, that question liketh me well!" quoth Mom. "With a *hey* down, *ho* down—"

"*Derry, derry, down*," Dad and she finished together.

So everybody changed cloths and ate lunch with no dawdling, and while Mom and Becky and I raced through the dishwashing, Dad dragged some straw bales outside and stacked them and painted a target on the top one. We three joined him with the quiver and bows.

"First we have to reestablish our handicaps," Dad announced.

"Why don't we just go out and take turns shooting?" I asked Mom once.

Mom smiled, to herself, it appeared to me. "Your father likes to be in control," she said. I wondered if she knew that when she takes his side against Becky's or my complaints, she says "your dad," and when she is not taking sides, she says "your father." (She never sides *against* him.) "Your father enjoys turning something into a game by making up rules," she added, smiling right at me this time. She got me to agree that doing something by a set of rules is more like a game than just doing it, and neither of us mentioned that Dad never asks anybody else to suggest a rule.

When the three of us joined Dad that extra-bright February afternoon, he was standing beside our target with the coffee can of powdered lime in his hand. He paced off a short distance and sprinkled Becky's toe mark, then he paced off another twenty yards and made mine. His and Mom's were even farther back. "That's where everybody was last time," he said. "Let's see what's happened to us in hibernation.

"Everybody gets five shots, starting with Becky. Remember: no going for shot arrows until everybody has shot. Three out of five bull's-eyes means a longer handicap: your line m–o–o–o–ves back."

Becky bustled up to her mark looking excited, proud, and embarrassed all at once. She hasn't had a bow very long. At first, she came with us in Mom's arms and lay on a blanket gurgling while we shot. Later she had to be held by the hand so as to be sure she wouldn't wander (or dash) between the archer and the target at just the wrong second. Eventually she graduated to Arrow Retriever, gathering our shot arrows and bringing them back to us. One day she asked if she could take a turn, using my bow. Dad explained to her that an archer should never assign himself a bow taller than himself. We all stood beside ours so she could see that none of us had. We let her try my bow, but as we'd warned her, she couldn't do a thing with it. That night Dad split a hickory stick with his axe and began to hew a fourth stave.

Now Becky does as well as I did when I was five. Her first

three arrows this February got nowhere and she looked over her shoulder at us anxiously.

"That's all right, honey, you're doing fine," Dad told her.

"We all had to begin," Mom said.

Becky shot again. "Good, that was better," Dad said, and maybe it was. "Keep your elbow lined up with your arrow. You're doing fine." Becky did shoot better the last time. Her arrow found the bottom bale. We all cheered, and it was my turn. I didn't get a single bull's-eye, which surprised me five times, but at least none of my arrows hit the ground. Everybody cheered for me, too, and it was Mom's turn.

Mom is quite a good shot—better than Dad, at short distances. If Mom stands at Dad's toe mark, she can't even get an arrow as far as the straw, but if Dad stands at Mom's toe mark and shoots turn for turn against her, she will beat him. By making himself stand farther from the target than Mom does, Dad can keep their scores pretty even. I asked Mom once why it didn't make her mad that he makes the rules so that she won't beat him. She laughed. "I'm not competing with your dad, Kate. I'm competing with myself. I'm trying to increase the distance I can stand from the target." Dad had said something just like that when he first handed down the rules. You don't catch those two giving me and Becky different answers.

After we'd been shooting for an hour, maybe, a hawk flew over. It circled above our heads, screaming its hungry hunting cry. "Marsh hawk," Mom said. Suddenly we all realized it was time we went in and had doughnuts.

Seeing the hawk from so close was as grand as hitting the bull's-eye, we all agreed. "Good thing, too," said Mom, laughing.

We didn't need to tally up to know that everybody's score

was down from last time. "Nobody," as Dad is fond of saying, "gets better in his sleep." Dad promised we would shoot again the next Sunday if we finished the end-of-February hoof-trimming on Saturday. (There's something that grows in sleep.)

Saturday we finished the sheep's monthly pedicure just in time for lunch. Dad went straight inside, but I walked around the house for the mail. There was a letter in the box from Ralston Purina. Since Dad didn't know I knew he was waiting for an answer from them, I had to walk it to him, not run. I made sure that letter was on top when I handed him the stack, though.

Mom and Becky were putting the soup on the table. I went to the bathroom and just swished my hands, waving them dry as I came back. Dad was reading his letter. Watching him, I stopped feeling hungry. Without a word, he handed the letter to Mom, crumpled up the envelope, and threw it at the wastebasket.

I might have known. After so many farmers like us sold all their cattle in the drought last year, a feed company like Ralston Purina needs fewer salesmen this year, not more.

Mom read the letter and gave it back. "Have some soup," she said. We all sat down and began to eat, but only Becky seemed to enjoy it. As soon as his bowl was empty, Dad got in the pickup and left. He didn't say where he was going.

Mom had errands to run, but the car wouldn't start. "I won't call Fred till we see if your dad can start it," she said. Fred Gulley is our serviceman. He has kept that car going for ten years.

Becky and I were setting the table and Mom was at the stove when Dad got home. I heard him park the truck and come across the back porch and into the kitchen. "I've got a job," he told Mom, "till early June." He didn't sound happy.

I wanted to dump all the knives and forks in a heap and hurry out to the kitchen, but I just set each one where it belonged as close to noiselessly as I could. Both my parents had been saying "Let's talk about it after supper" more than usual since the night of Orion.

"The night man at Wait'll Next Year Farm got kicked," Dad said. "They've got a barn full of foaling mares and need somebody to call the manager if one starts to deliver."

Becky began pulling all our chairs up to the table, scraping and bumping; the next words I could hear were Mom's. "So for minimum wage, you're going to sit up all night seven nights a week in an unheated barn, and then try to farm your own place next day." Dad answered something in a low voice, and Mom said, "Let's talk about it after supper."

After supper I did all my homework, and they were still arguing. They stopped once, while Mom made a telephone call, but they began again as soon as she hung up. They were still arguing when I fell asleep.

In the morning, Mom sat me and Becky down for a serious talk. "I'm going back to work tomorrow," she said.

Mom used to work for a lawyer in Clermont. After I was born, she took a year off to take care of me. Two months before Becky came, she quit completely. The call I'd heard her make was to her old boss. "I'll earn twice what those strip-mine millionaires would have paid your father to risk his health and abandon his farm," she told Becky and me.

"There's no way your father can run this place after he's sat up all night, and there's no way I can run it for him. I *can* get a job and leave him free to run it, and you can do a lot of things I do around here, Kate, and I'll be gone only five days a week. Becky can help by not being any trouble or worry to her dad while I'm at work and Kate is at school, can't you, Becky?" Becky didn't have any trouble agreeing to that, but Mom went on, "and be as much help to Kate when she gets home as you can. Kate is in charge when I'm gone and your dad isn't present."

Becky didn't look pleased about that. "Can I be in charge when Kate's at school?" she asked. Mom just laughed.

Mom hadn't used her shorthand since Becky was born. "I don't know if I can take dictation anymore," she fretted. She asked Dad to dictate a letter so she could practice, but he said he didn't have the time. I waited to offer till he went to the barn.

Mom claims she is much slower than she was five years ago, but she seemed fast to me. "Will you buy an ultrasuede suit for your job?" I asked her. Mrs. Culverhouse has one blue ultrasuede suit and one gray. I don't know which is more beautiful.

"I can still wear the skirts I was wearing before Becky was born," Mom bragged. "I don't need to buy a thing." She is saying that last part a lot these days.

When Dad came back from the barn he informed Mom that she would be going to church alone because he needed Becky and me to help him. "It's time we pulled that wool," he said.

Mom's eyes widened. She never used to question anything he said in front of Becky and me, but I saw the quick way she looked down at her lap. Dad must have seen it, too. "I know you think Becky is still a baby, but she eats. It's high time she started pulling her weight."

Becky looked from one to the other of us. She didn't know what Dad was talking about, but I had been dreading the wool-pulling. We normally shear in April, so those dogs had destroyed not just our lamb crop but also our wool crop. Any wool we could salvage, we needed, and I knew that Dad was right; the time had come. I hoped Becky would have the sense not to try to remind Dad of his promise about archery.

A dead sheep is so difficult to shear that no one tries to do it. If a sheep dies, the farmer drags it to where animals can't get at the body and waits till the skin begins to lose its grip on the wool, and the wool can be picked off easily by hand. From then on, putting the job off only makes it nastier. It isn't a hard job, just horrible. The sheep's eyes are bulging, and the smell of dead animal makes you take only shallow breaths. That's even if there's just one. We had many.

"Becky's got to learn the same as the rest of us," Dad said. His voice sounded like somebody else's. "It's a tough life. I'd love to make it different. I'd love to give her a world where dogs don't kill sheep, and dead animals don't rot, and a man who works all day, every day, all year, has something to show for it on New Year's Eve, and a man who is willing to work all day, every day, can get a job, but that's not the world we live in."

We bagged all the wool in one morning, partly because Mom didn't go to church. "The hymnals will keep," she said. "The sheep won't." I think she wanted to be there if Becky started to cry or throw up. Or maybe she thought the less time we had to spend pulling wool off a bloated ewe, the less we'd remember it. Speaking just for myself, she is wrong. When something is horrifying, I only have to glimpse it to remember it forever. After I finished the top side of my first sheep, I took hold of its stiff forelegs and tried to heave it over. It gurgled. I was so surprised, I screamed and jumped backward. Dad didn't say anything; he just came over and turned my sheep for me. Am I going to have nightmares about that gurgle the rest of my life?

Dad could have asked, "What kind of farmer do you think you could make?" but he didn't. He didn't say anything. I'm the one who's asking.

CHAPTER 12

Polaris

Monday morning I was able to spend a little longer than usual with Orphan Annie because Mom had promised to give me a lift to school. "Ordinarily I won't be going in soon enough for you," she said, "but I want to get to the office good and early my first day." Mr. Ormsby picks up children for miles and miles, and he has so many stops that no sooner does he have the bus back up to speed again after one of them than it's time to slow down for the next. Afternoons are just as slow. Hetty Anne says the bus takes us home like peristalsis.

Probably you think that was vulgar of Hetty Anne, but I laughed. Morgan Culverhouse says farm kids are vulgar. "I think you *like* manure!" she accused me one day. (I hadn't noticed that I had some on my shoes till she claimed that the smell was making her sick.) I felt angry when she said those things, but afterward I admitted just to myself that I guessed she was right about the vulgar part. Not being vulgar mostly means pretending that things don't happen, and farm kids don't get to do that much. When things happen on our farm, I am usually right in the middle of them.

Mom looked pretty good when she dressed for work,

even if her skirt was older than Becky. It was one that Madge Graith, a handweaver we know, had woven out of wool she'd bought from us and dyed a beautiful purple with raspberry Kool-Aid. I knew there was no chance that Mom had manure on her shoes, because she was wearing pumps. The only way Mom would ever wear pumps to the barn was if it were on fire with Becky or me or Dad inside it.

Mrs. Culverhouse puts special buckles on her pumps, handsomer than what comes on them. Once I hoped I could get Mom some special shoe buckles for her birthday. I thought Mrs. Culverhouse probably got hers somewhere in Lexington; she comes from there. When I asked Morgan, though, Morgan said, "New York, of course." I thought about that "of course," watching Mom's plain brown pump work the accelerator as she drove me to school her first job morning.

Riding to town with Mom, I missed talking to Hetty Anne till the trip home. "Here," she said as I sat down by her, "I promised I'd lend you this book." I had admitted, when she suggested naming one of our orphan lambs Jane Eyre, that I had never read *Jane Eyre*, and she had promised that she would get Ursel's permission to lend me Ursel's copy. Now I have read it, so I can warn you not to, or not on a cold rainy day, anyway—not unless you are a lot more like Hetty Anne than like me. The good part is that probably nothing so bad has ever happened to you as the things that happen to Jane and people she knows. Their parents die, or they die themselves, or they are so cold and lonely and hungry and browbeaten that they *wish* they were dead. They go crazy and get locked up in the attic with nobody to talk to but spiders. They burn to death. They go blind. I could see that, compared to Jane and her classmates, I was practically rich.

I guess that's what Hetty Anne means by the consolations of literature, something she is big on.

"Where will you live?" I asked her that awful day when she told me Morgan Culverhouse's father was going to foreclose on her family farm.

"Oh, I don't care a whole lot where I live," she pretended. "I'll always have the consolations of literature."

Now I am worried about where *I* am going to live.

When I got home Monday, there was no snack on the table, naturally, and I could tell that Becky had been crying. "Did you hurt yourself?" I asked her.

"Daddy's on the tractor and Mama's gone and you were at school."

"Well, I'm home now," I said. I put *Jane Eyre* under my pillow and hurried back down to the kitchen. I made two big onion sandwiches, and that cheered Becky up. There was a note fastened to the refrigerator telling me what Mom wanted me to do before she got home.

"Let's go pat lambs," I invited Becky.

The other lambs were sleeping, but Annie came running the minute she saw me. I let Becky hold an ear of corn for Sadie while I felt Sadie's udder. Sadie's udder wasn't tight, so I thought Annie must have nursed recently, but while Sadie stood scraping the kernels off Becky's cob, Annie shoved past me and nursed some more. Every few seconds she bumped Sadie with her head. That says "More! More!" in lamb language. I was pleased that Sadie didn't kick her, just went on eating corn. I knew how good the milk tasted to Annie by the way her little tail stump flipped back and forth.

My own family wasn't that appreciative of the supper I fed them, but I didn't blame them. None of us likes ground mutton. Mom had frozen a lot after Dad butchered the ewes not killed by the dogs but too hurt for us to try to make well. I know ten easy ways to cook mutton now. The trick is distracting your tongue with other, strong-tasting ingredients. Without the cinnamon and red pepper and Parmesan cheese, the moussaka I fixed that night would have tasted like burlap bags that have never been washed except when they were wrapping Lexington's Energy Tower during a rainfall. As it was, Becky took one bite and put her fork down.

Mom didn't miss that. "I know you'd all rather have fried chicken," she said, "but my freezer is full of ground mutton, and we're going to eat it." So she was saying "my" already then for things that were really both hers and Dad's. "Never mind," she added. "I get paid in two weeks, and I'll treat you all to fried chicken." Becky cheered. Dad didn't say anything.

Becky cleared the table, I washed, Mom dried. I used to hang back and let Mom beat me to the sink because drying is less work, since the last rackful gets to drip dry. That night, I made sure I got to the sink ahead of Mom, and I have continued to do this, not because she is so tired from her job—I am just as tired by suppertime as she is, and I still have my homework to do—but because she wastes water. (When she wants hot water, she just turns on the hot faucet and lets the water run down the drain till it comes hot, and we have to pay Kentucky American Water Company for every drop.) I cleaned an empty plastic gallon milk jug and set it beside the sink to catch the water in until the water begins to run scalding hot. I use that water all sorts of ways, like rinsing dishes, or making coffee, or if it has sat long enough to be room temperature, filling ice cube trays.

As soon as I put the last supper dish in the rack, I went up to my room to study. Through my front window I could see the little dipper. Just because I can't see men and animals made of stars doesn't mean I can't identify *anything* in the sky. The dippers are as plain as a Kentucky road map, and I can show you Polaris any night the sky is clear. "The name of the star at the end of the little dipper's handle," Dad told me one time, "is Polaris—because it is virtually exactly over the north pole. People in the northern hemisphere, like us, can always find due north so long as clouds aren't covering Polaris."

"I can locate north even on rainy nights," I said. "You just stand on the front porch and point toward the mailbox."

"Suppose you're not on the front porch," Dad suggested. "Suppose you were on a ship whose rations were running low and all you could see, in any direction you looked, was ocean, and you thought you might like to know whether you were going toward port or in circles? Then when dark came and you could see the stars and set your course by Polaris, don't you think you might sing one or two hymns?"

I could imagine blowing around all day, wondering if I were getting closer to home or to the sea monsters at the edge of the earth. I could imagine a sailor long ago seeing true and faithful Polaris brighten in the sky like the back-porch light Mom turns on to guide us home on nights we work in the barn. I looked at the stars, and they gave me a lost and found feeling at the same time. "Polaris has saved many a sailor's life," Dad said. "The other stars are like the moon—one place one time of night, another an hour later. In fact, they go in and out of our sight entirely. Orion is the brightest constellation in the winter sky, but by May he has vanished. But Polaris is always due north." He pointed. "Polaris is always there."

Jane Eyre was waiting for me under my pillow, so I meant

to get my homework over with as fast as possible, but I stood looking out the window. Looking out the top half, that is. The bottom was white with frost. It was the kind of sharp night when Dad used to call everybody out to see some constellation, but he had come in from checking the sheep's water and gone straight to bed without even telling Becky and me good-night. I pulled the shade down against the cold.

I had found out what Dad had been doing on the tractor while I was at school. With too many dead sheep to burn or bury, he had hitched the tractor to them, dragged them to the sinkhole farthest from the barn, dumped them in, and spread lime over them so they wouldn't attract *more* dogs. The job would have been a lot easier if he'd had a second person to help him. He keeps telling me that I'll make a farmer yet, but he must still be as worried about me as I am. I lay awake for a long time, feeling my train whistle feeling.

There's an excursion train that runs from Clermont to Maysville and back every summer. People take their children on it, just to give them an idea of what riding behind the old steam locomotives was like. The tracks used to belong to the L&N, but the L&N doesn't come here anymore. The company that owns them now uses them for nothing but hauling coal to Maysville, and, once a year, the excursion. Dad and Mom took Becky and me the first summer this train ran. A lot of people who weren't going to get on board turned out just to see the train. The last faces I saw as we pulled out were the Stanleys. I was glad they didn't board. J.M. was enough to spoil any excursion.

Becky was too little to know what was happening, and when that whistle blew, she howled. Mom had to comfort her. I was ashamed to admit that I needed comforting, too.

The lonely sound of that whistle made me think of all the gone trains and all the gone people who used to ride them. *No use,* it seemed to wail, *no yoo–oo–oose,* and underneath the train muttered *gone–gone–gone–gone–gone–gone–gone.* I've never wanted to take that ride again. To some kids, that whistle means fun and excitement, but I feel threatened when I hear it, and when I feel threatened, I hear it.

CHAPTER 13

Dress Review

"*H*ey, watch out with that firebrand!" a girl squawked. "You like to burnt somebody!"

Rubylee Barlow was trying to touch up her bangs and talk at the same time, and Rubylee always waves her hands when she talks. The Lowlands County Junior High girls' room wasn't designed to accommodate so many girls as were jammed in there changing clothes and primping for the annual Dress Review. "Oh," Rubylee exclaimed, "I'm *sor*-ry!"

"Whyncha fix your hair with a brush like everybody else?" the girl snarled. Everybody's nerves were strained. We had all toiled for weeks on the creations we were about to model for the strangers waiting in the auditorium. These strangers were mostly just our families, but 4-H has members in every school in Lowlands County. None of us knew everybody else's family.

That morning, everybody who had chosen Sewing as her spring 4-H project had turned in her garment at the County Extension Office to be judged for construction. The entries of those of us who also had signed up for Modeling were then sent over to the Junior High to be judged again, for how well they fit and how poised we were showing them off. We were supposed to walk out to the middle of the stage, show the audience front and back, walk the rest of the way across and then, hardest of all, turn around and walk the whole width of the stage back. Our parents would be sitting out front hoping our clothes wouldn't fall off us, hoping we wouldn't fall down, and three extension agents from UK would be sitting in none of us knew which seats, judging. None of us knew what the morning's sewing judges had ruled about our craftsmanship. We were all going to have to try to walk across that stage looking sure of ourselves, wearing a creation that, for all we knew, those judges had unanimously agreed was fit only for a car wash. Even the girls who pretended to be calm, like Hetty Anne, were jittery. "I'm getting a bump, of course," she had griped on the bus that morning.

Everything bad is *of course* with Hetty Anne, said not sourly but with a "What can you do?" grin. (I think it's from living on a horse farm. Somebody rich made an appointment to look at one of their yearlings, so *of course* the colt stuck his legs under the fence and hurt them. They bred their best mare to the best stallion they ever were able to take her to, so *of course* the foal came too early and died. Their youngest mare's two-year-old was favored to win an important race. *Of course* somebody burned the grandstand down the night before the race and the race was canceled.) I had looked closely at her chin. "No, you're not," I had said. "It's just a little pink. Makeup will hide it even from you. As for the audience, get serious."

"Maybe if I live on nothing but chewing gum and water all day, it'll go away," she had said more cheerfully. Now I saw her waiting her turn at the room's one mirror.

I didn't try to count how many there were of us trying not

to elbow each other in that narrow girls' room, but the only ones I knew were Hetty Anne, Rubylee, and Morgan Culverhouse. Hetty Anne had talked me into signing up for the Dress Review. "It makes no sense to model a tool apron for my dad," I had protested.

"The experience will be good for your self-confidence," Hetty Anne had disagreed. "Taxing your courage builds it, just the way lifting weights builds biceps. You can explain on your index card that the apron is for your dad."

Each of us had to print some stuff on an index card for Mrs. Roseberry, our County Home Extension Agent, to read to the audience while we were onstage. Hetty Anne typed mine for me. We weren't competing with each other, because Hetty Anne chose a much more advanced unit than I did. I took a pattern from Unit 4, but Hetty Anne's was from Unit 6. (Rubylee Barlow was a Unit Fiver, and Morgan Culverhouse was in Four, like me.) Not that there were hot prizes to compete for. The construction judges give every girl who hands in anything a ribbon and a diploma, and the modeling judges give a ribbon and diploma to every girl who makes it onto the stage. The ribbons do come in three different colors, and the diplomas don't all say the same thing. Also, each unit has one champion of construction and one of modeling. Those girls each get a plaque, and go on to compete with the winners from other Kentucky counties.

When the time had come to sign up for spring 4-H projects, I had expected Morgan to choose something like Patio Gardening, but she had put down Sewing-Modeling like Hetty Anne and Rubylee and me. She had made herself a green sundress. (I'd make myself a sundress, too, if I tanned like Morgan.) Rubylee had made a shiny purple evening gown, so low in front that I wondered if Mrs. Barlow would be getting her first glimpse of it when Rubylee appeared on stage. I also hoped Rubylee would get a short escort, not the basketball player she'd told me she was hoping for. (Every year, Mrs. Roseberry asks 4-H boys to volunteer for escort duty. After each girl has done her stage time, one of them ushers her to her seat in the models' section of the auditorium. "Who do you hope takes you?" Rubylee had asked me. "I choose that red-headed boy." I didn't care. Morgan had mentioned to me that Hume wasn't even able to come, let alone usher.)

Rubylee's evening gown was the reason I was in the girls' room. (I certainly didn't need privacy to put on a tool apron.) "Kate, honey, go with me and help me zip up my formal," Rubylee had pleaded. "LaNelle swore she would, but when Junior Thacker asked her to the movies, she went back on me, and I can't get Momma, because the baby screams if Momma gives her over to anybody."

I can believe what Rubylee said about LaNelle, but I was surprised to hear that the Barlow baby would cry if her own father held her. Then I saw Rubylee's dress, and I thought I understood. I felt ready to bet that Rubylee had never even asked her mother to help her.

It was a good thing I went with Rubylee, because she had made her dress so tight, she never could have zipped it for herself. ("Form-fitting," was how she described it on the index card she gave Mrs. Roseberry.)

Or maybe it's a bad thing I went. I didn't help Rubylee and leave; I hung around to see what everybody else put on. My staying contributed to the crowding that caused the accident. What makes it worse is that the main thing I was dying to see was Hetty Anne's coat. The one time she might have shown it to me before, we had (w)rapped with Cheops instead.

Hetty Anne makes practically all her own clothes. Even so, I had been surprised when she decided to tackle something so hard as a tailored coat, and white at that. I broke three of Mom's sewing machine needles on my heavy fabric, but my apron was still about fifty times easier to make. Mrs. Engle had brought Hetty Anne's box to our house the night before the judgings so that Mom could take it with mine to the Extension Office for us on her way to work. I had peeked in the box, but Hetty Anne had wrapped her coat in so many dry cleaner's bags that I couldn't see a thread of it. So, once I'd zipped up Rubylee, I hung around.

Morgan had chosen a simple pattern, but once she got the dress on, she looked like a *Seventeen* cover. When she caught sight of my apron, her face lit up. "Oh, Kate! An apron for your father! What a sweet idea!"

"What makes you think it's not for myself?" I asked.

Before Morgan could answer, that girl started squawking at Rubylee about her "firebrand."

"I tried to fix my bangs with a brush," Rubylee half wailed, "but when my heart gets to pounding like now, I just sweat so bad my bangs go limp on me every time, and a brush won't do a lick of good. That's why I always carry this thang—" she waved her hot curling iron again and a couple of us dodged. "And that's the littlest part of it." Rubylee finally laid down the iron to lift first one arm to the mirror, then the other. "I spend half my allowance on stuff to keep my clothes dry. I've tried every jar, tube, and spray sold in Clermont."

"Oh, you don't have to do that," said Morgan. "Just get your mother to give you some white vinegar." Rubylee and

RETA E. KING LIBRARY
CHADRON STATE COLLEGE
CHADRON, NE 69337

I stared at her. "Take a piece of cotton and scrub under your arms with vinegar every morning, and you'll never waste a dollar on any of that stinky store stuff again."

More of that *Consumerama* advice Morgan condescends to hand out to the less fortunate, I thought. I looked sideways at Rubylee, expecting her to cut Morgan down.

"*White* vinegar?" Rubylee repeated.

"They sell it at the supermarket," Hetty Anne put in. "Right beside the ordinary vinegar. Does that really work?" she asked Morgan.

"Works for me," said Morgan. "And Mother doesn't charge me for it." She grinned mischievously. "Antiperspirants come out of my allowance."

"Well," said Rubylee. "*White* vinegar. I'm sure gonna tell Momma she's got to get her some." She smiled brightly at Morgan and turned back to the mirror. The flip was restored to her bangs; she got out her mascara.

I'm sure Morgan gets a much bigger allowance than any of us. My wondering why she would pretend she needed to think of ways to stretch it was interrupted, because Hetty Anne finally took the wrappers off the dazzling white coat she had worked on every night, weekend, and holiday since we'd chosen our projects. I held my breath as she put it on. The buttons were mother-of-pearl. She left the top one unbuttoned and wound the blue silk scarf her boyfriend had given her for Christmas around her neck. It was just the color of her eyes and looked stunning.

Rubylee evidently thought so, too, because as she glimpsed Hetty Anne in the mirror, she gasped and turned toward her exclaiming, "Ohh, that's *beau*-tiful," and, of course, as Hetty Anne would say, *of course*, her arm flung out as she spoke, and *of course* she got mascara smeared on Hetty Anne's vision of a coat.

The swipe was at least two inches long, about halfway up Hetty Anne's left side. I leaned back against the wall. The coat was ruined, and Hetty Anne had never even got to wear it. "Oh, Hetty *Anne*," Rubylee moaned. You'd think Hetty Anne would be the one who would cry, but it was Rubylee's face the mascara started running down. (Maybe it's a good thing her neckline was so low, or her dress would have been ruined, too.)

"The dry cleaners will take that right out," Hetty Anne said quietly.

Some girls crowded forward to see what had happened. Others were retreating as far from the disaster as they could get. "Maybe you could try amyl acetate," Morgan whispered.

For a minute, my dismay turned to disgust. *Well, isn't that peachy, Miss Consumerama,* I wanted to say. *Got some amyl acetate in your pocket?* We all knew very well that there wouldn't be a drop in the whole Junior High building. Like Morgan, though, I could hardly speak.

"But what about to-*night?*" Rubylee wailed. "Now you can't *model* it. I've ruined *ev*-erything. Now—"

"Certainly I'm going to model it," said Hetty Anne. "I don't think anyone will see that mark from the audience."

We all looked away—at each other, at the floor, anywhere but at Hetty Anne. We all knew that everyone would see it instantly, and Hetty Anne did, too. "Stop crying and clean your face," she told Rubylee, "or they'll call your name and you won't be ready."

Hetty Anne turned away from Rubylee (*Can't bear to look at her,* I figured) and moved over beside me. "You aren't really going to model it, are you?" I whispered. That two-inch smear looked as big as the Black Sea to me.

Hetty Anne's face was a little pink and her lips were pressed together. I wondered if she really knew what she was doing, if she would forgive me, when morning rolled around, for letting her go out on that stage. My heart was in my throat; I tried to speak evenly. "Hetty Anne, it's a perfect coat, and you look like a dream in it, but I don't think the judges would feel they could get away giving somebody a prize with a big black smudge on her hip."

"So?" said Hetty Anne. Her color was beginning to fade back to normal. "There are ten girls competing in Unit Six, and nine of us aren't going to be champion. Why is that going to be any harder on me than on the other eight?"

I couldn't bring myself to say it, but not winning is one thing, and disgracing yourself is another. Would people laugh? Would they talk among themselves about "that strange Engle girl" the minute the show was over? "Listen," I started urgently.

"Kate, it will be *all right*."

I saw that Hetty Anne wanted to be left alone, that her disappointment was too great to face all of a sudden like that. I had no business in that crowded restroom anymore, anyway. Maybe if I hadn't come in the first place, having one fewer person in the room would have made the difference between everything for Hetty Anne and worse than nothing. That idea made me feel so bad, I left, the way Hetty Anne seemed to want me to.

Waiting in the wings, I kept my back to Morgan. I didn't want to have to talk about Hetty Anne. We couldn't see her, because Units One through Four were to the left of the stage and Units Five through Eight were to the right. I was glad.

Last Dress Review, she'd won Unit Five Honorable Mention, which means second only to the Champion. What she'd said to me then was, "Wait'll next year!" Now she was shrugging and telling me, "*Somebody* has to be the worst." If we were to catch sight of one another, I thought, one of us might start crying.

Showing off an apron, I had supposed, would be easy. I would go out with a big smile on my face and do like the stewardesses showing everybody exits and oxygen masks on the planes we take to Grandmom's. When Mrs. Roseberry read about the hammer loop, I would stick my thumb in it and mug, and so on. Now as I waited for Mrs. Roseberry to announce me, I was almost shaking. My gut was tight as a hickory nut, and my chest felt like an airplane hangar. The girl who'd snarled at Rubylee was leaning against the wall next to me wearing a fixed grin like a jack-o'-lantern. Back-stage was hot; my apron had never felt so heavy before. In spite of myself, I turned and cast an envious glance at Morgan's backless cotton. "My hands are freezing," Morgan whispered.

Don't ask me how I made it on and off, or whether Mrs. Roseberry read my index card or somebody else's. Don't ask me whether my family watched me or read magazines. All I can tell you is that at last I was back in the wings with my hand on the arm of a polite gawky boy I didn't know. As we walked to my seat I felt just the way I feel when I'm led to sit with Mom and Dad at weddings: half excited and half idiotic. I could at least be sure that nobody was staring at me anymore, because Mrs. Roseberry had called Morgan's name right after my exit, and Morgan was onstage. I glanced across the several rows that separated us at my parents and the Engles. They were all smiling at me. My insides twinged:

they didn't know about the Rubylee Barlow Memorial Inscription. Hetty Anne's boyfriend was sitting with the Engles. I hoped he'd be able to comfort Hetty Anne. I didn't know the judges, so I couldn't look for them. Rubylee had told me that one was a man; she'd seemed pleased.

I purposely didn't look at Mrs. Barlow when so much of Rubylee appeared onstage. Rubylee was nervous and walked too fast. Where she was supposed to turn around, she tripped on all the flounce she'd put around the hem. She didn't fall, but she stood in place for a couple of seconds looking so mortified that the audience laughed. I melted into my seat with embarrassment for her, but the laughter was sympathetic. Rubylee just gave the audience that same hopeless-me look she puts on when her arrows don't reach the target, and then smiled, and they gave her a nice hand.

The first Unit Six girl took Rubylee's tripping to heart, maybe a little too much. She walked so slowly, she could have been marching down the aisle to marry Frankenstein. Mrs. Roseberry finished reading her index card and this girl was still at the far side of the stage from where she was supposed to go off. She had to walk the whole stage width in silence; I would have died.

The second Unit Six girl was Hetty Anne.

Hetty Anne's head was high, her shoulders were back— and her left hand was on her hip. "Hetty Anne Engle is modeling a Lady Diana-style coat," Mrs. Roseberry read. Hetty Anne's hand stayed right where it was. With just the littlest smile—not the kind that shows your teeth, but the kind that shows you're thinking about something private that pleases you—she walked to center stage. ". . . made from Lowlands County wool woven by Madge Graith of Berea," Mrs. Roseberry read. Hetty Anne was turning in a slow circle. "The coat is lined with white satin," Mrs. Roseberry read. With her right hand, Hetty Anne held the coat open. The left hand stayed firmly on her hip. "Each cuff is tailored," Mrs. Roseberry read. Hetty Anne held her right hand in the air and twisted it deliberately to show the audience front and back. The left hand stayed in place. While Mrs. Roseberry read on about collar, seams, and placket, Hetty Anne finished her walk, putting each foot down in a straight line with the one behind it, just the way we'd been taught. (When I'd tried it, I'd felt like a teetering freak. Hetty Anne looked like the queen of England.) 4-H audiences always clap for everybody, but I thought this one clapped extra for Hetty Anne. I know those of us who had been in the girls' room with her did! That red-haired basketball player Rubylee admired escorted Hetty Anne to her seat a couple of rows in front of me, and I waited for Hetty Anne to turn and smile at me, but her neck was rigid. She sat staring straight ahead through all the rest of the modeling. When Mrs. Roseberry turned her microphone over to Mr. Estep to announce the winners, Hetty Anne never moved.

Dress Review is always the same. One at a time, starting with the Unit Ones, Mr. Estep recalls each of us to the stage. He gives each of us an envelope with a diploma and ribbon in it, and then we have to form rows starting at the back of the stage and stand there till all the girls have been called back. Some girls peek to see what color ribbon they got the minute they take their places in line, but Mom says I have a transparent face. (The first time Mom told me that, I thought she was talking about how fair my skin is.) I didn't want to look disappointed and have everybody in the audience think I must be conceited to have expected a better ribbon than I got, so instead of peeking, I kept my gaze fixed on Hetty Anne. What would she do when Mr. Estep called her name? I braced myself for an auditorium full of laughter if she came sashaying up the stage steps with that hand on that hip again.

Before Mr. Estep called her name, Hetty Anne had those mother-of-pearl buttons all unbuttoned. As she stood up, she slipped off her coat and flung it *Vogue*-ishly over one shoulder. She managed not to drop it when Mr. Estep handed her not just an envelope but also a plaque, and announced that she was Unit Six's Construction Champion. Her coat, he said, would go to the State Fair in August. This time Hetty Anne did flash me a smile as she took her place. The footlights, or maybe that blue scarf around her neck, made her eyes shine like sapphires.

Next Mr. Estep announced the Modeling Champions, starting with the Unit Oners. Come summer, those girls will go on to the biggest mall in Lexington and compete with the winning models from eight other counties. I didn't know the girl who won in Morgan's and my unit. The girl who won in Rubylee's had made a three-piece suit (and she hadn't tripped). The girl who won in Unit Six was Hetty Anne.

Hetty Anne's eyes turned almost black, and for a second, people in the back row could have heard that silk scarf if it had fallen to the floor. Then the audience began to clap. Hard as they clapped, they didn't scream for joy like some of us onstage. I could hardly wait to see the curtain come down. When I finally could throw my arms around Hetty Anne, her cheeks were the color of peonies, and she kept laughing. When she could stop she said breathlessly, "Now I know why some people shoplift. The closer I thought I was to being exposed, the harder my heart beat."

"You looked as if you didn't care," I said.

"I got to caring." Hetty Anne's face became serious. "I didn't care, going in, but I got to caring. I started to feel sort of—fascinated. Sort of the way Tom Allen says he felt when the Japanese flew over his barracks." Her face crumpled into a grin again. "Don't tell him I said so!" We both went off in the giggles at the thought of the disgusted look on Mr. Allen's face if some 4-H girl were to tell him that her modeling contest had taught her just how he had felt in a bombing raid.

"What color ribbon did you get?" Hetty Anne asked. I had forgotten all about my envelope. Blue.

CHAPTER 14

Foreclosure

In March, Mr. Engle's real estate agent advertised that he would sell the Engles' farm at auction. "I'm hoping he'll offer the farm separate from the house first," Hetty Anne told me, "because if we could get enough that way to pay off the bank, we wouldn't have to move." I had to lean toward her to hear her over our old school bus engine; it was as if she were half praying and thought that if anybody heard her but me and God, her prayer would be jinxed. "My parents would both get jobs and probably never work as hard again as we've all been working all my life trying to breed horses. I could sleep as late as Morgan Culverhouse, and my feet would be just as pink." I could tell she hated the whole idea.

Becky was in bed with a cold the Saturday of the auction, so Mom stayed home with her, and I was the only one who drove with Dad to Engles'. Dad didn't talk to me, which I understood. I didn't feel like making conversation myself. I just looked out my window.

The pastures were as brown as last year's abandoned corn. The sky was gray. Then as we turned onto the Engles' road, the sun fought through one small place, and the black crows flying across that single shaft of light turned to silver. *It's a good omen for Hetty Anne,* I decided to think. *Her father's black luck is going to turn to silver at this auction!* "Pops has eight thousand an acre in our farm, counting the barn and tool shed and fences and water fountains and not counting the house," Hetty Anne had told me as we rode to school the day before. "He's only got to get six thousand an acre to pay the bank off."

I had told my parents that at supper. "He won't," Dad had said. "He is three years too late."

"Oh, Rales," Mom had said.

By the time Dad and I got in sight of Engles' gate, the crows had settled black on a field of tan cornstalks. The dry leaves rattled, and I thought of the morning after the night of Orion. As Dad had begun dragging the first dead sheep out of the barnyard, I had heard a rattle like that in its throat.

A lot of cars and pickup trucks parked all along the Engles' driveway, and off it, too. Some were making deep muddy ruts right through Mrs. Engle's daffodils. I saw the man who owns the horse farm across the road from the Engles. "I guess Mr. Davis isn't too happy to see so many people," I suggested to Dad. I had heard him tell Mom that Mr. Davis was the likeliest one to bid. The Engles' land would be worth more attached to his land than it would be worth to somebody else. "With all this competition, he won't get the Engles' place cheap!"

"These people haven't all come to bid," Dad cautioned me. "Some come to sales like this just to see what land is bringing. Maybe they own a similar farm and wonder what they would get for it these days. Or maybe they've got one in mind to buy, and want to see if the price they've been quoted is in line. Some people come because they want to make the underbidder an offer on their own place before he gets back in his car.

"Some come because it's good for whatever their business is to be in crowds. See who's there, who's buying. Talk to people, listen. Get seen. Some people come just because it's something to do on a Saturday. And you can be sure the bank has people here, to make certain the farm brings as much as Engle owes them."

He was right about the bank; I saw Mr. Culverhouse, in a dark overcoat and galoshes, talking to a man wearing a camel's hair coat and a shiny green-and-red striped tie. I couldn't hear what they were saying. In fact, at first I thought Mr. Culverhouse was talking right through the man. If you make somebody mad, I wanted to tell Mr. Culverhouse, he'll go home and not bid! Mr. Culverhouse wasn't interrupting, though. The man wasn't talking, just chewing gum with his mouth open. I decided he was not a farmer come to bid but only one of those people Dad had said come to be seen. A farmer who chewed anything would have been chewing tobacco, which you can't do with your mouth open. Also, tobacco chewers have to spit. This man never spat.

Somebody who did was J. M. Stanley's father. I saw him and J.M over at the coffee table. Just as I was about to say so to Dad, Mr. Stanley spat, not two feet from the table, and J.M. put his knuckle to his nose and swiped clear to his wrist. I didn't know which of them disgusted me more. I turned away, and I didn't care whether they noticed, either.

There were a lot of men walking around that I didn't know. Some of them were talking, smiling. Others, like Mr. Davis, looked more like the poker players who sat around

Tom Allen's kitchen table every fourth Saturday night. They walked and looked, but they didn't let on if they were listening to the others, and they didn't speak to anybody.

Over to one side and sort of back, a small group was just standing—the Engles and some of their neighbors—the Allens, the Fletchers, the Barlows. One man I didn't recognize had his arm around Mrs. Engle. This group wasn't moving around, or talking, or smiling. They stood close together, like family at a burying. Dad and I walked over and joined them. Hetty Anne looked cold. Ursel wasn't there. Her boss gave her a day off for the yearling auction. I felt sure he would have given her one if she'd explained that her lifelong home was being auctioned.

Mr. Engle gave Dad a sort of stiff nod, but I could tell he thought it was friendly of Dad to be there with him. He introduced us to the man who had been standing with his arm around Hetty Anne's mother: "Rales Chidden, Frank Delk—Laura's brother."

Mr. Delk shook Dad's hand and put his arm back around Hetty Anne's mother. She said, "Good morning, Rales," and looked away fast; I thought she might be afraid she was going to cry.

Hetty Anne scowled, but not at me; she was just scowling. She didn't open her mouth. "I'm sorry about your mother's daffodils," I told her.

"They'll bloom again next year," she answered, and in a lower voice, "daffodils are like farmers. You can run right over them; give them a new season and they'll spring up again. Only way you can kill daffodils or farmers is to dig them up." I was glad nobody heard her but me.

Dad spoke to one or two of the other men and nodded to

their wives. Nobody was making conversation. It was "Morning, Rales," or just, "Rales." Then Dad said, "Any of you see the paper this morning?"

They all looked at him, whether they had or hadn't. "If you did, you saw where the pope died last night."

A few people looked surprised, me included, I imagine, but most looked as if they didn't think that was very interesting right at that moment. I was embarrassed for Dad.

"Yes, died in his sleep and went straight to heaven in time for breakfast," Dad said. "Didn't miss a meal. There was a man ahead of him at the gates, though—a banker, or so the pope heard him tell St. Peter." People shifted their feet when Dad said *banker*. Mr. Engle just looked at Dad. " 'I'll show you fellows your rooms,' St. Peter said, and the pope and the banker followed him—the banker first, because he got there first.

"The banker's room had a king-size bed and a VCR and a stereo and a beautiful cloud carpet, and the pope was thinking, *Wow, if he gets all this, what will my suite look like?* But where St. Peter led him, there was a narrow cot and an old AM radio and no rug on the floor, and the pope said, 'Goodness gracious,' or whatever popes say, 'are you sure you didn't get our assignments mixed? I'm the pope.'

" 'I know you are,' St. Peter told him, 'but you have to understand. We've got dozens of popes up here, but to get a *banker*, now *that* is *special*. It's a very rare century that puts a banker into heaven.' "

Mrs. Engle smiled. It was a grim smile, but Mr. Allen and Mr. Fletcher sort of laughed, and Hetty Anne's uncle laughed outright. Mr. Engle twisted up one corner of his mouth. "I've known J.H. all my life," he said to Dad. He was talking about Mr. Culverhouse; he and Dad have both known Mr.

Culverhouse all their lives. "My father did business with his grandfather." Dad nodded.

Then Hetty Anne's uncle Frank told a joke, too. It wasn't as good as Dad's, but at least you could see the group had relaxed a little, until the auctioneer said, "Folks, I'll read you our terms, and we'll get started."

First he would take bids on just the "dwelling and five acres." That meant the Engles' house plus Mrs. Engle's garden and Mr. Engle's orchard. I searched the sky for my crows, but I saw only that flat gray as far as I could look. A kildeer was screaming in the Engles' north pasture. A kildeer sounds like somebody who's been told that her children's school bus has rolled down a cliff into the cold river.

For a long time, nobody bid. Mr. Clay, the auctioneer, kept up a gabble that reminded me of the noise Dad's pickup truck makes when he's trying to get it going in January. About the time I had that awful cold-truck, old-truck thought, *It's not going to start,* the man in the camel coat scratched his ear.

For a second I thought nobody else was going to bid, and my heart started to thump. Then someone did, though I couldn't see who. I don't think the man in the camel coat could, either, because he looked all around and chewed harder than ever. I wished I had some gum, too. My mouth was dry. Camelcoat seemed to have to swallow every time anybody bid; his Adam's apple would bob up from behind that shiny tie and back down under it again. I could easily tell when *he* made a bid, because he hadn't worn gloves (maybe he expected the Engles' farm to have central heating), so any time he didn't need a hand, he kept it stuck deep in his pocket. But for noticing that, I would have forgotten how cold I was, I was concentrating so hard on trying to see who bid. Mr. Davis never moved; I don't think he even blinked. The other bidders were just as bad; I never did see who they were, even though the bidding was slow, like popcorn when the first few kernels begin to pop, now one here, now one on the other side of my pan, and I shake extra hard and get excited because once the first few start going . . . *pop* . . . *pop* . . . *pop,* I know that in a few seconds I'll start getting *pop-pop-pop-pop.* Mr. Clay tried to shake the bidders; he tried hard. I could see the worry in his eyes, because the *pop-pop-pop-pop* didn't come. I looked at Hetty Anne. She shrugged. Her lips were pushed together hard. I looked at Camelcoat and he raised his right hand from his deep pocket to his ear and stopped chewing. His mouth stayed open, but his jaw didn't move. To keep from passing out from worry I had taken to counting seconds between bids; Mr. Clay waited ten seconds for the final one. His own assistant made it, Dad told me later, under instructions from Mr. Culverhouse. When Camelcoat heard that last bid, both his hands came out of his pockets and stayed out. He balled them into fists and strode off toward the parked cars. He didn't even stay to listen to the next part, the bidding on the farm. I had been right; he was no farmer. I never was less pleased to be right.

I saw Tom Allen hurrying after Camelcoat, but I was too stunned to think anything of it. If it was hard for Mr. Clay to believe that Camelcoat's bid was the last he was going to get on the Engles' house, it was impossible for me. The figure seemed so low, I might have died right on the spot, if Hetty Anne hadn't explained to me earlier that whether her parents accepted the final bid on the house depended on what they were offered for the farm separate from the house, and what they were bid for the two together. I couldn't look at Hetty Anne. I just put my arm around her.

Mr. Clay didn't give the Engles any time to feel sick. He got busy describing the next option, everything *but* the house and its five acres. Mr. Davis was the first to nod. His mouth was clamped tight as a turtle's that has something he wants between his jaws and won't let go unless somebody chops his head off. He kept his back toward his neighbor, Mr. Engle. When the bidding would slow down, Mr. Clay would remind people of something, like how many stalls the Engles' barn has. Then someone would bid, and Mr. Davis would nod, and after a few seconds somebody else that I never did see would raise the figure, but by a number so small it was insulting to Mr. Engle. I tried to glance at Hetty Anne without letting her see me turn my head; her lips were white.

The higher the numbers got, the more Mr. Clay had to talk in between bids: how deep the Engles' topsoil was, and how much tobacco the government would let them grow if they wanted to, or how new some of the fences were. I figured he did that to make it look as if he were the one holding things up, and not that the bidders had to consider a long time whether to go another one hundred dollars an acre higher.

I knew that Mr. Engle's costs had come to him in thousands, not hundreds. I knew that Mr. Davis knew it, too.

Mr. Davis raised the per-acre bid one hundred dollars. His eyes glittered like a bull turtle's. Mr. Clay's urgent, anxious sing-song started up again. The men in the Engles' yard stood motionless. Under my arm, Hetty Anne was rigid. "Take your time," Mr. Clay said. "Anybody needs to go in the house, call his banker—get his wife's permission—we'll wait on you." Nothing. "This farm's been in the same family since the original military survey, two hundred years ago. Might be another two hundred years before you get another opportunity like this." No one moved but Mr. Engle, shifting his weight. "Folks," Mr. Clay said, "let me tell you about Matt Engle's alfalfa." He ran through the pounds and acres of corn and wheat and alfalfa the government allowed Mr. Engle to sell last year. Someone else bid, I never saw who. The glitter went out of Mr. Davis's eyes. Neither he nor anyone else answered Mr. Clay again.

A single crow flew over the house with a caw like laughter. The bidding was over on the farm part. I wanted to go away and lie down and put a blanket over my head. Dad was right. Even added to the last offer Mr. Clay had received for the house, the bid on the farm wasn't enough to pay off the bank, let alone leave the Engles anything at all. My arm around Hetty Anne couldn't even feel her anymore; I was numb. Mr. Clay was already asking for bids on the "total package."

He asked, and no one moved. I couldn't believe what was happening. Mr. Clay asked for a bid and nobody offered a thing. Finally Mr. Clay stopped asking. I looked at the Engles and their neighbors, but my mind's eye saw our barnyard the morning after the night of Orion, when I stood with Mom and Dad looking at our few remaining sheep standing huddled and stunned.

The last offer for the farm, we learned that day, also had come from someone bidding for Mr. Culverhouse's bank. Later that week Mr. Culverhouse told the Engles that they could stay on their farm for a very low rent until the bank got an acceptable offer for it. "Mr. Culverhouse is afraid the place will 'lose value' if it sits unoccupied," Hetty Anne said tonelessly. "Well, it gives me a chance to finish my school year here; they'll never find a buyer before June. It gives Pops more time to sell the horses and look for work.

"Meanwhile," her voice lightened, "we can hardly buy toothpaste. In fact, we aren't buying toothpaste; we're using baking soda." She paused and looked me in the eye. "Baking soda is better for your teeth, anyway. It doesn't contain abrasives."

She was trying to be her usual jokey self, and she is still trying, but I can't get that picture out of my mind—of people turned to sheep by misfortune; of people turned to sheep.

CHAPTER 15

Math Problems

I had been looking forward to Saturday, when I would be able to pay more attention to Annie. She had been running to her gate and bleating for me as I got off the school bus every afternoon, and Saturday I saw that she did the same thing every time I stepped into the backyard. Finally I realized that Annie never got to nurse except when I went in the field and offered Sadie an apple or an ear of corn. Yet whenever I felt Sadie's udder, it was slack.

You can force a ewe to let a stepchild nurse her, but you can't force her to have milk. We would lose money, Dad had said, trying to hand-raise even a ewe-orphan. It was too late to graft Annie onto any of Tom Allen's ewes. Would Dad send her to the market? I would take her under my arm and run away first, I thought wildly, knowing that was impossible. I went over to where Dad was attaching the wagon to the tractor so he could load all those branches I'd cut. He looked tired. "I'm afraid Sadie's drying up," I told him. "Could I give Annie extra milk?" I scraped my inside lower lip with my teeth to try to make my mouth less dry while I waited for his answer.

Dad had straightened up slowly as I began speaking. "It's up to you, Kate," he said, and bent over the hitch again.

I stood there looking at the back of his head. Usually Dad makes *all* the practical decisions about this farm. I was thrilled that he was going to let me do what I wanted, but his answer scared me. It was like what somebody would say who had given up.

Mom got me a lamb nipple and a twenty-five pound sack of milk replacer powder, and I taught Annie to drink from a Coke bottle.

I told Hetty Anne about it as we talked before church. "It's only for a few weeks," I said. "Annie will be three months old in April, and I'll be able to stop."

"Just as the evenings get pleasant, of course," said Hetty Anne. It *was* funny. Feeding Annie was like stargazing with Dad; I only got to do it when I was sure to be shivering.

I gave Hetty Anne back Ursel's *Jane Eyre*. For me, the trouble with the consolations of literature is that for other people to have worse troubles than mine doesn't comfort me a bit; it makes me miserable.

"You're supposed to feel inspired by how Jane bore her troubles," Hetty Anne said, "and triumphed in the end."

The trouble with that idea is that only a book's main character is sure to triumph in the end. Lots of less important characters in *Jane Eyre* fall over the cliff. Nothing good happens to them to comfort me for their sakes. For one thing, I don't feel like a main character myself. I picture at least half the dreadful things that happen to anybody in the book happening to me and my family, and no victory in the last chapter.

I certainly don't picture any sexy hero like Jane's Mr. Rochester going blind and coming to depend on *me*. Not that I would want Hume Culverhouse to go blind.

Hetty Anne laughed when I told her that I worry twice as

much about what will happen to my family now that I have read *Jane Eyre* as I did before. "You better just worry about sure things, like your math test tomorrow," she said.

The trouble with trying to study that night for my math test was that one set of numbers made me think of another, and no matter how hard I tried to forget the second set, I couldn't. Instead of reviewing the problems my class had worked for the last six weeks, I reviewed the bidding on the Engles' farm. I multiplied the top bid per acre they got times the number of acres we have, subtracted what we owe the bank, and studied *that* number. What kind of house would it buy? Before the Engles' auction, Hetty Anne had shown me an article in the *Lexington Herald-Leader* that reported what the average central Kentucky house costs. "Nobody but the Pentagon could pay that, of course," she had said. Certainly if nobody offered us more per acre for our land than the Engles were offered for theirs, *we* could not pay it. Hetty Anne and I had been studying the *Herald-Leader*'s Sunday real estate section all winter. Based on numbers, the "average house" was a shoebox on half an acre with a toothbrush stuck in front for landscaping. "Less to mow," said Hetty Anne. Mowing the Engles' pastures takes Mr. Engle two days a week, six months a year. Horses don't eat the way sheep do. Not that Dad doesn't have to mow, too. Not even a sheep eats ragweed and thistles.

Not even farmers who have lost their farms.

What such farmers can eat was the next question my mind reviewed instead of my homework. All our money was coming from Mom's job. What if, after we lost our farm and moved to a shoebox, Dad still couldn't find a job? Mr. Engle hadn't found one yet. Could we live on what Mom was making if we didn't have our shelves full of canned fruit and vegetables from our garden and orchard, and our freezer full of ground mutton?

My test was even tougher than Hetty Anne had warned. By the time Ms. Parish had it half on the board, kids were groaning all over the room. Not Morgan Culverhouse. She was done and handing in her paper before I was a third of the way through. When our papers came back, hers was marked ninety-three, and mine, sixty. I had never made below a B on my report card, but sixty meant that I was about to. I sat staring at my mistakes. "Oh, Kate!" Morgan exclaimed. "How could you miss the first three? They're taken *exactly* out of the book!"

Morgan gets straight A's. Morgan does her homework the minute she gets home. Morgan's mother is there to help her if she needs it. Even back when Mom was home, she was likelier to say, "The ox is in the ditch, Kate; drop everything," than, "Need any help with your homework, dear?" (We never had an ox, even before the drought. Mom is quoting the Bible. Jesus said if you had to choose between worship service and pulling your ox out of a ditch, it was okay to choose the ox.)

Why shouldn't Morgan know everything in the math book? I asked myself. Morgan doesn't spend the night before a test worrying about whether the bank is going to turn her family out on the road. My chest felt tight. "I guess I'm just nothing like as smart as you, Morgan," I said. When my Sunday School teacher told us about heaping coals of fire on the heads of those who give us a hard time, she intended us to use a sweetly meek tone of voice. Mine came out sarcastic, but it worked, anyhow. Morgan turned away without one more word and minded her own business. The Bible is full of good advice.

I don't know why Morgan goes to school in Clermont, anyhow. Her mother went to private school in Lexington when she was Morgan's age; she comes from Lexington. That's where Morgan got her name; Mrs. Culverhouse wanted everyone who met Morgan to know that that statue in front of the Lexington courthouse is of somebody kin to her. I guess Mrs. Culverhouse doesn't know how everybody laughs at that statue. It is of General John Hunt Morgan on a stallion. What's funny is that everybody in Kentucky knows that General Morgan rode a mare named Black Bess. The sculptor was an Italian; he didn't know any Kentuckians. "He just assumed a war horse had to be male," Mom says. "Men have a lot to learn, and not just Italians."

I think Morgan would be better for a boy's name than for a girl's, even if the Italian had sculpted General Morgan sitting in a rocking chair, but Morgan's brother had to be named Justin Hume, for his father and his grandfather. He is called Hume, because his grandfather is called Justin. (His father is called J.H.) Hume is so handsome it hurts to look at him; Hetty Anne admits it, although she has a boyfriend at Lowlands High. Whenever I wish Morgan would go to private school so I wouldn't have to see so much of her, I remember that if she did, Hume probably would, too.

CHAPTER 16

Package from Virginia

A couple of summers ago, Mom and Mrs. Tye finally figured out that I was old enough to look after little children. (I'd only been looking out for Becky for three years!) The telephone rang one day just as we were finishing lunch. Mrs. Tye wanted to speak to Mom, and I could tell from her voice that she was in a swivet.

Mr. Tye was killed when his Cessna crashed in the mountains in a thunderstorm. Mrs. Tye sold their big house in Clermont and moved into a subdivision that sprang up down the road from us three or four years ago. As soon as she had unpacked, she got a job. She is teller at our bank's drive-in window.

Mom came to the phone and we all heard her making soothing noises: "Oh, my" and "Oh, dear" and "I certainly agree with *that*," and so on—the way she talks to Dad when he's denouncing the government. Mrs. Tye was only working afternoons then. It was just about time for her to go to the bank, and her twins' baby-sitter hadn't shown up. "Sure, bring them right over," we heard Mom tell her.

Good, I thought. I had a new book. Becky was three that summer, and Fred and Nancy were four. With the twins to play with, I thought, Becky wouldn't be pestering me and I could read.

Trouble was, Fred and Nancy didn't want to go play quietly with Becky in her room. They wanted to play with me. It was four to one, because Mom and Becky both voted with the twins.

Baker's clay, I thought. I had a clear and lovely vision of three little heads bent over their modeling projects at one end of the front porch, and me with my book in a lawn chair at the other end.

How to make baker's clay: Mix three cups of flour with one cup of salt. *Gradually* stir in two cups of hot water. Knead fifteen minutes. Cool five minutes. You can add (1) coloring, (2) scent.

All the while I kneaded the clay, Fred stood by proclaiming what excellent rabbits and dogs and trucks he was going to make. When the time came, however, neither he nor either girl would make anything unless I sat on the porch floor with them and modeled right along. Then Fred said he was thirsty, and in the small time it took me to go inside for orange juice, Nancy told Becky that Becky's rabbit looked more like a cabbage, and Becky threw it over the porch rail and met me at the door saying she was tired of modeling and wouldn't I tell her a story.

Now that they'd made as big a mess of the porch as possible, half the fun had gone out of baker's clay for Fred and Nancy, anyhow, so they echoed Becky. At least I got to sit in my lawn chair. I told some of Grandmom's Buh Rabbit stories, like about the time Buh Frog had him treed, and he escaped by spitting tobacco juice in Buh Frog's eye. That was the last story, because I could see Fred looking thoughtfully at Nancy's eyes, and that caused me to think of something hazardous in every story I could remember. Besides, my throat was giving out. "How would you like to play cards?" I asked my masters.

"Slap Jack!" Fred cried instantly.

Nancy didn't look so eager. I wondered if Fred liked Slap Jack because it let him hit Nancy. "That's a two-player game," I pointed out. "Why don't the three of you play Old Maid?"

"You, too!" they chorused.

Without committing myself, I went inside and got a deck I thought might be nearly complete. By the time I got back, Fred was putting clay balls down Nancy's neck, and Becky was making him more. "Everybody wash hands!" I commanded. "First one whose hands pass inspection gets to deal." That proves how much I'd already learned about children just from taking care of Becky. I knew that if I merely said, "First one back gets to deal," they'd all come storming back without a clean hand among them. What I didn't know was that Becky, who *hates* to deal, who always makes me deal when we play together, would sit down in the middle of the staircase and cry because, being shorter than Fred and Nancy, she got left behind in the dash to the bathroom. What I didn't know was that Nancy, having beaten Fred to the basin, would scream at him because he didn't *wash* his hands, he merely towelled them vigorously while she was washing hers. So I had one child in tears of fury at herself for being little, one in tears of fury with her brother for "cheating," and one close to tears of fury with me for showing him the clay between the fingers he had breathlessly claimed were clean.

"I've got a better idea than cards," I said. "Let's make a squash horn band." Anything that sounded like noise struck

127

that trio as a good idea, even though they didn't know what I was talking about. (Becky wasn't born yet when Dad showed me how to make a squash horn.) I got a paring knife and out to the garden we all trooped.

How to make a squash horn: Take a big squash leaf and carefully trim it from the solid end of its stem without cutting into the opening. Slice short opening in hollow part of stem, close to solid end. Put solid end, including slit, into mouth. Blow.

The tone depends on the size of the stem, so I chose four different-sized leaves. Our first tries sounded more like J. M. Stanley giving somebody the raspberry than like the angel Gabriel, but I lengthened each slit and then we got genuine toots. We serenaded Mom in the kitchen and Dad in the barn. Joshua's army wasn't better pleased with its act than my band was with ours. I can say that we were unquestionably more musical than the same number of performers blowing on paper-wrapped combs. When Mrs. Tye arrived to take the twins home, everybody was flushed, three of us with joy.

Before many minutes, I was flushed with joy myself. "Kate," Mrs. Tye said, "I'm going to pay you just what I would have paid that sitter!"

Now I'm the twins' favorite sitter. My parents still don't allow me to sit for anyone else, or at night, or even for the Tyes, unless Dad or Mom is going to be in *our* house the whole time, where they can hear our telephone ring if I call. With all those restrictions, I really can't earn much. Sometimes that hurts worse than others, and this Easter was one of those times.

Waiting for the bus on Good Friday this March I was a little chilly, but the frost sparkled on the fence wire, the daffodils had rushed upward at least an inch since Wednesday, and suddenly I heard a birdsong that made me run for the house to tell everybody: the first red-winged blackbird was back!

I didn't get to tell Hetty Anne about the blackbird because she began talking the second I sat down. "Too bad our bus picks me up before you," she said. "We've got live entertainment in our front yard this morning." Then she stopped and waited for me to ask her what kind of live entertainment.

"What kind of live entertainment?" I asked.

"Well, we've got a new B&B." Any night the Engles have a B&B, they earn enough to pay the bank a week's rent. "He's a Bhagwasher. He wears only shades of lavender, even his boots, and he chants twice—"

"A *bog*washer," I interrupted. "How do you wash a *bog*?"

"He's not washing anything; Bhagwash is an Indian word, I guess—he spells it b-h-a-g-w-a-s-h. Bhagwash is his religion. Or rather, it's what he has instead of religion." She giggled. "Ursel calls it *hog*wash. He says religion is what you're programmed to have before you wake up to true enlightenment. His name is Swami Prem Neehar. Swami is his title; his leader, the Bhagwash, gave it to him when he joined the Beautifield."

"Joined the what?"

Hetty Anne's mouth was stretched like a toad's eating paste, but she pretended to answer seriously. "The Beautifield is the lovingness space the Bhagwashers bought for their leader in Tennessee so they can raise trout and chickens for him while he meditates. Swami Prem doesn't eat trout or chickens himself. Bhagwashers are vegetarians. He explained that to my mother over the phone when he made his reservation. He didn't tell her he was going to chant the sun up and down."

"Well, if Bhagwashers are vegetarians, what do they raise fish and chickens for?"

"Money. They sell them to people they haven't converted yet. If they managed to convert everybody, they wouldn't be able to sell them anymore, of course; they'd have to quit raising them. I asked Swami Prem what their time would go to then. He said, rejoicing and soybeans. Then he asked me what time my school bus came. If I'd known he was going to run out in the yard five minutes ahead of me and start dancing, I might have fibbed. You should have seen all the kids' heads sticking out the windows."

"What is a Bhagwasher swami doing in Lowlands County?" I asked. "And don't say *dancing*."

Hetty Anne grinned; she had been about to say *dancing*. "He's on his way up north to visit his parents. He used to be Stanley Edward Biddle III, before he moved beyond what he calls 'all that old stale programmed stuff' and woke up to enlightenment. He got a letter from his parents recently that his grandfather left him some money, but they wouldn't send it to him; he would have to come get it. They don't want the Beautifield to have it, he says. Everybody who joins the Beautifield takes a vow to be personally and materially nonpossessive. They give *all* their worldly *and* all their spiritual goods to the Beautifield. Swami Prem hasn't been home since he joined. He says his parents probably think that if they get him home, he'll stay, but he won't. He says he wouldn't even go, if the Beautifield didn't need money for an airstrip for the leader's jet. I asked him how many times he was going to stop and dance along the way. He said when-

130

ever spontaneous joy overtook him. You should have seen his necklace bounce when spontaneous joy overtook him five minutes ahead of the school bus."

I tried to picture somebody whose parents called him Stanley Edward Biddle III dancing his way north in three shades of lavender clothes, like a purple bird coming home for the summer—only this bird wasn't coming for the summer, he was coming for the money—Stanley Edward Biddle I's money.

Money and clothes: two things I especially didn't want to think about. I forgot my red-winged blackbird and Hetty Anne's weird Bhagwasher both, and thought about money and clothes. Hetty Anne must have been having some of the same thoughts, because after a minute she asked me, "What are you going to wear Sunday?"

Always before there were two sure things about my family's Easter preparations: Mom and Becky and I have gone to Miss Gravely's house to choose the new centerpiece egg, and Mom has made me and Becky beautiful dresses. This year I thought we might save money and use last year's centerpiece, but Mom said no, Miss Gravely counts on her regular customers. What with working for Mr. Watkins, though, Mom didn't have time for the dresses.

"I haven't decided," I answered Hetty Anne. Actually my parents were the ones I hoped hadn't decided. The best way to put it is that the question was hanging, but that was what Ms. Parish calls a "play on words," one that Hetty Anne couldn't have recognized, and explaining it was the last thing I wanted to do.

"I'm going to wear my pink organdy, of course," Hetty Anne said. "I took a piece of lace and sewed it all around the bottom, and I took a strip of organdy that was left over after I made the dress and sewed it all around under that lace, so the dress is long enough for me again."

Hetty Anne is tall. She is not quite the tallest person in our school, but she is easily the tallest on our bus. "That pink dress becomes you," I told her.

"The new organdy strip is a little darker than the rest, of course, but the lace keeps your eye from feeling quite sure of that. I hope. I wonder what Morgan will wear."

Morgan's mother takes her to Lexington to buy her clothes. Morgan never wears jeans to school, only dresses or skirts and sweaters. Thank goodness she doesn't go to our church.

I have one sweater as pretty as any of Morgan's; Grandmom sent it to me last Christmas. This sweater is the color of holly berries; I took it straight out of its box and put it on and we all agreed it was gorgeous. Pure wool, too; that pleased Dad. "Your mother was wearing a gorgeous sweater the first time I saw her," he told Becky and me. "That's why I noticed her—the gorgeousness of her sweater."

"Behave yourself," Mom said, and they both laughed. That was Christmas.

The Christmas sweater came from Woodward and Lothrop in Alexandria, Virginia, where Grandmom lives. When a big package addressed to Mom arrived from Woodward and Lothrop a couple of weeks before Good Friday, Becky and I didn't have to consult the FBI to guess it would be a present to somebody from Grandmom, so we could hardly wait for Mom to get home and open it.

I was feeding Annie in the pasture when Becky came looking for me. "Mama's on the telephone," she said.

"Can you fix supper, Kate?" Mom asked me. "We're

swamped in here. Every money-earner in Lowlands County seems to have put off filling out tax returns till the last gasp. Mr. Watkins wants me to work an extra hour, if you think you can manage."

I did have supper ready by the time darkness fell and Dad put the tractor away and came in, but we waited for Mom. When Mom finally came, though, Becky met her at the door with that package from Virginia. "Can you open it *now?*" Becky urged.

Mom didn't have her coat off yet. "I guess so," she told Becky with a big smile. Dad frowned and went in and sat at the table, but Mom didn't notice. I've thought how things could have been different umpteen times. I could have said, "What I've cooked needs to be served right away," for instance. It didn't, though, and I was just as eager to see what Grandmom was sending as Becky was, so we "three women," as Dad calls us sometimes when he's not crazy about what we're doing, gathered in the living room..

Woodward and Lothrop's box contained two dresses, one for me and one for Becky. We whooped for joy. The box was better than Christmas, because we hadn't been imagining fantastic possibilities for two months the way we do before Christmas. We hadn't been expecting anything. My dress was green with a deep hem and a sash that would hide letting out the waist, so I might still be able to wear it next year, and a pocket with a white lace handkerchief in it, the kind a fairy would sleep under. Becky's was yellow organdy. A shining yellow slip came with it—polyester, so nobody would ever have to iron it. Becky and I *ran* upstairs to try everything on.

Becky's dress zipped up the back, so I had to stop and help her, and then she insisted on putting on her patent leathers, which she insists on buckling herself even though she takes forever. (For one reason, they are too tight; she needs new.) I could have gone on down ahead of her, but I was looking at my dress in the mirror. It fit perfectly.

I started daydreaming that Hetty Anne and I were talking in the churchyard Easter Sunday and the Culverhouses drove by on their way to *their* church, and Hume was by the window, and he looked out. . . .

Finally Becky and I floated down the stairs and posed in the dining room, Becky pirouetting like a ballerina, I with my back straight as if I had on a slippery crown. (Hetty Anne says all crowns are slippery.)

Dad was sitting over his empty plate; Mom was standing behind him in the doorway to the living room, not seeing his expression. Becky stopped twirling and stood beside me beaming, waiting to be told how beautiful we were.

"Did you ask your mother for those?" Dad asked Mom.

"Goodness no," she said.

"Look how tight my shoes are," Becky said, sticking one leg straight out and pointing her toe like a dancer. "I have to have new before Easter."

"Are those the only shoes you've got?" Dad asked her.

"I have saddle oxfords," said Becky, "but they're for ordinary. I can't wear saddle oxfords with this dress."

"Time for ordinary clothes now," Mom said quietly. "Hang your dresses up carefully and come to supper."

Mom served what I had cooked: steamed cabbage and mackerel loaf. "No potatoes?" Dad said.

"Our carbohydrates are the bread crumbs in the fish loaf," I told him. We studied balanced meals in Health Class.

"I see," Dad said, and took a bite of cabbage. Mom always fixes vegetables like beans and cabbage his mother's way, which is boiled a long time with a hambone or bacon rind, but I was ready to explain about how boiling too long uses scads of electricity and kills vitamins, and about what fat does to your arteries. Dad didn't make a single complaint, though. "Interesting cabbage," he said. "Did you learn this way in Health Class?"

I felt proud of Dad for being willing to eat foods new ways. Many grown-ups' minds are closed.

Halfway through the meal I remembered that I was supposed to offer everybody vinegar with steamed cabbage. "I had my mind on Grandmom's box," I apologized. Nobody laughed with me.

When meals are as quiet as ours was that night, I go straight from washing dishes to my hot-air register. "Let Kate learn how to make herself a dress in Health class," I heard Dad say as I sat down. I couldn't hear what Mom answered. "Why does your mother think I can't clothe my own children?" Dad asked her. Mom murmured again. "This *gift* puts me right where your mother wants me, like a snake under a forked stick—can't turn either way. If I send my children to church on Easter in somebody else's clothes, I'm disgraced before all my friends, and if I won't, my children will hate me. So now it's special shoes for Becky, and next it will be new hats for both of them. I'll wind up paying out money I don't have, can't afford to borrow, and nobody will even thank me because it will be the marvelous new dresses that everybody notices, and I didn't buy those. Or were you planning to ask your mother for hats and shoes, too?"

"Not *too*," Mom had stopped murmuring. "I told you, I didn't say a word to Mother!"

Now it was Dad whose voice dropped too low for me, and Mom who broke in. "As for new hats, they don't need new hats; I can put new ribbons on their old hats. As for Becky's shoes, I get paid next Friday, and I can certainly afford to buy my daughter shoes." I heard Dad's chair scrape. I got to my desk in a hurry.

The next day when I got home from school the dresses were gone from our closets. "Mama hung them in the attic," Becky said. After I fed Annie, and while Becky and Dad were busy outside, I went up to see. There both dresses hung, more beautiful even than I had remembered. I stroked mine; it was smooth, smooth as a royal gown. I wanted to tell my grandmother that green is just the right color for a queen whose kingdom is pastures, but I had a feeling I'd better not write her anything right away.

Next morning Hetty Anne and I tried to name all the queens there ever have been named Katherine. We let the ones who used *C* count, too. Henry VIII married three Catherines, and Catherine the Great was the most famous queen ever of Russia, and Catherine de Medici was queen of France for more than fifty years, Hetty Anne said.

"There isn't any queen named Morgan," I mentioned.

"Morgan le Fay," Hetty Anne reminded me, "was queen of Avalon."

Morgan le Fay was King Arthur's sister. She was the cause of all his troubles. If it hadn't been for her son, Mordred, King Arthur's Knights of the Round Table would have gone right on doing noble deeds forever instead of fighting each other and wounding Arthur unto death. "Morgan le Fay was the wickedest woman in the whole King Arthur book."

"She's the one who took him away to nurse when he thought he was dying," Hetty Anne said. "She's the one who'll send him back to Britain if they're ever going to perish without him." We forgot about Queen Katherines, then, and argued all the rest of the way to school about how much good people have to do to be forgiven for the bad they do.

I wish we had come to an exact firm answer. I've gone on asking myself that question all spring. Grandmom's dresses were just the start.

CHAPTER 17

Ginger

Camelcoat's name was Irvin Scheeler, and he owned the biggest Chevrolet dealership in Miami, he told Dad. He gave Dad his card the day before Easter. "Honest Irv Scheeler, your Chevrolet dealer," it said, and listed three locations in Miami where you could choose one of his "INCREDIBLE WHEEL-DEAL STEALS." I'd gone back with Dad to the fence line we share with Tom Allen, because a rotten post needed replacing. I was holding the new post in place, and Dad was tamping the loose dirt around it with the heavy iron tamper when we saw Mr. Allen and Camelcoat heading toward us. This time Camelcoat was wearing gloves and a muffler, so at least he did come away with something from the Engles' auction, even if it was only a better idea of how to dress for Kentucky in winter. "Here's somebody I'd like you to know," Mr. Allen was saying as he came up to us, "the best neighbor a man could have."

Camelcoat didn't stop chewing his gum while he shook Dad's hand, but he stretched his mouth extra wide like a smile. Mr. Allen didn't think to introduce me, but Dad did, so I had to shake hands with Honest Irv also, in spite of his low bidding on the Engles' house. It was not, we learned, the first Bluegrass house he had tried to buy. "I've been explaining to Mr. Scheeler—" Mr. Allen began.

"*Irv*," Mr. Scheeler interrupted, "just call me *Irv*. Everybody in Miami calls me Honest Irv!" I saw Dad's expression not change.

"—explaining to Irv," Mr. Allen said, "that he's just not going to find the kind of house he wants without some land to it."

As a boy in Florida, Mr. Scheeler dreamed of a house with a fireplace where he could hang his stocking. Now that the car business had been good to him, he said, he could have it. The Allens' house had a fireplace in every room. Mr. Scheeler had no use, though, for a farm.

"That's what I thought when I was young," Mr. Allen said. "All I wanted was out of Lowlands County. Then the army took me. By VJ Day, I never wanted to breathe another man's air or take another man's orders. Land. Land of his own is the only thing that lets a man be a man—your own land, where you're the general, you call the shots."

"I'm looking for a place to get *away* from decisions," Mr. Scheeler protested, not altogether unhappily, I thought. "My business gives me all the decisions I need."

"Usually," Mr. Allen said thoughtfully, "a man gets land, he finds out he always wanted some."

Mr. Scheeler's laugh was confident. "What I want is a little place I can come, can't nobody telephone me I don't want to talk to. Place my friends can stop over with me sometimes. I got a lot of friends come down to Florida for the winter."

"This place is just fifteen minutes from I-75," Mr. Allen said. "Rales here is the man you should talk to. He owns all you can see there to your north. You might be able to cook up a deal with him, maybe lease him your acres. You've already got you a connecting gate. You couldn't find you a better man than Rales Chidden to do business with." I marveled at the way Mr. Allen talked to Mr. Scheeler as if Mr. Scheeler already owned the farm.

Mr. Scheeler's mouth automatically jerked wider when Mr. Allen spoke the word *deal*. I imagined his Adam's apple bobbing up and down behind his muffler. Dad just smiled without opening his mouth. "That wasn't the time," he explained to Mom later, "for me to volunteer that I couldn't lease a lawn mower. The more the man thinks about Tom's house as *his*, the harder he will find giving it up." Maybe, if they have to quit farming, Dad and Mr. Allen should sell cars in Miami.

After Mr. Allen and Mr. Scheeler left Dad and me to finish mending that fence, Dad let me drive the truck back to our garage. Shifting into reverse gave me a little trouble, but nothing else did. At first when Dad began to teach me, I had nightmares about the truck getting away with me at the wheel, as helpless as if I were riding Supernova bareback and a train was roaring straight at us (another of my nightmares), but now I can hardly wait to be old enough for a license.

Mom had been waiting for us to get home so I could go with her and Becky on our annual Lenten visit to Miss Gravely to choose our centerpiece Easter egg. "Maybe this year we could put all the Miss Gravely-eggs we already have in a bread basket and use that," I had suggested that morning. I was glad Mom's answer had been, "I don't think we should do that to Miss Gravely. She's counting on us."

Going to Miss Gravely's is like walking into a picture book. The house is red with lots of white trim everywhere there could be any. The trim is like the icing decorations Miss Gravely paints on the cookies she always has for customers. The red is like a barn. "Grandfather chose that color when he built," Miss Gravely says, "and that's the color the house has kept ever since. Doesn't need painting this year, thank goodness."

From February to November, something is always blooming in Miss Gravely's yard. In March, crocuses smile up from each side of the walk, white and yellow and purple and what Miss Gravely calls "variegated." In the sunshine they are wide open and full of happy bees, but in the shade they look like beautifully colored Easter eggs, smooth and closed. The house makes a lot of shade. Miss Gravely's grandfather built it for his bride, and he built an upstairs parlor and a downstairs parlor; stairs in the front for himself and Mrs. Gravely and all the children they were going to have, and stairs in the back for the cook and maid and butler and the nurse for all those children; bedrooms for himself and Mrs. Gravely and the butler and nurse and all those children, and a screened porch with a trapdoor to the basement. Miss Gravely's father was her grandmother's first child. He had three brothers and two sisters, but he and his wife had only Miss Gravely, and now she lives in the house all alone and it is hard to heat.

Miss Gravely was expecting us. She had this year's eggs spread out on the piano. "Might as well," she said. "I don't play now. Fingers just too stiff." More eggs were set out on little tables covered with embroidered cloths. "I embroidered those myself," Miss Gravely told me, "when I wasn't much older than you. Sharp eyes, then."

Mom says Miss Gravely never had a job; as a girl she cultivated her creative talents, so she would make a wife her husband could be proud of. She never married, but when her father died he left her his house and all his bank stock. Miss Gravely's grandfather founded our bank. His picture hangs on the wall there, and in Miss Gravely's downstairs parlor.

Mom and Becky and I take turns choosing our Easter eggs, and this year was my turn. I looked at every egg. Because of her trees, Miss Gravely's downstairs parlor is always dark, even though it has windows from the floor practically to the ceiling. "Used to have shutters," she says. Now the windows have long narrow lace curtains. "You can't buy such long ones now," she says. "I have to buy two and piece." She turned on some lamps so I could see her eggs better. "Won't have overhead light!" she declared. "We ladies need our beauty lights! Isn't that so, Helen?" Mom laughed with her.

There were blue eggs, pink eggs, any color eggs, many color eggs. There were eggs Miss Gravely had blown and dyed and etched with scenes, like a beautiful girl ice skating or a church on a hilltop. There were great big artificial eggs with scenes inside—last year Becky chose a mother hen with five little yellow chicks. Other eggs had things pasted on the outside like sequins or beads or lace or little flowers cut out of felt.

When light hits anything gold in a dark room, the gold blazes. The first egg I thought I would choose was like that: simple, just an extra-big egg—"Goose," said Miss Gravely— completely covered with gold sequins. "Glue," said Miss Gravely. Glow, was what I thought, and my fingers were spreading to pick up that one when my eye caught another one. It was dark green outside, the color of that dress Grandmom sent me, with a little white lace around the opening in one end, just the way Grandmom's dress was trimmed with white lace. Inside the egg was a little gray nest ("Spanish moss," said Miss Gravely) with six little eggs showing inside, each a different color, and sitting on these eggs, a little brown rabbit.

"Choose that one, Kate!" Becky urged, and I almost did.

In the end, I reminded Becky that she got to pick last year, and I took a hen's egg not even dyed much except for thin purple stripes. "I'm choosing this one because it reminds me of some of your crocus," I told Miss Gravely. I could almost imagine it opening if I set it in the sun; I could almost hear the honeybees that would come.

"*Crocus vernus*," Miss Gravely said. "Mother always had them. I made that egg with paraffin. Simple. Paint on your paraffin before you dye, and wherever you have paraffin, the dye doesn't take. I love that one, too, Kate; I'm glad you got it. Now everybody wash her hands and have some cookies."

Becky and I love to wash our hands at Miss Gravely's; the basins have pictures in them. "I speak for the doves!" said Becky. The basins are marble, and the pictures are dyed right in. The doves drinking at a fountain are in the downstairs bathroom. I went upstairs and washed my hands over a basket of flowers, all kinds of flowers I didn't recognize. No bees.

"Those are Italian flowers," Miss Gravely told me when I came back downstairs and asked. "The basins are nice, but the pipes keep me awake nights worrying. They are so old, and what will I do if . . . Have a cookie." She had brought in a big plateful shaped like rabbits. When we come back in December for a Christmas tree decoration (we buy one every year), she will have stars or reindeer or Santa Clauses. The flavor will be the same: ginger. "Ginger was my nickname when I was a girl," Miss Gravely said, "because of my hair." She opened the locket she wears on a chain around her neck and showed us. On one side, behind glass, was a piece of brown hair and on the other side, a piece of red hair. "The auburn was Father's," Miss Gravely said. "Mine was just that color when I was Kate's age.

"My parents gave each other a lock of hair when they became engaged. Mother put Father's in this locket with a piece of her own. She wore it till the day she died. Have another cookie."

"Thank you, Miss Gravely," Mom said, and looked at Becky and me.

"Thank you, Miss Gravely," Becky said quickly.

Miss Gravely sighed. "There are only three people left in Clermont who call me Ginger," she said.

I opened my mouth. Mom shot me a look. "Thank you, Miss Gravely," I said.

My hair is neither interesting nor beautiful; it is just a straw-colored ponytail. Not the shining golden straw my grandfather used to bale after he'd threshed his wheat, but the dark stuff Dad gets from combining. I can't think of anyone who would ever want me to give him a piece of my hair.

Hume Culverhouse's hair is black, like Morgan's.

I got to hold the egg in my lap driving home because this was my year to choose. "I don't see how," I objected to Mom, "Miss Gravely's fingers can be too stiff to play her piano when she makes all these beautiful eggs every Easter, and those grapevine baskets every summer, and those corn-husk door decorations at Thanksgiving, and those wreaths and tree decorations at Christmas time."

"I'm glad you didn't say so to her," Mom answered. "The

truth is, her piano needs tuning and the nearest piano tuner is in Lexington, and she can't afford the out-of-county service call."

I thought about that the rest of the way home.

After supper Mom said, "You read to Becky for me, and I'll wash the dishes, Kate." I knew that meant she wanted to talk to Dad, maybe about Grandmom's dresses. I hustled Becky into bed. I chose *Peter Rabbit* from her shelf, since the next day was Easter. First she read a few pages to me. Before Mom went back to work for Mr. Watkins, she was teaching Becky to read, and Becky does pretty well. Once I began, I made my voice monotonous, and she dropped off long before I got to the chamomile tea. I turned out Becky's light and hurried to my hot-air register, but too late to find out whether Dad was going to change his mind about Grandmom's dresses.

CHAPTER 18

Crying Over Spilt Milk

By day, the light in our attic comes from two square openings, one at each end, which Mom calls louvers. They look as if the builder meant to put in windows but never did, so somebody else nailed slats across them to keep out burglars. They have sills like our other windows, but they never have had any glass or screens. Mom says the builder meant the louvers for ventilation and put the slats there himself. "See how they slope?" she points out. "That's so they'll shed rain." It's true, rain never gets into the attic.

Easter morning I was still hoping Grandmom's dresses would come back downstairs for Becky and me to wear to church, but they didn't. I hadn't chosen Miss Gravely's lace-trimmed green egg because at the last moment I had thought that I might not be the only one it reminded of Grandmom's dress. I had reflected that it might make Dad angry if he were forced to look at it every time he went in the dining room. I wish now I had chosen it. Becky just loved that little nesting rabbit, and Dad stayed angry, anyway. After Easter I sneaked up to the attic a couple of times just to look at those dresses, they were so beautiful hanging there. The third time, both were gone.

"Usually," Hetty Anne says, "if you can't have one thing,

you can have another. It helps to concentrate on that." For a few moments I stood staring at where the dresses had been. Then I walked over to one of those louvers to look for something to concentrate on. That's when I heard a sheep's distress call. I dashed across the attic, downstairs, and outside.

Nothing terrible was wrong. Eudora had knelt and pushed her head through the fence wire to nibble grass, and couldn't remember how to get herself free again. "I'm coming," I called. That didn't seem to make a bit of difference to Eudora, but Annie came trotting to the gate.

When Annie saw that I had no bottle and wasn't even going to stop and pat her, she maneuvered in front of me so that I almost fell over her. "Just keep it up," I told her. "I'll wean you early."

If only I had weaned her that day!

I knelt beside Eudora and told her to relax. Then I tried to turn her head sideways, the way I knew she had to have turned it to get it through the fence wire in the first place. Thank goodness Dad was out on the tractor: I was in no mood for his helpless-sheep lecture. "Sheep can be a lesson to us," Dad tells Becky and me. "For thousands of years, shepherds have taken such good care of their flocks that just as many lambs grew up who didn't have the sense to take care of themselves as grew up that did have the sense. The result is the sheep you see: helpless. Remember that, when you want somebody else to solve your problems for you. You let somebody else protect and take care of you long enough, and you'll turn into sheep."

"I'd rather have Mama stay home and take care of me than be the smartest person in Kentucky," Becky had said, last time we got this talk.

"Then you will be sheared and eaten," Dad told her.

That's what Eudora seemed to feel was about to happen to her. Her eyes were huge and scared, and she pulled against me with all her strength.

Annie, on the other hand, was not scared. She kept bumping me with her head, rubbing me with her shoulder, doing everything but carry a poster saying PLAY WITH ME. "Back off," I told her, but she seemed to think I had said, "Nice Annie." I was on knees and elbows struggling with Eudora when I felt four little hooves land on my back.

Lambs aren't so heavy as they look, because a lot of what you see is wool. Annie's hooves tapped on my shoulder blades, keeping her balanced. Before I could tilt her off, she began chewing the end of my ponytail. "That does it," I told her, and stood up. She landed lightly and skipped around, trying to make it look to the other lambs as if jumping down had been her idea. I climbed over the fence so I could work without Annie's help. Once I managed to free Eudora, I forgave Annie for gumming my ponytail and promised her a bedtime bottle as usual.

Back in the house, Becky helped me with my hair. I didn't take the rubber band off. I just backed up to the basin and Becky ran tap water as far up as Annie had chewed. Becky wrapped a towel around the wet end and rubbed it as dry as she could, but I felt a cold spot between my shoulder blades the rest of the afternoon. Probably to a lamb on your back, a ponytail is the most inviting way you could wear your hair, I thought regretfully—all gathered up and presented. A page-boy, which is what Morgan Culverhouse says I should wear, would fall away.

One day right before class my rubber band broke, and my hair fell to my shoulders. I always have a spare in my pocket, but before I could dig it out, Morgan took hold of my hair with both hands, one on each side of my face. She turned the ends up and cocked her head, studying me. "You would look cute with an end permanent and a page-boy," she said.

My family can eat for a week for what an end permanent costs. "I thought I was pretty cute already," I said, and shook my hair free. I don't think so at all, but Morgan sounded so know-it-all, I wanted to push her.

"Oh, I didn't mean it like that!" she wailed. I didn't have to say "Did, too." Class had begun, so she had to knock off the crocodile tears and smug advice both.

Morgan has to go to the Magic Mirror at least every four weeks to keep her hair the way it is. Mom cuts mine, and I fasten it with a rubber band saved from the Sunday *Herald-Leader*, so mine doesn't cost anything except for shampoo and water, and since the night of Orion, I am very sparing of both. Even contorting myself to get my ponytail under the bathroom tap, I figured on keeping it.

I fed Annie her full formula ration as usual that night and next morning. Formula is expensive, and Annie was getting to be good-sized (just ask somebody whose back she tap-danced on), but she still lacked a couple of weeks of three months. My plan was to wean her at three months like the other lambs. Dad and Becky were in the house when I got home from school that afternoon. "Kate," Dad said, "as soon as you've had your snack and fed Annie, come find me in the woods. I'm going to cut firewood and I could use a loader."

"I can help, too," Becky said. "I can come with you now. I'm not hungry." Becky loves to drop wood into the truck bed, one of the few clattery things she can do without Mom telling her to tone the racket down.

The trouble was, Mom wasn't going to be there. "I'd rather you stayed here," Dad told Becky, "so you can tell your mother where we are when she gets home."

I hoped Becky wouldn't think of telling Dad he could leave Mom a note, because I had an idea he was just being safety conscious. I could keep Becky from running into his chain saw if he wanted to tell her just to wait and come with me, but farmers have to be extra cautious types. Fortunately Becky was proud enough of having an important message not to argue. "I'll hurry," I promised.

Annie was waiting for me at the gate. All March she had come running whenever she saw the bus bringing me home. "Look," I told her, "there goes Dad in the truck. I'm going to have to walk all the way to the woods because of having to stay and feed you. I hope you appreciate me." Actually I would rather walk than ride on this farm. You can't hear the birds over the truck engine. All the birds are singing in April—and even if they weren't, the mockingbird would make you think they were.

Annie didn't pay any attention to anything I said; she just attacked the bottle. Her little tail flipped faster and faster as she guzzled and grunted and bounced that bottle back and forth. "Calm down!" I told her. Actually I enjoyed doing anything for her that she liked so much, and I didn't have very many more days to do it. Maybe meditating about how nice it had been, having Annie think I was her mother, I didn't pay attention to how rough Annie was getting with her bottle. I remembered her in a hurry when she suddenly gave a tremendous pull and the nipple popped off. The formula came splashing out all over the ground—plus all over my jacket, jeans, and boots. The bottle was in my outstretched hand, open and dripping. My mouth was open, too, but not Annie's. She had the nipple in hers.

"Give me that!" I commanded. My voice sounded hoarse. Whether you believe sheep laugh or not (I think they do), Annie couldn't with that nipple in her mouth—she would have dropped it. I prayed she *would* drop it! Even crawling on my hands and knees in mud and manure to find it would be millions of times better than having her swallow it. I jammed the bottle in my pocket so I'd have two hands to grab her with. She had the nipple between her jaws now. She chewed and chewed like somebody with a big wad of fresh bubble gum, and danced away from me. I was trying to keep her from dying, and she thought it was a game.

I tried to make my movements calm and gradual so Annie would relax and stand still, but she stayed just far enough away that my fingers couldn't hook on her collar. All I could see in my mind was that nipple getting stuck in her throat and choking her to death right there in front of me, or getting swallowed and corking her up inside somewhere so she first would have days of agony and then would die in convulsions. I made one quick lunge at her, but not quick enough. I fell flat on my face on the wet grass and whatever else was there, and Annie skipped away, chewing.

I was lucky; Becky heard me scream for help. She came running, and together we cornered Annie. Then as soon as Becky got both hands on Annie's collar, I put my left hand on one side of Annie's head and began to try to wiggle the fingers of my right hand into the other side of her mouth. She had stopped chewing and her jaws were clamped shut. (I think if I'd remembered that Coke bottle in my pocket, I might have considered hitting her right between the eyes with it. Would the nipple have dropped out of her mouth, or would she have gasped it right down her throat?) I kept pushing and wiggling my fingers and finally got them into her mouth. For a second all I felt was her stubborn tongue and my heart plunged. Then in almost the same instant I felt the nipple, still there. I pulled it out.

"What's all the screaming?" Dad asked.

We'd had our minds so completely on Annie, Becky and I hadn't noticed the truck coming back. A part had broken on the chain saw, I learned later, so probably Dad was already in a dark mood before he got to us.

We are never, repeat never, supposed to run near sheep. If one sheep runs, the others run after it, and when sheep run, they are liable to take fright, maybe even run themselves to death. I've known this since before I was Becky's age, but when I had picked myself up off the ground and had seen Annie skipping away with that nipple still between her teeth, I'd torn after her. I'd paused just long enough to scream for Becky and had taken off.

Now Dad looked at the combination of things on my front side. "You were running," he said. "Both of you."

I showed him the wet sticky nipple. He held out his hand. He didn't look at us while he inspected the nipple. I knew there weren't any missing pieces—I had looked already—but I let him see for himself that Annie hadn't swallowed anything. He put the nipple in his pocket. "Wean that lamb," he said.

"Yes, sir," I answered.

As he turned to leave, his eye caught sight of the bottle in my pocket. *"Katherine."* Uh-oh. "You were running, in a field full of sheep. You were running, with a glass bottle in your pocket. You could have fallen—you did fall—you could have fallen on that bottle and gashed yourself badly. How many times have I told—"

"It wouldn't break if I fell on it, Dad. Coke bottles are strong as baseball bats, see?" I pulled the bottle out and showed him what thick walls it had.

"Always got an answer, haven't you? I tell you not to run in a field full of sheep, and you tell me Coke bottles are made of thick glass. I tell you not to raise a cosset lamb, and you tell me it's a ewe. *I tell you, a lamb raised on a bottle costs more than it is ever worth*, and what do you do?"

I stared at him. "You said it was up to me."

"It was up to you, whether you wanted to disregard my advice. You knew what I thought. I had told you. Knowing I was against all this, you chose to do it, anyway. Now you listen to me carefully. This is my farm, my father's before me. You three women are not going to take charge of it while I'm alive. *I* am going to say what is to be done here. That lamb has sucked her last bottle. Is that understood?"

"Yes, sir."

"What about you, Becky: you got that straight, too?"

"Yes, sir," said Becky.

I couldn't believe Dad could be so unfair. Nothing he said was just the way things were; he was twisting everything. It was true that back in February, he had explained why he wasn't going to let me try to bottle-raise any of our orphans. It was true that the morning after the night of Orion he had said, "A hand-raised orphan never makes a good-looking lamb. It grows up pot-bellied and poor every time, and so mixed-up it doesn't even know it's a sheep." We didn't put Annie on the bottle then. That came later, after I'd named her and everything, and Sadie turned out not to have enough milk for her, and that was different, and he did give me permission. And Annie didn't need to be a super-looking lamb, because we weren't going to sell her. We were raising her to be a mother. And she played with the other lambs all day, and she had been sleeping curled up against Sadie's side every night. She never thought she was human. She thought I was a *sheep*.

It isn't fair, I thought. He changes the rules. First it's okay to feed Annie and then it's not; first Grandmom's presents are lovely and then they're insulting. First he wants me always to think like a farmer and then he wants me never to think, period. What's the matter with him? I knew, though.

Dad got back in his truck and drove off. He was taking his chain saw to be fixed, but Becky and I didn't know that till later. I remembered Mom complaining to him recently, "Sometimes I don't know whether you have left for half an hour or for the rest of the day."

"I am not a child, and you are not my mother," he had told her then. Hearing him talk that way made my stomach hurt, the way it was hurting now. He used to think she was perfect.

Becky and I trudged back toward the house. Dad hadn't offered us a ride. Becky started to take one of our old short-cuts, but I stopped her. I pointed to where the spring weeds were already showing green down the middle of our road. "Every one we step on means that much less weed killer we have to spray on them later," I said. "Weed killer is expensive. We have to save money so we can pay off the bank, and they won't take our farm."

"Dad's farm," said Becky.

That Sunday our minister preached on the Twenty-third Psalm—the one that talks about the still waters; the one that says, "The Lord is my shepherd"—that one. The one that says, "I will fear no evil: for thou art with me." I thought about it so long, Hetty Anne asked me why I was so quiet Monday, but I didn't tell her. Monday night Mom made meat loaf out of ground mutton again, and while it baked, she and I folded clean clothes. Dad and Becky were watching the news. The TV is a long way from the laundry, so I asked Mom the question I had been asking myself: "Was Dad a good shepherd when he slaughtered those ewes the dogs bit?"

Mom looked distressed, but she didn't hesitate. "Yes, he was. The ewes were suffering, and they were too badly off to recover. Your dad could not save them, but he could end their pain."

I thought about that while I sorted the socks into pairs. "So then," I asked, "Is Mr. Culverhouse a good shepherd if he takes the farm away from Dad so as to let us quit suffering, trying to make it pay, even if it kills Dad to lose it?"

Mom snatched up the towels she had folded. "*Kate*," she parted her teeth just enough to say, "I have been up since dawn, and I have not stopped to rest since, and I am exhausted. I do not have the strength to play little smarty-pants games with you!" She stamped across the porch and banged the kitchen door after her. She never has answered me.

CHAPTER 19

An Ocean of Air

After Hetty Anne told me the story of Anne Frank, I pretended for a while that the Engles had to hide from Mr. Culverhouse in our attic. I was the one who took them their food, and I took Hetty Anne her homework assignments, so she would have all her work done waiting to be graded when it was finally safe for her to come out, and could graduate on time.

Pretending to be brave is easy.

One Saturday morning when I was alone in the house, I heard scuffling in the attic. For a second I couldn't move. Then I grabbed the broom and ran upstairs.

In the upstairs hall, I slowed down. More than a hundred years ago, some Lowlands County houses were stations on the Underground Railroad. I never heard that ours was. Besides, I reminded myself, I do not believe in ghosts. My feet didn't hear me.

I crept up the first few attic stairs. I am not afraid of bats, either, I encouraged myself. In the twilight, when the first stars are just beginning to admit they're in the sky, bats swooping overhead are beautiful. They can't help how hideous they are up close. I put one foot on the next step and then the other foot on the same step. My heart beat so fast it hurt.

Bats don't come here so early as April, I remembered. They have to wait till the insects are back. So what was in our attic? Maybe nothing; maybe I had imagined everything.

Again I heard scuffling. I froze and listened. Finally I lifted the attic trapdoor just enough to peer in.

No one was there. I couldn't see a thing out of place, but the attic was so dark, I couldn't feel certain. Slowly I finished lifting the big square overhead door and set it to one side. I was going to have to walk all the way to the middle of the room to turn on a light. My feet moved stiffly. The attic's one light bulb works by a chain that I have to stretch to reach, but neither of my arms wanted to go out into the air alone and leave my ribs unprotected. As I finally pulled the chain, I heard rustling. I almost screamed.

The rustling was from the south louver: English sparrows had built their nest on the sill. The mother flew out between the louver slats as I walked toward her. She had one brown-splashed egg.

We are careful of songbirds on this farm. One time a wren built her nest in Dad's workshop ragbag and none of us tried to get one rag out of that bag that whole season. Dad used paper towels. English sparrows, though, are even messier than chickens (for one thing, they fly), and they don't sing, and what's worse, they kill the babies of birds like cardinals and bluebirds that do sing. That's why it was okay for me to take the sparrow's egg out of our attic.

I used it for lunch that very day. The closer April 15 came, the more work there was for everybody in Mom's office, filling in clients' tax forms. Finally Mr. Watkins asked

Mom if she could work Saturdays. ("Only this Saturday and next," I heard Mom tell Dad, "and then it will all be over till next year." Dad said something about next year, but I couldn't hear what.) Mom's working Saturday meant that I fixed lunch. The day I found the sparrow nest, I made egg sandwiches. I put one fried chicken egg in Dad's, two-thirds of a fried chicken egg in Becky's, and one-third of a fried chicken egg plus the sparrow egg in mine.

Lying in the pan, the sparrow egg had looked just like a hen egg, only tinier. "You know what a sparrow egg tastes like?" I asked Mom that night. She was sitting at the dining room table putting patches on the knees of Becky's jeans. Becky was asleep and Dad was in the living room watching the Reds play the Cards.

"Like a tiny hen's egg?" Mom asked.

"How did you know?"

"Just guessed. How did *you* know?"

I told her about my find.

"My goodness, Kate, what is there a child won't try?" Mom squinted at the needle she was threading. "What took you up to the attic?" she asked quietly.

"I thought I heard something. It must have been the sparrows."

That was when Mom told me that she had sent the dresses back to Grandmom to exchange for "something more appropriate to the kind of life we lead. Your grandmother sent you the kind of dresses I wore when I was your age, but I don't have a servant to do my washing and ironing the way she did. And dry cleaning is very expensive." I do as much of the washing and ironing around here as she does. "I hope you cleaned the nest off the sill," she said. I wonder if mothers think children don't notice when they change the subject.

"We could have worn the dresses once. Even if nobody ever had *any* time or *any* money, we could have worn them for Easter."

I saw the pain on Mom's face before she could turn her head away. "Yes, you could have worn them once."

The reason we couldn't have those dresses was that Dad didn't want us to have anything that he didn't give us, and she always gives him the last word. "You could have waited a while to see if Dad would change his mind."

"Kate, I had to get them back to Grandmom while Woodward and Lothrop was still willing to exchange something for them. Letting them hang here no good to anybody was no guarantee that your father would ever change his mind."

"Becky cried." I didn't admit that I had cried a little, too. "And I bet Grandmom's feelings were hurt."

"Don't worry about your grandmother's feelings. She understood. What we need to worry about right now is birds in the attic. Did you get rid of that nest?"

"No. I thought maybe the sparrow would lay some more eggs. We could use them in meat loaf or something."

"Dear Kate! Next you'll be serving us boiled dandelion greens. Excuse me: *steamed* dandelion greens. Anybody would think you were afraid we were all going to starve to death." I didn't open my mouth, but my face must have said something, because she said "Dear Kate!" again. "Dear Kate! Don't you know I'll always feed my children?" Dad came in about then, on his way to the refrigerator, so I didn't have to answer. Dad didn't say anything, either, not one word. In fact, he didn't even look at us.

He heard her, I thought. She didn't give him the last word about her going back to work for Mr. Watkins. She likes to be in control almost as much as he does. Maybe it's just where Becky and I are concerned that she always gives him the last word.

Next day I pushed the sparrows' nest off the attic sill. I bet they start another by tomorrow, I thought. I don't know whether I was right or not. "Tomorrow" was the day of the storm.

There's been a lot of talk since the storm about why the school didn't send us home early. Where was the weather bureau? My classroom did get a little darkish toward the end of last period, but I only remembered that later. Nobody said anything about it at the time. Kentuckians are used to cloudy Aprils.

When we stepped outside at three o'clock, the western sky was a strange smoky yellow, but overhead was just ordinary overcast. I remember deciding that if it did rain, I would take off my nice leather gloves and keep them dry in my pocket.

Hetty Anne gets the window seat because I get off ahead of her, and pretty soon she and I were talking so hard, I wasn't giving the weather any thought. Then J. M. Stanley called out, "Lookit them clouds travel, man!" and we looked out.

Even from the aisle seat, I could see that the sky had darkened and that clouds were passing over us faster than any clouds I had ever seen. "I hope we beat the rain home," I told Hetty Anne. "I don't remember how I left the barn door this morning."

Some rains that would drench you and me roll right off an unsheared sheep. On the other hand, the kind of drenching that would make you and me laugh and run to change clothes can give an unsheared sheep pneumonia. Sheep can't run and change their thick wool, and if the wool is wet to the skin, they lose heat through it faster than they can make more. Not many sheep live through pneumonia. "A down sheep is a dead sheep," Dad says. He says his dad always said that, and that it's true. "Once a sheep is too sick to stand up, you might as well quit giving it food or medicine either one: A down sheep is a dead sheep."

Every morning, Dad and I put out hay and ground corn for the lambs and nursing mothers, and last one out of the barn is responsible for the sliding door. I couldn't even remember whether that had been me or Dad that day. I peered worriedly out the bus window.

"Looks like rain, sure enough," Hetty Anne said gloomily, "but at least it's not windy." Wind gets horses all excited, Hetty Anne says, and makes them tear around and maybe hurt themselves. We argue sometimes about which has less sense, a horse or a sheep. (I always win.)

Hetty Anne turned her shoulder to the window, more to see the gray sky less than to see me better, I thought. "Pops finished plowing the cornfield too late to get fertilizer down yesterday. If he spread it this morning, rain now would be perfect. If he didn't—uh-oh."

"My dad was going to plow winter wheat," I told her. I didn't need to add that rain would put an end to any plowing. I said something instead about how lonesome Becky gets when Mom's at work and I'm at school and Dad's out on the tractor. Then we talked about Becky, and how we are going to take care of our children when we have them, and I forgot the darkening weather until J. M. Stanley yelled, "Hey, Mr. Ormsby, what's that? What's that in the road? Ain't that a *tornado*? Ain't it?"

"Sit down, J.M.!" Mr. Ormsby snapped. "Everybody sit down!"

I didn't jump up when J.M. yelled, because J.M. is always trying to stir things up. He is the kind of boy who puts both hands behind his back with a dead bird in one of them, and goes around asking girls, "Which hand do you think has the peppermint?" Once he let a jarful of white-nose bumblebees loose in class. White-nose bumblebees don't sting, but no-body reached out and grabbed any of J.M.'s to see what color their noses were. When J.M. said "tornado," Hetty Anne and I did quit talking, but that was just a reflex. We didn't believe him a bit. Then we felt the bus slowing down.

For a second we looked at each other. Then we looked out.

Way down the road ahead of us, a big black sort of funnel-shaped cloud that came down out of the highest sky all the way to the very dirt, was traveling quietly toward us along the road. It didn't make a sound that we could hear; the bus engine was louder. The kids on the bus were louder still. "Sit down and get quiet!" Mr. Ormsby roared, pulling over. "Storm Drill. Hetty Anne Engle, back door."

Hetty Anne looked a little pink. I swung my legs out of her way and she pushed past me. The front door has steps, but in Storm Drill, everybody who sits in the back half of the bus has to get out the back door. Hetty Anne is the tallest one on our bus, and her Storm Drill job is to be the first person through the back door, to help the little ones down, to count everybody who gets off after her, and to *remember how many she has counted.*

Hetty Anne went to the rear as fast as she could without running—we are not to run—and jumped out. She wasn't as fast as J. M. Stanley; he had whooped and dashed down the aisle the second Mr. Ormsby said, "Storm Drill." Hetty Anne swears J. M. didn't behave that way because he is a coward. He and Hetty Anne are in the same grade, and she thinks he just can't bear that she is taller than he is. "J.M. would shrivel up and blow away if anybody even thought about helping him off the bus," Hetty Anne says.

I made myself wait my turn. The light had gone all queer; it made the kids ahead of me look yellow. I was the last one out the back door. "You're thirty-one," Hetty Anne told me. "Help me remember."

I looked around for where to take cover and saw the sky just sucking the funnel-shaped cloud back up. In five seconds every foot—every *inch*—of that threat was gone.

I never had time to feel grateful and safe. The wind suddenly began to blow as if our particular bus and everybody who had come out of it were its personal enemies. I thought I was going to be blown away.

There wasn't a house in sight, not even a barn. We would all have to lie in the ditch along the road. We've practiced that, too, and we're supposed to get away from the bus so that if it blows over, it won't land on us. Kids were doing their best to run in spite of the wind that pushed us so, but Nancy Tye was just standing in the road screaming and sobbing, and Fred was standing with his arms around her, trying to comfort her. Mr. Ormsby saw them the same time I did, and he had Fred by the hand by the time I got there. I grabbed Nancy, and Mr. Ormsby and I just dragged the two of them to the ditch. I pulled Nancy down with me and lay halfway on top of her to be sure she didn't jump up. There was no use trying to talk to her; the wind was too loud.

Once we lie down, we are not supposed to look up. We

are supposed to keep our faces to the ground, and our fingers linked behind our heads to remind us to keep them to the ground. Also so that anything the storm dumps on us will smash our knuckles instead of our brains, I guess. I only looked up once, just the instant before Nancy and I tumbled together into the ditch, but I'll remember what I saw all my life.

I know how the ocean roars; I hear it every time I visit my grandmother. Looking from her upstairs windows, I have seen the ocean storm; I have felt my hair prinkle across my scalp, have flinched and shuddered even though I was warm and safe and dry. That day I looked *up* and saw a storming ocean, looked up from its very bottom. I felt as if the world had turned upside down. All the roaring and surging and swirling was high over my head. No nightmare has ever been so unreal.

In the ditch, I lay as flat as I could. Since I was lying partly on top of Nancy with one arm around her, I had only one hand for the back of my head. Alone like that, my hand felt terrified. I pushed my forehead hard against the cold grass; that left just enough air around my nose to let me breathe. Always before, in Storm Drill, the thing I've worried most about has been keeping my clothes clean, and I've sort of squatted, but that day I tried to be, not something laid on the earth, but part of the earth.

The storm roared over us, as fast and loud and heedless as a freight train. Why would Mr. Ormsby make such a point of telling Hetty Anne to remember how many kids she counted, I thought, if he didn't think some of us might blow away, if he didn't think the police and the Red Cross and everybody else would need to know how many to look for? How many bodies. Hetty Anne knows that; she thinks what

I think, I thought, and turned colder. She hadn't asked me to help her remember because she was afraid she might forget; she would not forget. She, too, was afraid of getting blown away. If two of us knew that number, there was twice as good a chance somebody would be around to tell it, after this was all over.

CHAPTER 20

Tornado

One second I was dry. The next second I was soaked, even the side of my body that faced the ground—my shoes full of water, my hair a weight on my head. I knew Nancy had to be thinking about her father. I didn't know if she was still crying or not; I couldn't have heard her if she had yelled, but my arm could feel the tension in her shoulders. *I* was too scared to cry. We weren't just being wet, we were being pounded. I had a vision of Annie battered to the ground in a puddle, struggling not to drown. My right hand held Nancy's right hand on top of her head—*if Becky were one year older, she would be here*—I gripped tighter. Then hail started bouncing all over me. I was lucky to have forgotten all about taking off my gloves: even sopping, they kept my hands from getting cut. My heart was pounding. I have read in the paper that this rain and hail lasted eight minutes. It seemed like eight months. Even with my face pressed into the grass, I could see flashes of light. The thunder came so fast after some flashes, I squinched my eyes and kept them squinched to keep from knowing how close the lightning was. For a while, all I thought was, What next? What next? Then I was just concentrating on getting through, not even thinking.

The storm didn't die out, it stopped. Nancy and I waited. After a little bit, stiffly, we stood up. Then both of us looked around to be sure the sky wasn't just about to come at us again. Nancy was the first to move; she clung to me, wet as we were. Then she saw Fred and ran straight to him. Nancy hadn't made a sound, but Fred was waving his arms and jabbering. He turned when Nancy pointed in my direction and, blue-cold as he was, grinned and waved.

I was dazed. "You okay?" Hetty Anne asked me. Water was dripping down her face from her hair. I hadn't seen her stand up. I couldn't believe I was okay. I couldn't believe the roaring had stopped. Our bus was standing right where Mr. Ormsby had parked it. The trees, the fences, all were right where they had been. All along the road, kids were picking themselves up out of the ditch. Some just stood. Looking at them, you'd have had to wonder if they would ever remember how to talk again. Some kids couldn't keep their mouths shut. "Lookit that ol' bus," J. M. Stanley protested. "We could of set right in her and stayed dry!" I didn't remind him he had been the first one off. Hetty Anne went to report to Mr. Ormsby. I was shivering. Worry was replacing the wind and rain and the hail and lightning. Had Dad made it to shelter somewhere? Had Becky been alone through all that terror? Had Mom been safe in the basement of her office building, or had she started home early and been caught?

Mr. Ormsby began herding us onto the bus. Hetty Anne stood by the front door, counting. The first car since we'd stopped came along and pulled over. The driver got out and asked Mr. Ormsby if we needed any help, if anybody was hurt. The worst we had to report was chattering teeth. (I felt like a sheep that can't take its wet wool off.) Two more cars came along and did the same thing, but finally we were all in our seats, and Mr. Ormsby had walked down the aisle and counted us again and reported on his radio to Mr. Rankin, our principal, that we were all okay and he was taking us home. "Report when you're empty," Mr Rankin told him. "Report if you run into any problems. Word here is that the twister put down somewhere not too far west of Clermont." We all heard Mr. Rankin say that, and the bus got very quiet. West of Clermont is our homes.

Mom caught up with the bus at the first stop, Fletchers'. Mr. Ormsby let me get off with the Fletcher kids. I was so excited to see Mom that I forgot I was cold for at least a minute. I completely forgot how muddy I was, and she didn't seem to notice; we gave each other a huge hug. Fred and Nancy and Hetty Anne and J. M. Stanley were all waving and calling to Mom out the bus windows. I heard Mr. Ormsby growling, "Sit down, J.M.!" The bus lumbered on.

By the time I opened our car door, I was recovering my brain. "I won't sit down," I told Mom, "I'd soak the seat."

"You sit down and buckle up," Mom said. She got the engine started and the heater going, then groped in her pocketbook and reached me out a granola bar. I tore off the wrapper. Granola bars come in two pieces; I offered her one. "Eat both," she said. "They'll help you get warm."

"Have you talked to Dad?" I asked. Then I took a big bite.

"Phone's dead." She had almost cried while she was hugging me; now her face was stiff. That's when I remembered that all those drivers who had stopped to offer to help Mr. Ormsby, all the cars that had passed the bus after we got going, all had come from the direction of town. No car had come from the other direction—west—the direction Mom and I (and Mr. Ormsby) were driving.

I had already been wishing that I could share my granola

bar with Hetty Anne. Now I didn't even want the first half. *Let him be all right!* I thought. *I forgive him for the dress.* "Eat that!" said Mom, not taking her eyes off the road. We weren't meeting any cars, and the way she was driving, nobody had passed us. We didn't say anything else to each other all the way home.

Dad and Becky came running out to meet our car. Dad hadn't even been able to get a radio report, because not only the telephone was dead, we had no electricity. First he hugged Mom, then me, and then Mom and I both hugged Becky. "It didn't put down in Clermont," Mom told him. His eyebrows went way up, and he took a deep breath.

Annie was all right. "The sheep didn't even get rained on," Dad said. "We can thank Kate for that. Around two-thirty, the sky looked so bad I put the tractor away and then stood in the barn door and called Annie. She came running, and the others just followed right along."

That's the closest Dad ever seems to be able to get to apologizing after he has been unfair. He doesn't say, "I was wrong. I'm sorry," or even just, "I'm sorry" (these are not the same). He just says something extra appreciative to let you know. I am used to my dad, so I felt warm from what he said, even soaking wet the way I was.

"We were lucky," Dad said. "The worst thing here was that that biggest locust came down smack on the back field fence; also you'll see some window damage."

Hail had broken every pane on the west side of the house. Inch-thick ice stones lay all over the yard, glistening, because now the sun was back. The sun was shining, entirely unconcerned by all that had happened to us while he abandoned us.

I wanted to run right out and see Annie. "You get those

wet clothes off before you go anywhere, young lady!" Mom said. "What she needs," she said to Dad, "is a hot shower and a big mug of cocoa, but if there's no power. . ."

"I've lit a kerosene heater in the bathroom," Dad answered. Dad looks ahead.

I dumped my wet clothes in the tub and roasted myself in front of the heater a little before I put on dry. I towelled my hair with all my vigor, but when I ran downstairs, Mom said I couldn't go see Annie till she worked on it some more, and by the time she was satisfied, Dad said, "Helen, I'm going to drive back to Allens' and on, just to make sure." He didn't have to finish his sentence. With the telephone and radio both out, we had no way of knowing whether our neighbors had been as fortunate as we. "I'd like to take Kate along. Don't know what we'll find. Might call for two." Mom frowned and her chin started rising, but before she could object, Dad said, "Kate's got a cool head."

That's one time I was glad Mom gave him the last word.

Mr. Allen was standing beside his electric fence. "Lightning traveled right down the length of it, Rales," he said, "right to where the wire was nailed onto the chicken house. Set it afire."

The terrible rain hadn't saved the chickens; their house had burned to the ground. Mr. Allen's sheep were all right, though. Like us, he has lightning rods on his barn. "Last call from Honest Irv, he was pretty close to my price," Mr. Allen said. "You don't think he'd back out over a chicken house, do you?" His voice said he was joking.

"He'll probably think it's one worry less," Dad said.

After the Allens, the Stanleys live up one side road, the Engles another. I was glad Dad chose the Engles' road first.

Mrs. Engle came to the door in her coat; the Engles' house

must have been cold, too. "Matt's out in the barn," she told us. "The roof lifted right off." Hetty Anne was in bed sneezing, she said, so I went with Dad.

I expected a barn full of hysterical horses, but Mr. Engle had quieted them somehow. He was standing in the middle of the aisle, looking up at the sky. The roof was all in a jumble about a hundred yards away, rafters, sheeting, shingles and all messed up together like a giant sparrow's nest. Tom Allen had spoken of his barnyard as looking as if a couple of Japanese Zeroes had paid him a visit. What would he have said about Engles'? "Patched that roof last summer," Mr. Engle told us, laughing. "Put on a hundred dollars' worth of new shingles." He laughed even harder and shook his head. "Wish I'd let her leak! Don't tell J.H. I said so."

"Horses?" Dad asked.

"Didn't lose one yet." Mr. Engle shrugged. I knew he'd sit with his pregnant mares all night. "Scrapes," Mr. Engle said, "but nobody's limping."

"Heard anything about anybody beyond you?" Dad asked.

Mr. Engle shook his head. "Laura wanted to call you and Jim Stanley, but the lines are down."

Dad nodded. "Kate and I will drive on over there now, if we don't find the road blocked. We'll stop and give you the word on our way home."

All that was on Monday.

Tornadoes don't share their destruction equally among neighbors. If they did, the first call we got after the telephone lines were repaired Tuesday afternoon wouldn't have been to tell us that Mr. Stanley was dead.

Driving up Stanleys' lane Monday, Dad slowed way down. He was staring, and so was I. When the truck finally stopped, Dad turned off the ignition, but we didn't get out.

Dad's face looked the way I imagine it looking if we got out of bed one morning and the radio told us this country was at war.

Mrs. Stanley wasn't home; the Stanleys' *house* wasn't home. The barn was flat. Trees were down everywhere; one lay across what had been Mr. Stanley's tractor. Mr. Stanley was standing beside it, just standing. We walked slowly over to him. J.M. and two of his brothers were in the back field counting cattle, Mr. Stanley told us; Mrs. Stanley had taken the littlest Stanleys to her sister's. "I'm ruined, Rales," he said. "I'm ruined."

"Wait in the truck, Kate," Dad said.

The look in Mr. Stanley's eyes was terrible. I see his eyes in my dreams. "I haven't paid the bank in eighteen months," he said, "They've been riding with me, but now—they'll take everything I own. I'm ruined, Rales."

"In the *truck*, Kate," Dad said. I moved a little faster. The last thing I could hear was Dad saying something about insurance, and Mr. Stanley almost yelling that he'd had to let his insurance lapse; he'd had no money in two years. Dad talked to him for a long time.

Not everything had been destroyed. The hen house had not been touched. The Stanleys' car and truck were both in the garage, dry. The garage was not quite untouched. Walking reluctantly back to the truck, I saw the strangest sight of all the terrible sights the storm had created for us. A straw, an ordinary straw, pale, flimsy—the kind I might tickle Becky with, the kind you could blow away as easily as you might blow the bangs out of your eyes, a straw that you could double back on itself between your thumb and forefinger—had been driven like a nail half an inch into the garage wall. When the Tuesday phone call came, I remembered that straw, and shuddered. Suddenly it seemed as if the storm had been marking its prey.

"Where will they sleep?" I asked Dad as we drove back toward Engles'. I didn't know I was holding my breath till he answered, and I let it out.

Mrs. Stanley and the small children would stay at her sister's in North Middletown, he told me, and Mr. Stanley and his older sons would stay at his brother's. Mr. Stanley's brother tenant-farms the next place over. "It'll be easiest for Jim and the boys to go back and forth from there," Dad reassured Mom when she asked the same question, "and the cattle and chickens still have to be fed."

Mrs. Stanley had driven the car to her sister's, but I think that now she must wish the garage had collapsed like the barn, collapsed or been blown with everything in it beyond the Mississippi, to the shores of the Pacific and beyond. Especially everything in it. Tuesday afternoon we got our telephone service back, and the first call told us that Mr. Stanley's truck had stopped the Seaboard System's northbound coal train.

The Seaboard's engineer had seen the truck motionless on his track, and he had braked, but not soon enough, our caller said, to save either the truck or the man behind its wheel, Mr. Stanley.

CHAPTER 21

Morgan

After that Tuesday telephone call, I just wanted to get out of the house. As soon as I could, I went out and sat in Annie's pasture. Annie trotted over and laid her head in my lap the way she liked to when she was sleepy, and I gripped her wool with my fists. We stayed like that a long time.

Kids on the bus Wednesday morning talked in whispers. By that time, everybody knew that Mr. Stanley wasn't dead, but in a coma that he might never come out of. Hetty Anne and I didn't talk. We couldn't even look at each other. Maybe she was wondering about Mr. Engle what I was wondering about Dad. I was ashamed for wondering such a thing. "Suicide is always cowardly," Dad had always said. Mr. Ormsby didn't stop at J.M.'s corner.

You'd think everything would shut down, maybe forever, but there we all were, going to school as if nothing had happened, or as if we didn't care. Feeling guilty made me angry. I think maybe Mom felt the same way. "She shouldn't have driven off and left him alone so *soon!*" she said, meaning Mrs. Stanley taking the little Stanleys to her sister's.

"Seems to me he's the one who left her," Dad answered.

I was too sorry for both Mr. and Mrs. Stanley to be angry with either of them, but I was confused about J.M. At the same time I was sorry for him, I was glad he could stay with his uncle, and we didn't have to invite him to stay with us. This kind of confusion does strain my temper.

Wednesday morning I walked into homeroom holding on to the soles of my saddle oxfords with my toes to keep them from flapping. (I didn't want to tell Mom that they needed to go to the cobbler.) There was Morgan Culverhouse in her green plaid skirt and her gorgeous green sweater with the big black-and-white panda woven into the front. Her father gave her that sweater for Christmas. I thought about J.M. sleeping on a cot and wearing just whatever his cousins could lend him and I hated her. It wasn't fair. Mr. Culverhouse would take the Stanleys' farm for his bank, and Morgan would get lots more gorgeous clothes, and nobody I'd listened to through hot-air registers or anywhere else had any idea what would become of J.M. and his sisters and brothers.

I hung up my coat and slid into my desk next to Morgan's. She didn't look up and that made me mad, too. She didn't have anything to be so snooty about. "How does your father feel now, Morgan?" I asked. "Everything working out right for him?" My toes gripped my shoe soles.

I hadn't made my voice nasty. I figured Morgan would know very well what I meant without that. Her head turned first halfway, then all the way toward me. For a second she just stared. Then her face crumpled. It's high time you realized what your cashmeres cost! I thought. "Oh, Kate," she said, as well as she could; she was weeping. "You're the only one who's asked!" I thought one of us had lost her mind. "I thought you hated my father like everybody else!"

Her father felt some better that morning, she said. The doctors thought he would be coming home quite soon. It was my turn to stare.

Mr. Culverhouse was in the hospital. I hadn't known that. The heart attack he'd suffered after people told him about Mr. Stanley was his second. I'd never heard about either one. He had known what was happening in time to tell Hume to drive him to the hospital at once, and Hume had driven the speed limit all the way. By the time they'd reached Emergency, Mr. Culverhouse couldn't talk. "We're lucky he's alive!" Morgan declared. She had stopped crying, and she wiped her face as if she meant to push any more tears back in with her fingers. If she noticed that I was stunned speechless, she apparently mistook it for simple concern. Her words rushed on all the faster. "It's a wonder it didn't happen sooner! Hume and I have been dreading it ever since Tinsley Mills closed. All those people who thought they'd have their homes paid for by the time they retired—they practically all have their mortgages at Daddy's bank, and how can they make their payments now? Daddy was already half sick with worry, and then that idiot has to come running in telling him Mr. Stanley shot himself!"

Mr. Stanley had not shot himself, but he had been in Intensive Care in a wordless coma ever since the Seaboard's freight train had hit his truck.

"They say he thought Daddy would take his farm, and some kids aren't even speaking to me. Do they think Daddy wants the Stanleys' farm? If Mr. Stanley couldn't make money on it, why does anybody think the bank can? If Mr. Stanley couldn't sell it for enough to pay off his mortgage, why does anybody think the bank can? Half the farms in this county are for sale. Have you heard of one selling in the past three years? Why couldn't Mr. Stanley have kept his nerve and helped Daddy work something out? I know I ought to feel sorry for him and I do, I feel terribly sorry for him, but to me, if my father had died, Mr. Stanley would have been a murderer!"

Ms. Parish had arrived, and I noticed her looking at Morgan and me. Morgan's words just kept coming, low and passionate. "What is Daddy supposed to do? He has to figure out a way for the bank to take in as much money as it puts out, or it will go under just like anybody else. If the borrower's end of the boat leaks, the banker's end fills up with water, too. If the bank doesn't stay afloat, everybody who owes the bank money will go under with it. *You* understand that, Kate. Why doesn't anybody else? Why doesn't *everybody*?"

The bell rang for first period, and I still hadn't spoken a word.

About the time I got home that afternoon, Mr. Estep showed up. I put on coffee, and he and Dad sat down to drink a cup while Becky and I ate our snack. Supposedly Mr. Estep had come to talk to Dad about cover crops, but it didn't take long for him to start in on what was really on their minds. "Trouble comes to everybody," he said, stirring a third spoonful of sugar into his coffee. "That's when a man is tested; that's when you find out what a man is worth, and Jim never has been worth much. I mean, you know, Rales, none of the Stanleys—"

"He wouldn't have destroyed the truck," Dad said. "It was about all his family had left. He wouldn't have done that to his family. He had a shotgun."

LaNelle Barlow had told everybody on the bus that Mr. Stanley's shotgun had been found in the wreckage that the train had thrown around. I believed her, because a lot of farmers around here install a rack in their trucks, and keep a loaded gun in it always, so they can shoot stray dogs on sight.

Mr. Estep set his spoon in his saucer and picked up his cup. "Takes nerve to put a loaded gun in your mouth and—"

The look Dad turned on him, I didn't want to see. "Sometimes it takes nerve not to," he said.

"Come and help me pick asparagus!" I told Becky. I kept her busy outside until Mr. Estep drove away.

Mom had left me a note to say which of the casseroles she had put in the freezer over the weekend I should set to thaw. When she got home, she took out a second. "One of us should take this to Louise," she told Dad. Louise is Mr. Stanley's sister-in-law, the one J.M. and two of his brothers were staying with.

Dad was all sweaty and dusty. "You're clean," he said.

"You don't have to go in," Mom told him. "Just tell Louise to tell Roszella I'll try to come see her at the hospital Saturday." In the end, though, she heated our casserole in the oven and took it to Mr. Stanley's brother's house. Through my register that night I heard her telling Dad about it. "Louise just says it was the Lord's will." Mom sounded impatient. "She says Jim's boys say he loaded all the eggs and set out to that farmer's market in Lexington and just never did get there."

Dad didn't speak right away. Then he said, "Jim would not have filled the truck bed with egg crates just so he could go sit in front of the Seaboard."

I was dreaming something when Becky woke me Wednesday night, but I forgot it as I opened my eyes. She had come to tell me she had wet her bed. She hadn't done that in two years.

Neither of us got back to sleep very soon. How am I supposed to stay awake in school?

CHAPTER 22

An Accident

Dad was right: Mr. Estep telephoned him Thursday evening to admit it. Dad began telling us as he hung up. "The Seaboard's engineer states that he saw Jim Stanley jump out of the cab before the collision, Jack says. He says he saw the truck just sitting with its nose on the tracks. He braked, but he couldn't stop in time. He thinks the truck might have broadsided Jim as the train struck it, or maybe a piece flew off and hit him."

Friday morning, that was all over the bus. "So he didn't, after all," Hetty Anne said.

Everybody knew just what she meant. "Oh," LaNelle Barlow said, "he meant to, though. He just lost his nerve."

Hetty Anne's face started getting the red it turns when she's really mad.

"Yeah," said Rubylee. "What was he a'settin' there for?"

I was glad Hetty Anne managed to hold on. I have never seen her cry.

I didn't have a lot of time after school to sit around brooding about what LaNelle Barlow said or Mr. Stanley did. Dad was shearing, and with Mom at Mr. Watkins's office, Becky did my job and I did Mom's. I would catch a ewe and have her waiting so that Dad could simply turn from the one he'd just shorn and grab mine. He'd set her on her bottom with her forelegs sticking out in front as if she meant to play the piano and *brrrr*: ten minutes later, she'd step away from a one-piece fleece.

Becky tied each fleece and bagged it, according to how Dad judged its quality. Our imperfect fleeces go in a huge burlap bag to the big manufacturers. Each fleece good enough for hand-spinning goes into its own plastic bag. Dad has sold our best wool to the same outfit for years—Graith and Daughters, of Berea, Kentucky. Madge Graith and her two daughters are hand-spinners, and hand-spinners are the pickiest buyers alive. For them, the wool's got to look as if the sheep lived right here in the house with us, and every fiber in the whole fleece has to be the same strength for its entire length. For *that*, a sheep has to eat just right every day of the year. The part of a fiber that grows while she's sick, or isn't being given the proper food, or has been too scared to eat it, might be thinner than what grew before and after. Most producers around here can't satisfy hand-spinners and soon quit trying, even though hand-spinners pay about twenty times as much per pound as the big manufacturers.

This April we not only had fewer sheep to shear, we had to put more of what we did get into the burlap bag. Before, Dad was too proud to offer any fleece to Madge Graith that he didn't know she would accept. This year, we had so few like that, he decided he'd better offer her any he thought she *might* accept. I heard him explain this to her, before she started inspecting. "I know you count on me for a certain amount, and I haven't got that much," he said. "See what you can use."

Madge had never turned down a fleece Dad offered her before. She worked her way slowly through our bags, not speaking or looking at any of us. Then she straightened up and turned to Dad. "Rales," she began. Dad smiled and shook his head. She nodded, sighed, and pointed to those bags she would take.

The wool we pulled in February went to a company that makes insulation: They paid the least per pound of all. We knew in February that we'd make a lot less on our wool this year than last, but when April came, we got even less than Dad had expected. Through my register, I heard him and Mom talking about our June interest payment. "It's just not there," I heard Dad say.

I went to the bathroom and brushed my teeth, ten strokes apiece on each side. Then I got under my covers, head and all.

I should have remembered that not having enough air is liable to give me a nightmare. That night's was one I've dreamed again and again since the train hit Mr. Stanley's unmoving truck. First Dad says, "You think like a farmer, Kate; you'll be all right." Then Mom says, "Take care of Becky." Then I don't see them again.

The house was quiet when I woke—so quiet I wanted to scream for Dad and Mom to tell me they were there. Finally I tiptoed to their door and listened till I heard them breathing.

For some reason my mouth always tastes awful after I've had a nightmare. I brushed each of my teeth ten times on each side again.

Back in bed, I lay awake worrying so long I was almost wishing Becky would wake up and come crowding into my bed. At breakfast, I had trouble staying awake.

Dad didn't go to church with us. Mom hadn't gone to the hospital Saturday the way she had planned because Mr.

Watkins had kept her at work way late. I think she was planning to go Sunday afternoon. I believe she was as surprised as Becky and I were when about the time we should have been starting to town, Dad, who was all cleaned up and shaved like every other Sunday morning, told Mom he was going to Lexington to the hospital. "You can have the car," he said. "I'll take the truck. It's time one of us visited with Roszella."

Mom's face got three or four expressions, one right after the other. Driving to town, though, it kept just one: stony. Becky and I didn't say word one the whole way.

Hetty Anne must have been watching for us. She practically met me at the car door. "Pops has a job," she announced. "The chain Uncle Frank works for is opening a branch in Lexington, and the guy who's been his assistant is going to manage it." Mrs. Engle's brother manages a huge store in Louisville. "Uncle Frank told him about Mom and Pops, and they'll both get jobs—Pops in hardware and Mom in dresses."

"I guess you'll move," I said.

Hetty Anne studied our car's front tire. "Not before school's out, anyway, that's sure. The store opening won't be till late summer. If it's on schedule, though, I'll be able to work there a few weeks, too." She looked right at me and stretched her mouth as if it were smiling. "I'll be able to get a discount on all my 'Back-to-School Clothing.' " Before she finished the sentence, she really was smiling. Hetty Anne makes practically all her clothes ("of course").

I tried to grin back at her. "Do all these jobs mean you'll be able to go to Transy after all?" I asked. Transylvania University, in Lexington, is the oldest college west of the Allegheny Mountains. Hetty Anne's mother went there, and

Hetty Anne had always planned to go there, too, before Mr. Culverhouse's auction.

"Maybe I'll go to Berea College," she said. "All Berea students work their way through; it's required. Holding a job is part of your education, they think."

Hetty Anne and I visited Berea together, one autumn. Our 4-H Club drove down there for the Kentucky Guild of Artists and Craftsmen's fair, and then toured all the interesting places—Graith and Daughters was the best. I remember a ginkgo tree on campus big as a chapel and pure gold. I was about to say something Hetty-Anne cheerful about that when it was time to go in to church.

Dad was waiting for us with his own news when we got home: "Roszella says Jim knew her last night."

"Oh, Rales!" Mom said.

"He knew her, and this morning he told her what he remembered of the accident."

"Accident," Mom repeated.

"Accident," Dad repeated firmly. "He doesn't remember being struck. The last thing he remembers is jumping out of the cab. The train wasn't even in sight when the truck stalled, he told Roszella. Slowing down so as not to crack any eggs going over the tracks was what did it, he said. She says the truck had been doing that in low gear lately.

"Jim told her he was sitting with just his front wheels on the rails trying to get her going again when he saw the train. He didn't jump right away because he couldn't believe he couldn't get the engine to fire; he kept thinking just one more pump would do it."

"Well," Mom said.

"Roszella thinks he'll be home before too long," Dad finished.

Whatever home meant for the Stanleys now. J.M. and the older boys were still staying with their uncle next door to their farm, if you could still call it their farm. No one could imagine that the bank could afford to lend them any more money. Mrs. Stanley and the younger children were still staying with her sister in North Middletown.

If pity went by numbers, I should have been even sorrier for the Stanleys than I was for the Engles, there were so many more of them. I had been ashamed of how much pleasanter I found riding the bus without J.M.'s loud trashy talk. I *was* sorry for Mr. Stanley, so sorry my stomach got knots in it when I thought about him, especially when I would see his eyes again as he said, "I'm ruined, Rales. I'm ruined." When it came to comparing J.M. and Hetty Anne, though, I couldn't help thinking that one place was like another to J.M. His family had lived on three farms already just since he was born, whereas the Engles . . . Hetty Anne had mentioned to me what her mother was going to do with different things when they found a place to move, "because it'll be a lot smaller, of course."

"How can you bear it?" I asked her. "Your family have *always* lived in that house!"

"They certainly have not," Hetty Anne retorted. "My great-great-great-grandfather's great-grandfather was born in South Carolina. He came out here to claim his land grant because his Tory neighbors had burnt his trading post while he was away fighting Redcoats, and they told him straight out that if he tried to build it back, they'd burn it again. As for his wife, the day she married him, she moved out of her father's house on one of the prettiest streets in Charleston. If she and Great-to-the-someteenth-grandfather could pack up and come to the wilds of Kentucky and learn how to raise every bite they ever ate, you certainly don't expect me to lie on the bus floor and wail about moving to a Lexington subdivision with sidewalks and central heating, do you? After all, my best friend is going to visit my store every time she buys *anything*, right? When Great-times-something-grandmother came to Kentucky, there was no mail, no telephone, no visits from home. So far as her Charleston friends were concerned, she could have fallen into an abyss."

I shivered. When I tried to imagine my family's future, my mental screen just went black. Mom didn't have a brother in a big department store chain, any more than Mrs. Stanley did. Were we to fall over the edge, there was nobody I could think of to throw us a rope.

CHAPTER 23

The Pond

Monday afternoon, I held each ewe by the collar as Dad trimmed her hooves. Then Becky held the clippers while Dad helped me catch the next ewe. He could have put the clippers down, but having Becky work with us kept her from getting lonesome. We all saw Mom arrive home. She marched straight to the barnyard, still in town shoes! I kept hold of the sheep Dad was working on, but Dad set her hoof down. Mom looked so happy, I thought she was going to tell us that Mr. Engle had found a horse farm to manage after all.

"Mr. Watkins gave me a raise," she said. "It's a start, Rales." I knew what that meant. The raise wouldn't be enough to pay the bank in June. "It's a sign our luck is changing." Usually Mom looks older at the end of the workday than she does at breakfast, but that day she looked younger. "The next thing that happens will be even better."

"Think so?" Dad answered. "Well, be sure to come and tell me about it."

"I brought home a roast to celebrate," Mom told him.

"Good for you," Dad said shortly, and picked up my sheep's hoof again.

Mom fixed the roast with wine and mustard and bayberry

leaves from our own bushes, and when she brought it to the table, it smelled like Christmas. Mom was beaming. Dad wasn't hungry, but Becky and I ate seconds. I slept better than I had slept since the tornado and was wakened next morning by the first bluebird.

Most kids like summer best, because school is out, but there's a lot to be said for spring. The sun just croons at the earth, and everything smiles like a baby whose mother is rocking it. Little flowers sparkle in the grass, and the orchard turns into pink and white clouds, and wren babies leave their nest in the bayberry bush and hop up and down on the branches.

Usually by summer the earth has learned the words to the sun's song and sings along. Of course (as Hetty Anne would say), last summer was the exception. Last summer the sun roared, and when the sun roars at the earth, the earth gets quiet. The day after all our cows and steers were hauled away was so quiet, I thought my heart would freeze. The lowing and bawling stopped abruptly; then slowly I realized how many other things were still. Things like the pond, which usually croaks and chirks all summer, and the chimney, which usually hisses and twitters till almost Thanksgiving. The chimney swifts, the frogs had vanished. The pond was dried to a cracked cake, like a can of dark shoe polish I've forgotten to close.

I knew the swifts had only flown south and would give us another chance in the spring. I knew the pond would some day be full of water again. I believed the frogs had died. I believed that our beautiful pond might be songless forever.

The day after Mom told us about her raise, Dad sawed up the big locust the tornado had dropped on our fence. Becky and I were hanging the laundry when he got back. "I stopped by the pond," he told us, "and lo! Safe again from a foreign shore, your frogs send you greetings. 'Tell those daughters of yours we're back!' they said."

Becky cheered. I was so glad, I couldn't say a word.

The pond bank used to be my favorite place to read fairy tales, because it's like fairyland itself. I used to sit beside its still waters and feel my soul being restored, the way King David says. After Hetty Anne and I watched "Anne of Green Gables," she'd joked, "When they write my biography, it will be called 'Hetty Anne of Clean Stables.'" I'd laughed with her. Mine, I thought, would be "Kate of Still Waters," but I didn't say so. Even from Hetty Anne, the pond was my secret place.

The pond is at the bottom of the only slope on our farm steep enough to slide a sled down, and water has always collected there. One July day a few years ago when the temperature in the shade was about 90 degrees, Dad told Mom and me that the afternoon project was to deepen that place so the cattle could drink there. After lunch, Mom put a couple of spades in the back of our pickup truck and took Becky on her lap in the front seat. I got to sit over the wheels in the back, which I like best because it is jouncy, and I see everything, and the cool breeze blows my hair back, and I pretend I'm riding the winner at Churchill Downs.

As soon as the truck stopped, my face naturally felt hotter than ever. Mom reached for one of the spades. "No," Dad announced: "A woman's job is to feed workers and look after babies. Kate and I are going to do the digging."

I was tickled because I had thought I was going to have to look after Becky. Mom laughed. "You know what that claim makes you, don't you?" she asked Dad. She sat down on the moss with her back against a holly tree, and Becky started crawling around beside her.

"A *male chau*-vinist *pig*," Dad said cheerfully, digging.

The mud felt heavenly between my bare toes. I dumped a spadeful where Dad wanted the bank built up. "Dad is an MCP," I sang.

"Right!" he shouted, and smacked the water's surface with the flat side of his spade. Water sprayed up. "Wicked Dad! Fright-ful Dad!"

"MCP! MCP!" I yelled, so he would do it again. The cool water felt lovely. Becky and I splashed each other and laughed and shrieked. We were so muddy by the time we went home, Mom hosed us off in the yard before she would allow us in.

That very summer, like magic, frogs appeared. As I'd walk down the slope, I'd hear them: *Plop! Plop-plop! Plop! Plop! Plop!* By the time I'd be close enough to see one, there wouldn't be one, but I used to sit and never move until they forgot me. First eyes would appear. Finally a frog would take a chance. He would hop back up on the bank and sit, looking around. Finally there would be many. Once I sat so still my head fell asleep. (When people say, "I fell asleep," I picture bodies falling over, which mine did not do. I know my head sort of fell, though, because I felt it jerk back up; that's how I realized it had been asleep.) Probably hearing something is what had wakened me, because now I heard rustling in the hawthorn thicket on the opposite bank. I stared hard and saw nothing, but the frogs were all plopping back into the pond. I shut my eyes, then looked as hard as I could at the moss between my knees, to focus my eyes. When I raised my head again, I saw a different color, reddish brown, among the hawthorn branches. I was just deciding that this was probably a seedling oak that had kept its old leaves all winter, not anything that could have made the noise, when the reddish brown moved.

I didn't blink; I didn't breathe. A deer poked its head out from the hawthorns. It was a buck; I could see two bumps where antlers were coming. Showers of brown bud sheaves fluttered from the bushes he disturbed as he looked left and right, but never at me, sitting right across the pond. Then he emerged the rest of the way and picked his way to the water's edge, silent as a wraith. I used to read fairy tales all the time and halfway believed in them. That tree roots hosted elves and streams hosted wraiths seemed as natural to me as that clouds host angels. Just for maybe less than a second I thought this was the kind of deer that your hand would go right through if you tried to pat it. (I can just hear Hetty Anne. "Of course. All deer vanish if you try to pat them, Kate, I guarantee you.") I soon knew this was a real buck because the water rippled when he drank.

I had to breathe. I can't believe he could have heard me, but his head jerked up. I could see the crystal droplets fall back from his chin into the pond. I was rigid. The buck looked intently in my direction. I didn't even blink, but I swallowed. He snorted, wheeled, and bounded away. He was beautiful, beautiful as a prince under a witch's enchantment.

That's what Becky won't grow up seeing if we lose our farm—a woods shimmering with holly and dogwood blossoms, and singing frogs, and sometimes magic, like that buck.

"You'll both see other things," says Hetty Anne.

I'm not just thinking about us losing the farm, though,

but about the farm losing us. Dad doesn't allow hunting on our place. Maybe the one who got it from us would shoot the doves and quail; maybe he would hunt deer. Maybe his wife wouldn't have any better sense than to pick lady slippers and trillium, that don't come back if you break off their flowers. Maybe if we can't stay here, the magic can't, either.

Look how much magic just the fear of losing it has cost us. "I'm sure that your father didn't mean to be cruel," Mom had said when I told her how Becky cried over Grandmom's dresses.

"I'm not," I had retorted.

She pressed her lips together and I thought that she was revving up to chew me out, but though there was a glint in her eyes, when she spoke, it was to recall a conversation we'd had months before. "Your father is a saint of patience if he is in control," she'd said then. (I'd commented on the way Dad will whittle for hours to give us each our own bow, and then not let us shoot without *explicit* instructions from him.) "And not patient at all if he can't be."

As Mom reminded me of this, I thought how Dad had shaken me when I didn't instantly watch him puncture that cow, and then had taken all the time in the world to explain the trocar to me when I did watch. I also thought about the way she says "my stove," "my freezer"—"my children," even. You like to be in control yourself, I thought. It was confusing. I hadn't liked hearing her defend Dad, and now I didn't like to hear her criticize him.

"As long as he is looked to to run the show, he will never give a bad performance," Mom said. "But not to be in control of the situation is more than he can bear. At times like that, it's our turn to be patient."

"But Becky," I started angrily—

"Turn about's fair play, Kate," she interrupted me. "Your dad can't help not being in control of the weather. We have to help him through times like this, the way you told me he helped Sheena deliver Annie: patiently.

"Yes, life would be smoother if your dad were always sweet and easygoing. But let me tell you something. In times like these, sweet easygoing men lose their homes!"

I must have looked stricken, because she seemed to read my mind. "Kate, I am not saying that they're the only kind who do. Nothing could be less true. And I can't guarantee you that your dad will save ours. But I can guarantee you that the same pride that makes him behave the way we agree he behaved at Easter will make him nearly kill himself trying. So give him time. Kate, your dad has always taken care of us, and it makes him furious that he can't right now.

"You didn't like his attitude at Easter. I didn't like it. But it's that fury that will drive him to do something for us all. He will think of something. When he does, you'll know your dad again, the one who whittles you arrows. In the meantime, no, Kate, he will not always be fit to know."

That night I dreamed that I yelled at Dad, something I have never done, something I have never heard anyone do. "You're jealous!" I yelled. "You're jealous of Mom! You're jealous of Grandmom!"

I don't know what Dad would have done in real life. In my dream, he laughed. "You're so jealous of Morgan Culverhouse, your face is as green as a frog," he taunted.

"No!" I screamed. I forgot being furious with him; I begged him to believe me. "I used to be, but I'm not anymore!" I had been asking Morgan about her father every day. I had even told her I was glad, the morning she said he was getting out of the hospital. I had even walked to the girls' room with her both times she asked me (so she wouldn't be by herself if anybody said something to her about Mr. Stanley).

Dad laughed. He laughed and kept on laughing till it woke me up.

When I was little, I used to get a neck ache (like our city visitors) trying to count the stars in the Milky Way because Dad had told me I could never do it. He said not even scholars knew how many there were. When I finally gave up I was so frustrated, I stamped my foot till I hurt my ankle. Then I told myself, After I die, I'll know. If heaven is perfect, I reasoned, then we'll be able to learn anything we want to know, once we get there. J. M. Stanley claims we won't have to wait that long. He claims that soon astronauts will take a computer along programmed to bring us back the answer. Even before Mr. Stanley got hurt, J.M. wanted to quit school because he sees no reason to study, he says, "when computers can tell us everything we want to know." I think he might be partly right. Computers tell us how much money we're going to owe the bank now that we've lost our lamb crop and our wool crop; they ought to be able to tell us how many stars there are in the Milky Way.

J.M. is wrong about that "everything," though. Computers can't tell you how to make somebody keep on loving somebody.

CHAPTER 24

A Down Sheep

A truck came, and Dad and the driver loaded all the male lambs into the back, and the driver took them to market. The ewes that were losing their lambs ran bleating after the truck as far as their pasture fence would let them, and their lambs answered till they were out of hearing. Becky and I went inside. Late that night Becky came to my room in tears. "Shh, you'll wake Mom and Dad," I whispered. I took her under my covers.

When Becky had calmed down enough, she told me what she had dreamed. "Mr. Culverhouse came in his truck and took Mama and Dad away," she sobbed. "Mama was crying."

"Shh," I whispered into the top of her head, and hugged her harder. "That was only a dream. Mom and Dad are asleep in bed, and nobody's going to take them away." I let her put her cold little feet between my legs to warm them. I had to sleep on my side all night to make room for her.

I can't blame my bad night's sleep entirely on Becky. After the lamb truck left, Dad walked the length and breadth of our farm, inspecting what the drought had done to our pastures. Spring had come, but not spring's grasses. At supper Dad told Mom, "The roots are dead. No matter how much rain we get now, the grass will not come back."

Mom looked scared. "Can you reseed?"

"*I* can't. It takes a renovator." Mom looked blank. "A special rig that drills the ground as it releases your seed. Otherwise the seed just lies on top of the dirt and the first wind blows it away. Renovating costs seventeen dollars an acre, plus seed, plus fertilizer."

"Well," said Mom, "this is a good year for the man who owns a renovator."

"It's an even better year for the bank," Dad said. "I will have to borrow the money, and then if we don't get rain, it will all be to do over."

That conversation was already giving me a bad night even before Becky came. I was half stupid in school all the next day, and when I got home and Annie didn't meet me at her gate, I was dumb, dumb, dumb, about thinking where to look for her.

Dad says all the sheep drink at the pond, and it's not my fault, what happened to Annie. I try to believe him, and sometimes I start to, but before long I'm having to try all over again. I was the one who had wasted time I should have spent working. This house is a permanent mess since Mom took that job, but I wasted time walking down to the pond with my homework. (I could just as well study beside the pond as in the house, I had told myself, leaving out the question of the time I would spend walking there and back, time that could have gone to window washing or spiderwebs.) I wanted to see whether the columbine was blooming yet, and the little blue-eyed grass. They were, and the moss was all fuzzy, as soft as ashes. I sat on some beside the pond, and Annie came and laid her head in my lap and slept. We were both happy. That's why I'm afraid she was looking for me when she went to the pond. I wasn't there; I was in school, and she waded in, and she didn't wade out.

If she hadn't lost her mother the night of Orion, her mother would have stood on the bank and called her to come out. Maybe they would have waded in together in the first place, and the ewe would have shown her how to turn around. That old Sadie didn't care if Annie drowned or died of pneumonia or dropped through a hole in the earth.

Dad says sheep don't wander off alone, but I think Annie had gone looking for me, and that no other sheep was in sight when she waded in to get a drink. She waded in till the water touched her belly, all cold and wet, and that astonished and frightened her so, she stopped right where she was. Dad agrees about that part. She could have walked right across the pond and come out the other side, but she was too scared. She probably just stood there bleating for me for who knows how much of the afternoon, till I got off the school bus and saw she wasn't waiting for me at her gate and put on my coveralls right over my school jeans and went looking for her. The pond wasn't the first place I looked. Why didn't I hear her and run straight to her? Dad says she may have been too scared even to call for help.

Dad says if I had found Annie any later, she would have fallen over and drowned right where she was. As it was, she waited to give up till I had her on the bank. Then she just went heavy on me. I couldn't make her walk—I couldn't even make her stand up—and I couldn't lift and carry her. I yelled for help, but I knew nobody could hear me. I took off my coveralls and laid them on the ground beside her, took her by her feet and turned her onto her other side so that she fell on the coveralls, and dragged her homeward. I counted my steps: every five steps I called for Dad. When I heard the truck coming, I knew he had heard me.

As soon as Dad stepped out of the truck, I began to cry. I didn't want him to waste time hugging me, though. I ran to put the tailgate down so he could load Annie. I couldn't stop crying. I started to climb in after Annie, but, "You ride with me!" Dad ordered. I think he was afraid Annie would die before we even got her to the barn.

I didn't want to slow us down by arguing, so I got in the cab. "I'm sorry, Katie," Dad said. "I knew this cosset lamb business was a mistake. You get to forgetting it's just a lamb."

I stopped crying. "She's not dead yet!" I said.

Dad shook his head. "A down sheep is a dead sheep, honey. I'll show you what to try, but I warn you, nothing works."

Becky ran to meet us at the barn. Dad laid Annie on the straw in a claiming pen. "The shock has sickened her," he said. "She has quit—just like those lambs that died in February after those dogs chased them, even though the dogs never touched them. Sheep are mortal cowards."

"Annie's not a coward," I said. "She didn't die after those dogs chased her. They killed her own mother, but she didn't die."

Dad sighed. "All right. See if you can get her to drink something. If she'll drink, see if she'll eat. Rub her." Becky and I didn't wait for him to finish; we started rubbing. "Not her sides," Dad said. "She won't feel you through her wool. Rub her legs; rub her head; rub her ears. The idea is to get her blood circulating. Work her legs." Becky and I knelt beside Annie; Becky rubbed her ears and face while I took one leg in each hand and worked both back and forth while we listened to the rest of Dad's instructions. At the end he said, "A down sheep is a dead sheep. When you're ready to accept that, come inside."

After he'd driven the truck to the garage, I remembered my coveralls lying in its back. They were too wet to put on again, anyway. My jeans were wet, too, and it was too late to worry about getting them dirty. *I do the laundry around here anyhow,* I told myself. *And if my knees get stained forever, too bad.* Once I would have been ashamed to sit beside Morgan Culverhouse in stained jeans.

Annie wouldn't respond to crushed grain, so I ran to the house and put some water on the stove. While it heated, I got out of my squishy shoes. I fixed Annie's bottle with hot water and molasses. Back in the barn, I shifted Becky from rubbing Annie's face to rubbing Annie's legs so I could put the nipple in Annie's mouth. Annie's eyes were glassy; she didn't look at me. I told her I would make her well, not to worry. Then I remembered the funny way Dad looks when Mom says, "I'll always feed my children."

"Becky and I are here," I told Annie. "*We'll* take care of you."

At first I thought Annie was drinking and my heart filled up tight, but then I saw that the molasses water was just running out of the underneath side of her mouth. She also wouldn't bite hay. I put a sugar cube in her mouth, and it rolled out. I shifted Becky back to massaging Annie's face, and I went back to working her legs. When Becky complained that she was tired, I suggested that she work the foreleg, and I would work just the hind leg. I was tired, too. After awhile I started to sing one of those songs Grandmom has taught Becky and me that Virginia slaves used to sing, songs that had rhythms that made the work go easier. Becky sang with me. I thought our singing might encourage Annie, too, might reassure her. I think farm animals know that people don't sing when something terrible is happening. "My *mas*-ter *give* me a *hol*-i-*day*," I sang, and Becky, too. We went back with Annie's legs on "*mas*-" and forth with "ter," back with "*give*" and forth with "me," and so on. Annie just stared, and not even at us. At nothing.

We were singing and working like that when Dad came back into the barn. He stood and looked at us for a moment, then said: "You've been out here an hour. Time to turn her over."

"Her," not "Annie." Dad hadn't called Annie by name once since he found the two of us soaking wet in the woods, and Annie not walking.

If an animal lies still too long, he told us, its lungs start to fill with fluid. Annie had to be turned over every hour so she wouldn't get pneumonia. That is, we hoped she wouldn't.

Turning her wasn't hard; I just took hold of her ankles and heaved. The hard part was the way she just thumped over and didn't rouse. I sent Becky back to the house with Dad to ask Mom for an alarm clock, and I tried the bottle again. Annie stared without seeing me, and I could put the nipple in and out of her mouth all I wanted, nudge her with it all I wanted, she wouldn't suckle. When Becky came back with the clock, she had an old foot rug also. "Mom says put this rug under Annie's head. We have to protect Annie's eyes from getting scratched or getting grit in them. And she says supper is six-thirty as usual."

If Mom were sure a down sheep was a dead sheep, I

thought, she wouldn't bother about Annie's eyes. "Let's take turns going for supper," I suggested. "You can go first. Hold Annie's head up for me while I spread this rug."

About quarter past six, Mom showed up with our suppers. Annie had shut her eyes after we had put the rug under her head. "Has she suckled?" Mom asked.

"No," Becky admitted, and I thought she was going to cry.

"Not *yet*," I said.

Mom felt the bottle. "I'll reheat this," she said. "You can pick it up when you bring in your supper things. Bedtimes are as usual," she warned, and left before we could argue.

We looked at each other. That gave us just three hours. When I'd smelled Mom's stew, I'd changed my mind about keeping on working while Becky ate: all of a sudden I'd felt too hungry. Now, in just as quick a switch, I couldn't eat. "Let's try to get her up," I said.

Becky set down her stew without complaint. We lifted Annie and held her in an upright position, my arms under her chest and Becky's under her belly. She hardly even held her head up. Her feet wouldn't do a thing to help us. After a few seconds of grunting and puffing I saw from the color of Becky's face that we'd have to put Annie down or drop her, so we laid her carefully down. She had never even opened her eyes. I took my stew and sat so my thigh was against the back of her neck, so she'd get some of my warmth, and so she'd know she wasn't abandoned.

When I finished my stew and stood up, Annie looked at me. "Sit here in my place!" I told Becky. I ran all the way back to the house.

Dad and Mom were still at table. "I'm sure she's getting better," I pleaded. "Her eyes followed me when I left. That's the first time. If we go off and leave her all night, she'll die!"

"You may not miss school for a down sheep," Dad said, "and you can't go to school on no sleep."

Why can't I do the way we do in lambing time? I started to ask, but stopped in time. When I say, "Why can't I?" to Dad, he thinks of three answers before I've swallowed, so that is not the way to begin. "Could I take my sleeping bag the way I do when we're lambing?" I asked. "I won't stay awake. I'll just turn Annie over once every hour, and go right back to sleep."

Mom and Dad looked at each other, then Dad looked away. "We'll talk about it at nine o'clock," Mom said.

I went back out with the warm molasses water, sure Annie would be so glad to see me come back, she would drink, sure she would feel so much better after she drank, she would at least lift her head, maybe even scrabble her feet as if she at least *wanted* to get up. Nothing.

At seven-twenty, we turned her over again and I set the clock for eight-twenty.

At nine o'clock Becky went to take her bath, and I reheated Annie's molasses water and carried it and my sleeping bag out to the barn. My first look at Annie hit me in the chest; I thought she had died. I dropped the bag and fell to one knee in the same second, but even before I could get my hand on her, I saw her ribcage lift and then subside. So she wasn't dead. Her eyes were closed again, probably because I had left, but she was breathing. However, I might as well have been putting a cold shrimp in her mouth as that lovely warm nipple. I laid my bag beside her. I wanted her to be able to hear me and feel me there all night.

At ten-twenty the alarm clock went off like the Fourth of July. I turned Annie, offered her her bottle, reset the clock, and crawled back in my bag. It seemed as if I'd just zipped

201

RETA E. KING LIBRARY
CHADRON STATE COLLEGE
CHADRON, NE 69337

it up when the eleven-twenty alarm went off. I felt bad offering Annie a cold bottle, but I knew better than to make noise in the kitchen. In any case, her lips never moved.

At three-twenty my head ached and I felt stupid for ever thinking a lamb that wouldn't drink warm water would drink cold. Setting the clock for four-twenty would be dumb, and setting it for three-twenty, two-twenty, and so on back had been dumb. The moon was so bright I turned Annie over and brought her her bottle without even turning on the light. I knelt beside her and put the bottle under my arm to see if that might make it any warmer. Then I fell asleep without knowing it and started to topple over on her, so I went ahead and put the nipple in her mouth. She began to drink.

"I knew you would!" I jabbered. "I knew you would!" My nose started running. "Good Annie! Dear Annie! Drink it all," I crooned. "Drink, little Annie, drink it all." Stuff like that. Nothing I'd want on a tape recording. When she quit swallowing, I buried my face in her wool and whispered to her.

She drank a little more at four-thirty, and at five-thirty, I was able to fix her some warm.

At breakfast I tried to pretend not to be sleepy. Maybe if I'd let my chin hit my chest a few times they would have let me stay home. "I'm making progress," I urged. I remembered all Becky's rubbing and leg-working and singing. "We've made real progress," I said. "But if we quit, she'll backslide, and Becky's not strong enough to turn her."

"No," Dad said. "You know the rules and you know the reasons. No."

"Just one day? Even Mr. Rankin wouldn't pretend that my brains would all spill out of my head like sawdust if I missed one day of school. Couldn't I just—"

"Kate," Dad said, "if I have to tell you no again, I will get up from this table and cut that lamb's throat. It would be kinder to her and to you than prolonging this any further."

I swallowed carefully. "Will you turn her till I get home?" I asked him.

His expression was all the answer I needed. "I have a farm to work," he said. "I cannot abandon an entire farm full of hungry animals, including two sentimental little girls, for one down sheep."

"I'll turn her the last thing before I leave," Mom promised. "And Becky can keep her company and feed her all she'll eat." None of us wanted to look at each other.

After breakfast I turned Annie one last time. I whispered in her ear that I loved her. She mouthed a little hay. I told her good-bye.

CHAPTER 25

Hume

I napped some on the bus going to school. I wouldn't have wanted to talk to Hetty Anne about Annie much even if I hadn't been sleepy. My plan was to put my head on my desk and see if I could doze a few more minutes before first bell, but Morgan was already in her seat and watching for me. "Kate!" she cried before I even laid my books on my desk. "*Guess* what's happened! Tom Allen called Daddy last night, and what do you think? Somebody from Florida is buying his farm, and it's enough to pay the bank, and then some! Isn't that grand? Kate? What's the matter? Are you sick?"

"Just a little strung out. That *is* grand." I tried to think only of Tom and Mary Allen and look as happy as I should have looked.

Morgan frowned. "Why 'strung out'?" She squinted at me. "You haven't gone and taken something *dumb,* have you?"

Anybody who knows me ought to know better. Before Mr. Culverhouse went to the hospital, and everything, if Morgan had asked me that, I would have snapped at her. Now I told her about what a sheep-killer pneumonia is, and how Annie was lying in the barn with her lungs probably filling up right that minute, and nobody to turn her "till whenever that poky bus finally gets me home."

"Oh, the poor little thing," Morgan exclaimed. "You probably won't hear a thing Ms. Parish says all day. I'd be so worried, I wouldn't be able to read word one. Listen, Hume's picking me up after school. I'll just tell him we've got to go to your place first. That'll at least help *some*. Mother and I drove behind that old bus you ride one day last week. It never got above thirty miles per hour, and every time it turned a corner, it stopped again. I didn't know there were as many kids in this whole school as got off that bus of yours while we sat there waiting for them to quit waving bye-bye and get on out of the road. If I'd had a sick lamb waiting for me, I would have gone right into orbit."

For an instant, my mental movie camera had shown me something besides Annie. Hume Culverhouse drive me home? Maybe *Morgan* thought that suggestion would help me concentrate! I have always found it really strange to hear the casual way she talks about Hume, as if doing things with him, like eating breakfast and supper right across the table from him, were ordinary and natural and not even very interesting. Ride home in Hume Culverhouse's black Camaro? If I hadn't been so worried about Annie, I would have turned into a butterfly and flown right out the window.

I managed to tell Morgan thank you, to say that if Hume would do that, it would be very kind of both of them. "I have to give Ms. Parish a note," I said. I wanted to turn my back on Morgan because I could feel my face changing color.

Dad had written Ms. Parish a note because I hadn't done any homework. Hetty Anne and I had read this note on the bus. I'm sure Dad wanted me to read it; he hadn't sealed it. "My daughter spent the night nursing a down sheep," he had written. "I believe this experience will teach her as much as she would have learned from her neglected school-work. Rales Chidden."

Reading that, I had felt hot. He wants her to die, I had thought, feeling the idea seep down my neck and all the way through my legs. He'd rather prove he's right than save Annie's life! He would win, too, I reflected, as soon as the shock of Morgan's suggestion wore off. Even in Hume's Camaro, I wouldn't get home till after three, and that would be too late.

Ms. Parish read Dad's note. "I'll expect you to make up the work, Kate," she said. "How is the sheep?"

"A down sheep is a dead sheep," I said. She looked concerned. I shrugged and went back to my desk.

Now besides worrying about Annie, I was worrying about whether Hume would be on time, and about what he would say. What if he were so late the bus passed our house before I got home, and I was later getting to Annie than I would have been taking the bus? What if she died during just those minutes?

What if Hume already had other plans and couldn't take me home, or said he did, because he didn't want to take me? I couldn't tell Mr. Ormsby I had a ride home till I was sure I did, and what if the bus had to leave before I was sure? All these questions made me worry about Annie even more. I remembered how cold and stiff those other lambs had been the morning after the night of Orion. It's a scene I mostly manage to keep out of my mind. Now I pictured Annie lying like that in her pen. Before Morgan's offer, I'd felt helpless and almost hopeless, but at least if you're helpless and hopeless, there's no use fretting. Now, though, I had a decision to make, and I didn't know what the right one was. I only knew what I wanted it to be.

In the end, Hume was on time, and when Morgan told him about Annie he said, "Sure, hop in." I didn't, though. I had to run tell Mr. Ormsby that I wouldn't be on the bus. I couldn't help wondering if the second I was out of hearing, Hume started saying something to Morgan about making promises for him and his car without asking him first, maybe even something about me in particular. As I came back, neither of them was talking, just watching me come. I'm weak from hunger by three o'clock every day, anyhow. Having Hume Culverhouse watch me walk all the way across the parking lot nearly made my knees wobble.

Morgan and I got in the back. "This is a neat car," I said.

Morgan stroked the seat. "Daddy gave it to him for his birthday. Daddy promised to give him a car as soon as he was old enough to get his license, on condition that he pass his exam his first try. 'Do I get the same terms when it's my turn?' I asked him. 'We'll talk about it then,' he told me. Good old Daddy! Well, it was better than no, anyway."

I had meant to be speaking to both of them when I complimented the car, but I couldn't be positive Hume had heard me. He didn't say anything. He did reach up and adjust the mirror and smile at me, or I should say at us, or maybe just at Morgan. I tried to think what else I could say. He is on the swimming team, but I was not about to say anything that might remind him of that awful day that Hetty Anne made me struggle across the 4-H camp pool beside him. I thought about asking what kind of mileage the car gave; that's what Dad always asks his friends about their trucks. I didn't, though. I was embarrassed to mention miles per gallon to somebody who was driving miles out of his way to do me a favor. I stared out the window, hoping something I saw would give me an idea of something I could say that wouldn't sound foolish to a boy as much older than I am as Hume Culverhouse is, but all I could see was Annie lying on her straw with her eyes closed. Then we passed Fremit Brothers' feed store.

Fremit Brothers is where Dad has his account, which I've heard him tell Mom they are "carrying." Sitting there beside Morgan, I started remembering something she had told me the morning I learned about her father being in the hospital. "Half the Fremit Brothers' regular customers can't pay their bills!" she had declared. "The Fremits have been clients of Daddy's bank since before Daddy was born. Do you think he enjoys telling them there's a limit? McIlvains' Implements is the same story. Mr. McIlvain couldn't sell anybody in Lowlands County a new tractor at cost with a ham thrown in." Driving through town, Hume and Morgan were as quiet as I was.

"What's going to become of people like Miss Gravely," Morgan had challenged me, "if the bank stops paying her dividends? Where will Mrs. Tye get a job if the bank has to let people go? She's told Mother and me herself, she doesn't know how to do *anything*. About as much as Miss Gravely! Where do people think dividends come from—a greenhouse in Daddy's backyard that grows dollars? Oh, Kate, Mother and Hume and I are so worried! Daddy's going to make it this time, but what about next? He just worries, worries, worries, and there's no relief in sight. Every week another farmer walks in and says he can't pay. What's Daddy supposed to do?"

If anyone had asked me before that day what riding in Hume Culverhouse's car would be like, I would have said heaven, but I was miserable. I was miserable even before the realization hit me that I had made an awful mistake. Those of us who ride buses are let out of class ten minutes ahead of the others. Why hadn't I used my ten minutes to call home, instead of just waiting at my desk with Morgan? There wasn't any use dragging her and Hume into the act if Annie had died an hour ago.

Then Hume said, "I sure hope your lamb makes it, Kate. I know how you feel. Morgan and I lost a pet once. It was a baby rabbit. A tomcat got it."

Morgan shook her head and looked out her window, and I was sorry for her, and certainly for the rabbit, but I was resentful, too. *Annie is more than a pet,* I wanted to say. *Annie is one of a handful of animals that stand between me and your father taking my father and mother away in a truck.* Talk about confused. All day I'd been hating Dad. All day my determination to save Annie if I could because I loved her had been only half the story, and the other half had been determination to save her to spite my hateful father.

About that time Hume turned on the radio, so I didn't have to worry anymore about saying anything. I stared straight ahead, willing the road to pass under Hume's car ever faster, willing us to reach Annie before it was too late.

When we got to my place, I suggested that we drive straight to the barn. I didn't have to explain. I think Morgan was almost as eager as I was.

Hume parked close to the gate, and I was unlatching it before he and Morgan were even out of the car. I ran to the barn and my heart was pounding as if I'd run a mile. I don't think I was swallowing or blinking or seeing anything: my whole body was just concentrated on whether Annie's sides would be moving.

"Kate?" Dad sounded surprised. "You're early."

"Kate!" exclaimed Becky. Her face about split, grinning.

Annie was standing in the middle of the claiming pen eating crushed grain mash out of a pie pan in Dad's hand. I leaned against the barn door, staring at him. "We were lucky this time," he said. "Come and take this, now that you're here."

"This is twice we've stood her up!" Becky said. "Once was an hour ago and twice is now!"

I threw myself to my knees beside Annie and put my arms around her neck. She stopped eating and wiped mash all over my cheek. Hume and Morgan were coming in the door. I had forgotten them. I stood up and took Dad's pan and introduced Hume and Morgan as if I hadn't forgotten them, and Hume shook hands with Dad like a grown man. When he told Becky "Hi," her eyes got wide.

"Isn't she *sweet,*" Morgan said. I think she was talking about Annie, who was folding up her knees to lie down again.

"Her name is Annie," Becky told Morgan. "She waded in our pond and got almost deaded. Dad and I came at lunchtime, but Annie still wouldn't stand up, but after we ate, we came back and said, 'Now get up, Annie,' and 'Come on, Annie, get up,' and all like that, and he *picked* her up and *held* her on her feet, and I held the pan, and pretty soon Annie ate some and Dad . . ."

Dad and Hume were talking, and I heard Hume say "1987A."

Hume? 1987A, Dad has read to Mom and Becky and me, is the first supernova visible to the naked eye in over a hundred years. An astronomer in Chile discovered it just before he quit work for breakfast on February 24, 1987. Dad was excited about it, even though it's not visible to the naked eye or any other kind of eye in Kentucky. You have to go to the southern hemisphere to see Supernova 1987A. What Kentuckians see in the sky in February is Orion. Dad hadn't dragged any of us out to look at stars since February.

"My father gave me a telescope a few years ago," Hume was telling Dad, "and it's incredible, what you can see with it. I have to drive out in the country to use it, though. There's too much light in town. I'm always wondering if I'm going to get shot, setting up my weird contraption in strange places on the darkest nights."

Yes, Hume. Hume Culverhouse was interested in stars. I could have said something in the car about stars. All those miles I didn't say one word, couldn't think of one thing, and all the time . . . I would never have another chance. I stood in Annie's pen with my hand on her head. I felt absolutely hollow.

"We don't get as dark out here as we did when I was a boy," Dad was telling Hume, "because too many farmers burn outdoor lights all night, but we see a lot, even without a telescope. We watched the last lunar eclipse, didn't we, Kate?"

"Did you?" Hume looked at me as if he and I were in the same grade. "I misset my radio alarm for a station that turned out not to start broadcasting till sunrise, and I slept through the whole thing!"

"It was really interesting," I said. That much was true, and if Dad guessed how I'd hated his coming to roust me out of bed to risk frostbite to see it, he didn't let on.

"Bring your telescope out here any time you want to," Dad told Hume. "I'll show you the highest point, or Kate can. You'll find Polaris with your back to our front door and your face toward the mailbox."

211

Hume grinned. "I tried to teach Morgan left from right by Polaris when she was little. Remember?" he asked her.

"Do I! Good old Hume! 'Just stick your arms straight out like a scarecrow and face Polaris,' he tells me. 'Your left arm will be the one pointing west and your right arm will be the one pointing east.' All little Morgan had to know was west from east and sure enough, if it was dark, and if somebody was there to show her Polaris, she could give you her right hand." We all laughed, and then Hume and Morgan had to hurry away, because Morgan reminded Hume that their mother would be getting home very soon. (I'd always pictured Mrs. Culverhouse *there* when Morgan got home from school, but Morgan says she's usually doing volunteer work somewhere. Except when she's at the monthly meetings of the Garden Club—she's the treasurer—or the D.A.R.—she's a Regent. Tuesdays she waits on people in her church's old-clothes store, Morgan says.)

When Mom got home, Becky told her about Annie before Dad or I had a chance. "Dad *picked* her up and I fedded her and then Kate came home, and she fedded her some more, and Annie wagged her tail."

Mom held out both arms to hug Becky and me, one with each arm. "I have good children!" she said.

I straightened away from her. "We're Dad's children, too," I said. Mom gave me a long look.

CHAPTER 26

Scared Sweat

Dad seemed very pleased at supper. Since he'd just saved Annie's life, that didn't alert my curiosity a bit. There was more to it than Annie, though.

At breakfast, Dad had said nothing specific about his immediate plans. He'd just said that he was too busy to yo-yo to the barn all day and turn Annie. Soon after Mom left for work, he drove the pickup truck to the barn, collected Becky, and took her to Mabel's Country Kitchen. He bought her a bowl of chocolate and vanilla and peppermint ice cream, one scoop each, and told her to talk to Mabel till he came back for her. Then he went to keep an appointment at the bank that none of us knew he had. At supper, he waited for the rejoicing over Annie to quiet down to make his announcement.

"Well, I'm going into business with the bank." Even Becky stopped eating and waited for him to explain. "They're going to rent me a renovator. I'm going to do our work, and with what I earn doing other people's, I'll pay that rent and still make a profit. Might tide us through."

"Oh, Rales, that is marvelous," Mom said, but I wasn't so sure that Dad hadn't lost touch with the world. The bank, rent out a renovator?

Dad grinned at Mom's astonishment. "You get most of the credit," he told her. "You're the one gave me the idea." Mom looked blank. " 'A good year for the man who owns a renovator,' " he quoted back at her, doing a pretty good job of imitating her Virginia way of talking, too. "I got to thinking, maybe I should be that man. I called Jack Estep to get his advice, whether he thought I could get enough work to come out ahead borrowing the money to buy the rig. He told me that the bank had repossessed one last fall and hasn't been able to sell it, this being the kind of year it's been for everybody around here. 'See if J.H. will rent it to you reasonable,' he said. He's put me on to several farms he knows as bad hit as ours or worse, owners he knows would be good for the pay."

Becky and Dad had come straight to the barn from Mabel's, Becky told me, and turned Annie over. "Might tide us through," Dad had said. That meant it might not, too. Evidently Mom was wrong, a little bit. Evidently Dad doesn't insist on being 100 percent in control. He just can't stand to be 100 percent *not* in control.

Dad's first customer was Tom Allen, which is to say, Mr. Scheeler. Honest Irv had had to do some more driving around, learn for himself that what Mr. Allen told him about affordable pre–Confederate War houses was true, but in May, as Morgan had been the first to tell me, the Allens' farm became Honest Irv's. "People from up north just love white columns," Mrs. Allen had told Mom when they were first talking about what kind of prayer she and Dorothy, the Allens' daughter, might have of selling that farm out from under Mr. Allen "before it worries him to death." It's sort of a joke on her that Mr. Scheeler is from down south ("Well, Florida," she says, as if Florida didn't rightly count), and that what he saw as he drove up was four chimneys. He never said a word about the columns.

The final "deal" was that the Allens would sell Mr. Scheeler their house and farm and then stay on to manage both for him until he could hire somebody permanent. They would continue to live right where they had lived all my life, but the bedroom with the biggest fireplace would be Mr. Scheeler's and the bedroom with the best view would be for his visitors. This was no problem to the Allens. They'd had most of the house shut off to save heat even before their last child had left home.

I don't have anything against the Allens, but I couldn't help thinking that if Mr. Scheeler had bought the Engles' place, Mr. Engle would have stayed on just as long as Mr. Scheeler liked. Dad must have read my mind. "Takes a lot less capital to go into sheep than horses," he said. "A man can buy all the sheep in this end of Lowlands County for what Matt Engle's got in fences alone." Horses have to have special fences. They would injure themselves on the kind of wire we put around our sheep. "I know what Matt paid just to enclose that front field, and for the same money you could buy a hundred prime ewes." Which, in the end, is what Honest Irv did. Mr. Allen tagged their ears and put them right in with those he had preserved on the night of Orion.

"It's enough to make a man change his mind about retiring," Mr. Allen told Dad. "Now I'm farming the way a man wants to farm—money to pay for what the flock needs, don't have to cheat the dentist and the preacher to buy it."

Mary Allen wasn't so pleased. "I wanted Tom to do less, not more," she fretted. "I wonder if men would be as happy as they are making themselves sick if they didn't know women would take care of them once they collapsed."

"If Japs couldn't kill me, sheep aren't going to," Mr. Allen said. Mr. Allen was in his barracks at Fort Mears, Alaska, when the Japanese dropped a bomb right on top of it. The bomb killed twenty-five soldiers and put twenty-six more in the hospital, but Mr. Allen wasn't even hurt. I heard Dad tell Mom once that he believed Tom Allen wished he had been a little hurt, so he'd have a scar to show. As it was, the best he could do was have Mrs. Allen give him an army-style flattop every ten days.

"Some of the place is pretty good," Mr. Allen told Dad when he arranged to have Dad renovate. "The clover in that field next to you is good as I've seen it, but you'll see for yourself, there ain't nothing but ragweed in my biggest field. If I had to pay for the work myself, I couldn't have it done."

Mary and Dorothy Allen's plans had been to get Mr. Allen into a Louisville condominium, where he could watch TV between racing dates at Churchill Downs and basketball games at the university. The trouble was that once somebody else started paying the bills, Mr. Allen no longer wanted to leave Lowlands County. "For the first time in my life," he said to Dad, "I can farm the best I know how."

Dad couldn't shake his head, because he *did* know what Mr. Allen meant, but he didn't dare nod, because Mrs. Allen was so upset. Mr. Allen reminded her of those bombs that missed him in 1942, and I thought she wanted to hit him herself.

About a week after Dad renovated Mr. Allen's big south field, Mr. Allen poured himself a cup of coffee at the kitchen stove, and fell down. The doctors said he'd had a stroke. He could not speak, or even chew. Mrs. Allen hired J. M. Stanley to help her with Mr. Allen's work four days a week, since J.M. had quit school for this year, anyway. Dorothy came over from Louisville to help out, but with a job and family of her own, she couldn't stay forever. After she was gone, Mom made a lot of cream soups to share with Mary Allen.

"If Mr. Scheeler had bought horses instead of sheep," I pointed out, "the Allens would be in Louisville already." And I would have Hetty Anne next door, instead of Snotnose Stanley, I added, though only to myself.

Dad's third customer was the farmer across the road from the Engles, the one who'd tried to buy their farm for next to nothing. "I hate for Dad to take Mr. Davis's money," I said to Hetty Anne, "after the low bid Mr. Davis made on your place!"

"Well, Kate, Mr. Davis probably bid all that he could. It wouldn't have helped us a bit for him not to bid at all. Personally, I hope your dad gets to renovate half the farms in Lowlands County."

The day Dad did Mr. Davis's work, the sky was the color of old sidewalks. As I stood at the dining room window watching Dad drive away, a last-year's leaf skittered across the porch. I hoped for Dad and Mr. Davis's sakes that the weather forecast was right and the rain would hold off till evening. After a minute Mom glanced through the kitchen doorway and noticed me standing around. I knew she'd say something about that. "Take a quart of this soup to Mary Allen," was what she said. "Tell her I used the blender."

I got a pot to set the soup jar in. Dad's truck on this farm's roads gives a sloshy ride. The sheep just went on grazing as I drove by. Not even Annie raised her head. We always count the flock when we pass them, to make sure no sheep is in trouble somewhere (like standing in a pond). With all the male lambs gone now, I scarcely had to slow down for the count. "Margin of profit is *small,*" Tom Allen had instructed Honest Irv first thing. "It's no use to go into the sheep business with any fewer than a hundred." We hadn't had a hundred ewes even before the night of Orion.

The mothers of the lambs we'd sent to market seemed to have forgotten them, and I was beginning not to dream about them myself. When Dad was my age, he points out, he had to help Granddad butcher lambs. I haven't told him, but not only is that one bit of toughening up I am never going to ask of myself, Becky and I are not even going to send them off for somebody else to do it. We are going to switch completely from meat sheep to wool sheep. Madge Graith says if we advertise in weaving magazines we'll have customers writing us from Maine to Japan. I thought about this as I bumped along with Mom's split pea soup. There's always going to be the occasional sick or injured animal, if animal husbandry is your profession, but for somebody as weak stomached as I am to make it, I told myself, she will need to insulate herself from pain and death all she can. I, I promised myself, am certainly going to. I got that sinking feeling in my stomach at the question that always came next: what am I going to do those times when I *can't* insulate myself? That's when I looked across our back line fence and saw probably thirty sheep on their sides with their legs stuck out straight as Noah's Ark pieces and their bodies swollen like roasting marshmallows.

Two more ewes had sunk to their knees before I could depress the clutch and brake. I looked around to see if anybody knew what was happening and saw J.M. running toward the sheep's field from the Allens' barn. I jumped out and ran toward him.

There was a tool in J.M.'s hand; I recognized it. "They've got bloat, don't they?" I gasped. "Shall I go tell Mrs. Allen to call Doc Spivey?" I could feel the sweat break out on my forehead. I wanted to get away before J.M. went to work.

"Done told her," J.M. answered. He stuck Mr. Allen's trocar at me. "You've helped your daddy use these thangs," he said.

Why on earth had I bragged to J. M. Stanley that I had helped Dad save a bloated cow? Was there anyone in Lowlands County whose opinion I more despised? Over his shoulder I saw another sheep go down. My brain was too stunned even to remember just how exaggerated my boasting might have been. "That was a year ago!" I protested.

"Bloat ain't changed none," said J.M. "You take this; I've got a knife." One hand went into his pocket even as the other urged the pointed steel tube on me.

I recoiled. "All I did was watch," I jabbered. "And it was a cow, not a sheep."

"I'll *show* you," J.M. said. *"Take* it."

I put both hands behind my back. "I can't!" I cried. "I *can't!"* The look J.M. gave me dried my tears before they showed. "I'll try," I whispered.

J.M. was flipping the first sheep over before I realized he had moved. "Make sure you always punch 'em on the *left* side," he told me. "That's where her paunch is. Put the heel of your left hand against her hip bone and the heel of your right hand against her backbone. Let your thumbs meet, and where your forefinger knuckles comes together, that's where to stick her." He had already done so as he spoke; green foam spewed upward. The moment it stopped, he removed the trocar and moved to the next sheep, without even glancing to see if I had understood. "Point toward her right knee," he said, "or you'll stick her in the stomach and kill her." I felt cold sweat glaze my armpits. J.M. was holding the slimy trocar toward me. My hand shook as I took it. "You cain't make thangs no worse," he said. "I cain't do 'em all before they start a'dying."

"Remember when you're dealing with bloat," Dad had said, "you can't kill an animal that wouldn't have died anyway, without you, and you might save one."

J.M. was already at work on the next nearest ewe. I blinked a few times, swiped my eyes and nose with the back of my hand, and chose my sheep. She was glassy-eyed with pain, her breath coming quick and shallow. I placed my hands on her flank the way first Dad, then J.M., had shown me. I could feel no bones at all. She was so distended, I had to guess where they should be. In her agony, the ewe ground her teeth, and foam bubbled at her lips. I took a deep breath and rammed the shining steel into her side.

I could hear the ewe's labored breathing relax. Can I get it out? I was asking myself wildly. I needed as much courage to withdraw the trocar as I had needed to jab it in. Then when it came (I gasped with relief), I had to move on at once to another ewe. It was all to do over again. My knees seemed to have weights tied to them. You got through the wool pulling, I reminded myself.

But there were fewer to do, myself answered. *And I couldn't hurt them. They were already dead.* All the while I was dragging my feet to the next suffering animal, grabbing her ankles, and turning her left side up. He did say *left* side? I turned in a panic to see what J.M. was doing. J.M.'s movements were regular and unceasing as the movements of a man on an assembly line. He never glanced my way. With something like anger—how dare he expect so much of me?—I turned my face and stabbed.

I did not count how many times I leaned away from my

lance and watched the green guck shoot up. Each time I felt the taut skin give under my lance, I prayed that when I withdrew the lance, I would see that no more sheep remained to be treated, but for what seemed like forever, they were falling faster than J.M. and I could work. My ears hummed, and my elbows ached. The palm of my hand grew pitifully sore. J.M.'s lips were pulled back from his set teeth; his eyes were narrowed. His pace never flagged.

At first I kept myself going by promising myself that if I would take care of just one more, Doc Spivey would arrive and take over. At last I could not believe that the nightmare might after all be ending. I stood exhausted as the final horror shrank back into a sheep under my hand, rose, shook herself, and belched. J.M. came over to me. "Well, Prissface," he said, "we done 'em all."

My back was clammy. I knew how my nose would wrinkle as I took my shirt off. Scared sweat stinks. "Here," I told J.M., reaching him the mucky trocar with a steady hand. "Who's paying me to mind your business?"

His grin got downright friendly. I felt my own face grinning back.

CHAPTER 27

Star Light, Star Bright

I set the supper table using mostly my left hand, because of how sore the trocar had made my right hand. Mom was just about to help our plates when the telephone rang. She put her serving spoon down, and Dad answered. "Hello," we all listened to him saying. "Yes, hel*lo.*" Mom would have said, "Hello, so-and-so," to tip Dad off who it was so he could go on about his business, get ready to come to the telephone, or flee, depending on what he expected from so-and-so. "Yes?" Dad was saying. "No! Well!" All Dad's telephone conversations are like that. "Yes, yes," he said. Becky's stomach growled, and Mom looked at me. *"Yes,"* Dad said. Mom put her chin in her hand.

The phone caller turned out to be Mrs. Allen telling Dad about J.M. and me saving Mr. Scheeler's sheep.

I hadn't left the minute J.M. and I had them all back on their feet. "We should iodine the wounds, shouldn't we?" I had suggested. J.M. had looked surprised, but I remembered Dad daubing iodine on that cow, and then smearing her cut with Vaseline to keep flies away. J.M. hadn't figured I would stick around to help him do that, but we found cotton and strong iodine and a jar of Vaseline in Mr. Allen's barn medicine cupboard, and J.M. swabbed every punctured ewe with iodine, and I followed up with the Vaseline. Of course, I had already told Dad and Mom all about it, but Mrs. Allen's comments made Dad downright jovial. Doc Spivey had arrived soon after I left, she said, and he and J.M. had given all the punctured ewes antibiotic shots. *Brave* and *tough* was what Doc Spivey had called me; "brave and tough," Dad repeated proudly.

When is a down sheep not a dead sheep? When it has bloat. How I wished all my problems had one-step dramatic solutions. A trocar to the flank, *whap!* Your farm is safe. *Whap!* Your family will never lose it. You, brave and tough, will farm it forever. *Whap!* Your parents love each other, and you. *Whap!* They will always love each other, and you.

Actually, I think my parents are like what I remember Dad telling me once about planets. The distance between any two planets is always changing, he said—first increasing, then decreasing, then increasing again. I guess Becky and I will just have to remember, when we notice Dad and Mom moving away from each other, that so far, every time they've moved just so far apart, they've turned and moved together again. Maybe that goes for us, too. Since Dad saved Annie, we've tried to forget our Easter dresses.

There's a sadness that comes right when a person is happiest and realizes that life will never be this way forever. Hetty Anne says the word for it is *rueful.* Underneath that sadness, though, I still felt good. One of my favorite books is about a girl who answers an advertisement for a wife. The letter she writes tells about herself and finishes, "and I am plain, and tall." I imagined myself writing such an answer. Some of what I would tell about myself would be *rueful,* but I would finish, "and I am brave, and tough."

It's easier for me to talk about things like this to Hetty

Anne than to Mom. For a change, I actually felt impatient for the school bus to come. Hetty Anne was the only one I could tell how I felt as I compared what I've always thought of J. M. Stanley with what I used to think about Morgan Culverhouse. I described to Hetty Anne how cool J.M. had been, surrounded by fallen and falling sheep. "I hated Morgan for being a snob, which she was not, and *I was,* the way I despised J.M. I wonder if he ever hated me the way I hated Morgan."

"Oh, cheer up, Kate," Hetty Anne told me, as usual. "I bet J.M. is having exactly the same kind of thoughts. You've discovered it's possible for somebody who wipes his nose on his sleeve and says *ain't* to be a hero in a showdown. I'll bet J.M.'s just as surprised to find out that somebody who is compulsive about grammar and pocket handkerchiefs can be a pretty reliable ally in a pinch."

Thing is, Hetty Anne was just too full of her own good news to be as concerned about my character flaws as I was feeling. Around the same time Mary Allen was talking to Dad Saturday night, Mr. Engle was learning that Super had just won one of those races that gives the winner's breeder a bonus. "And it's all going straight into my college savings account," Hetty Anne told me, "because Pops says Super wouldn't be alive if you and I hadn't caught him that day he crashed into his gate."

Mr. Engle's bonus will be enough to pay for almost a whole semester at Transylvania, which Hetty Anne has gone back to hoping she will attend. Mrs. Culverhouse has promised to nominate her for a D.A.R. scholarship and help her get supporting letters when the time comes, and Miss Gravely has already talked to Transylvania's admissions counselor. He told her that Hetty Anne was a good candidate for a Transy scholarship, if her grades don't slip. Miss Gravely knows Transy's administration well because her father was a member of their board for years. "I've promised them Father's library," she says, "but I haven't promised them my house yet."

What Hetty Anne has to do is *study,* but that's not all. Scholarship applicants have to be in extracurricular activities. For Hetty Anne, that is 4-H. We go to meetings together.

4-H is helping Hetty Anne toward Transy in more ways than one. When she told the manager of the store that she'll be going to work for in August about being Unit 6 Dress Review Modeling Champion, he suggested she might do a little modeling at the store sometimes. "Pays extra," says Hetty Anne. The cleaners did get Rubylee's mascara out of her coat, so it will be perfect for her to model at the 4-H Area Competition at Fayette Mall, and Hetty Anne says the manager will be there.

Hetty Anne's latest project was a pleated skirt, and mine was a cushion shaped like a lamb to give Becky for her birthday. I designed it myself, cut out the cloth, sewed it together, and stuffed it. Hetty Anne helped with the ears.

Hetty Anne also took the cushion home and hid it for me till presentation time. "Look who's waiting for me in the front yard," I pointed out to her as the bus approached my stop on Becky's birthday. "Good thing it was raining this morning." My raincoat was over my arm; the day had turned beautiful about noon. I smuggled the cushion into the house under my raincoat, while Hetty Anne waved distractingly to Becky through the bus window, calling "Many happy returns, Rebecca!" Becky adores Hetty Anne. If Becky could give scholarships, Hetty Anne would get six.

I can remember when Becky was born; she was red and round. Mom called her "my little apple." (So Mom was already saying "my." Maybe if Dad would remember that, he wouldn't read so much into it now as I think he does.) Becky is still round some places—her tummy and her bottom and her face—but she is "ranging out," as Hetty Anne calls it. She'll be ready for school in August.

"Do you think Grandmom remembers next week is my birthday?" she asked me one night.

What could I say? She brings the mail in, except on Saturdays, when Mom does. Chances are she would know if a package came from Virginia. If I said, "Grandmom would never forget your birthday," then wouldn't not getting a present be even worse than if I had said, "Well, Grandmom's getting old," and shrugged a little? I had been worrying, too. I was afraid that Mom was wrong and that Grandmom's feelings *were* hurt on account of those beautiful dresses going back to Woodward and Lothrop. Maybe she just wouldn't send Becky a birthday gift. "Mom and Dad haven't forgotten, and I know what they're giving you," I told Becky.

"What?"

"Oh, that's for me to know and you to find out."

"Tell. Please tell. I won't tell them you told me, promise."

"You can have three guesses, yes or no answers only, and that's all. After three questions, no answers."

"Is it to eat?"

"No. That's one."

"Is it a doll?"

"No. That's two."

Becky thought a moment and looked less eager. "Is it useful?"

"Yes," I said, and she sighed. "It's pretty, though," I added.

"Pretty. Pink socks?"

"The sun shines bright," I began to sing, "on my old Kentucky home—" At least she'd forgotten for the moment about no mail from Grandmom.

This year, Becky blew the birthday candles out with one breath. I was wishing it were my wish, not hers, because I knew what I would have wished, whereas six is young enough to wish for something that doesn't really help. Becky looked pretty serious, though.

The birthday girl has to cut the cake, and everybody watches while she opens her presents. Nobody gets a bite till she's through. Dad and Mom's box was on top of the stack. Becky opened it carefully. (I had explained to her before supper about saving gift wrapping.) "Red sneakers!" she exclaimed. "Oh boy, thanks a lot!" She beamed at Mom and Dad. "I was afraid it would be *socks*."

Mom and Dad looked startled for a moment, but then they looked at each other and laughed. Becky never noticed. She was too busy opening Grandmom's present. Mom had been hiding it for a week. It was a book. On the cover, a very satisfied-looking redheaded boy was resting his feet on a hog. The hog looked just as satisfied. I was right on the point of asking Becky if she could read the book's title (which was *A Regular Rolling Noah*), but I didn't. Becky is so proud of being able to read some, she might have decided to give us a long demonstration immediately. I wanted her to hurry up and take a bite of cake so I could. I also wanted her to open *my* present.

"It's *Annie*," she cried. "Oh, Kate!"

"I did a lot of stuffing," I told her. "I felt like that mother goat cramming the old wolf's belly with rocks and then stitching him up."

227

"She's not an ol' wolf; she's Cushion-Annie," Becky said firmly, and gave my present a hug before she tucked it under her left arm and began to eat.

Cushion-Annie has spent every day since that night propped against Becky's bed pillows. Whenever I see her there, I feel encouraged. I remember that I am not a sailor sailing chartless who will go over the edge of the world if the wrong winds blow, over the edge of the world into the unimaginable abyss where no one will throw him a rope. I am a resourceful farmer's daughter, brave and tough. Maybe I'll found my own cottage industry, if I have to; put a Cushion-Annie in every bedroom in America, maybe; why not?

Usually these days I wash the supper dishes, and Becky puts them away, but I told her that she didn't have to help on her birthday. I expected her to say "Yippee!" and go off in a corner with her new book, but she insisted on helping. "You need plenty of time for your homework," she said.

Becky is very conscious that being six means she is old enough to go to school like the Tye twins. She has begun thinking about homework. "I'll have all evening—" I began.

"Less nobility and more dishwashing," Dad said.

"I'll help you both," Mom announced, "because it's Becky's birthday." She went straight to the sink and started letting the cooled water in the hot water pipe run right down the drain. A month ago my stomach would have plunged, and I would have seen auction signs all over the farm, but I just rubbed my teeth front and back with my tongue and went back to the dining room for another load of dishes.

Dad was still sitting at his place. He had Becky's book open to a big picture of that same redhead, sleeping between a cow and a horse. A minute later when I came for a third load, Dad was leaning back with a grin on his face. He got up and followed me to the kitchen door. "Becky," he asked, "would you like me to read you your grandmom's book?"

I listened, too. The regular rolling Noah is a Kentucky boy who had to milk a cow and make chicken nesting boxes and things like that which Dad did when he was my age, and he also does some other things that were a surprise even to Dad.

"When you write to thank your grandmother," I heard Mom tell Becky as she was tucking Becky into bed, "be sure to tell her that we *all* enjoyed her gift."

Next morning Becky let me take a piece of her cake to school for myself and one for Hetty Anne. "Oh, joy," Hetty Anne said. "I knew this was going to be a good week! We got a new B&B yesterday."

I sat back to hear about this one.

"He teaches Visual Arts someplace up north, and he's come to give a demonstration at Transy. He's going to dress up thirteen art students in nineteenth-century French clothes and then have them coat themselves with liquid clay—clothes, hair, faces, and all. Then they'll all go outside and pose on Haupt Plaza like the dancers in a famous painting by a French artist named Renoir. The students will pose like the couples in that painting as long as they can stand it, to show the other Transy students what the painting would have looked like if Renoir had sculpted it instead."

"He must be nuts!" I protested.

"I think it sounds like fun," said Hetty Anne.

"It sounds like anything but fun to me. I bet those students are going to wish your B&B had run out of gas somewhere north of Cincinnati and found out how much *he* likes just standing around. Who needs it?"

"What if your partner were Hume Culverhouse?" Hetty Anne teased. I felt my forehead prickle, right about where the hair starts. "I heard from the wind that he thinks you are an unusual girl."

"Unusual. Is that good, or bad?"

"It's a start," said Hetty Anne.

Supper was late that night because Dad had been planting corn and didn't quit till dark. Then as he unfolded his napkin, the telephone rang. Pushing his chair back from the table, he wasn't smiling. "Hello," he answered. "Yes. Ye-es." Mom and I looked at each other, and I put Dad's hash in the warming oven. "Yes, yes," Dad said. "Well, yes." I tiptoed back to the table. "Yes," Dad said. "That Stanley boy's father is looking for a place."

I put down my fork.

"Yes, that one. Well, he taught the boy all the *boy* knows. I would say so, yes. Well, that last tornado pretty much wiped him out. Can't blame him for that. No, he's not. Yes, I do—strongly. Yes. Well, just a minute, I can give you the number." He read off Mr. Stanley's brother's telephone number. "Yes, well, I hope so. Any time. That's all right, any time." Dad hung up and sat down, and I brought him his plate. "That was Irv Scheeler," he told Mom. "He's going to talk to Jim Stanley about maybe managing his farm."

"Oh, Rales," Mom said. "Oh, that's wonderful."

"It is wonderful," Dad agreed. "So are your biscuits. Please pass me some more."

I ate extra fast. I wanted to be the one to tell Hetty Anne how J.M.'s steady nerve had landed his father a job. I could hear things I would have said once, if I'd been informed that the Stanleys would be moving into the Allens' big house. Things like: Maybe J.M. will learn to wipe his nose on toilet paper, now that he's going to have indoor plumbing. Certainly I never thought I'd be cheerful about the news that he was going to be my next-door neighbor, and I still wasn't eager to wind up sitting next to him on the bus every day after Hetty Anne moves, if he decides to come back to school in the fall. Hetty Anne says, "The important thing you've learned is that just because you can't imagine you'll ever want to dance with J.M. doesn't mean you two couldn't help each other tote water to a grass fire."

"Put the heel on your left hand against her hip bone and the heel of your right hand against her backbone," J.M. had told me, as I shook in my sneakers. "Let your thumbs meet, and where your forefinger knuckles comes together, that's where to stick her." Who knows? There might be more tricks about farming he could teach me.

I finished eating before anyone else, excused myself, and went up the stairs two at a time. I had just uncapped my toothpaste when Dad called after me not to dawdle. "Dishes can wait," he was telling Mom. "I need all you women to help me look for shooting stars." I dropped the toothpaste tube and raced downstairs.

It was May: Orion and his dogs had vanished from our sky. The mockingbird was singing on our chimney. As the front door thwacked shut behind us, he stopped and flew somewhere. The air smelled like honeysuckle, so sweet I almost thought I could taste it. Dad lifted the binoculars. "You want to focus on Hercules," he instructed all us women, "and watch for streaks." Mom and Becky stared where he was pointing, but I noticed that Becky's jacket was buttoned crooked and bent to fix it. " 'Shooting star' is a misnomer," Dad lectured. "What we're actually looking for are not stars but meteors. Meteors travel forty miles per second. They look like the writing you girls do with your sparklers on the Fourth of July."

I am going to remember that description so I can use it if I'm ever showing any visitor our night sky. Because Dad is right, I do know where the best place for a telescope is.

Meanwhile, I unbuttoned all Becky's buttons and started fresh. Becky made a face. "I'm just doing this so you won't get chilly," I told her.

Becky saw Mom looking at her. "Thanks," she told me, grudgingly.

"You're *welcome*," I answered, letting my tone of voice tell her that I thought she should appreciate me.

Mom patted each of us on one shoulder at the same time, which is her way of saying, "Smooth your feathers," and usually makes mine ruffle worse, but just then the mockingbird started singing again from the big cedar tree, one different bird's call after another, and Becky and I looked at each other and grinned. "We have good children," Mom said, putting her arm through Dad's.

Dad lowered his binoculars and looked at her. "We do," he said, handing the binoculars to me for my turn. "And we're going to leave them *our* farm for their children."

Nobody said anything. I don't know what Becky was thinking, but probably Mom and I were thinking the same thing, and maybe Dad himself was thinking it, too. What he had said sounded more like praying than promising. I didn't shut my eyes, though. I pointed our binoculars north, to Polaris. It will always be there.